MISTER O

by Lauren Blakely

ALSO BY
LAUREN BLAKELY

The Caught Up in Love Series (Each book in this series follows a different couple so each book can be read separately, or enjoyed as a series since characters crossover)

Caught Up in Her (A short prequel novella
    to *Caught Up in Us*)
Caught Up In Us
Pretending He's Mine
Trophy Husband
Stars in Their Eyes

Standalone Novels

BIG ROCK
Mister O
Well Hung (Fall 2016)
Far Too Tempting
21 Stolen Kisses
Playing With Her Heart (A standalone SEDUCTIVE
    NIGHTS spin-off novel about Jill and Davis)

The No Regrets Series

The Thrill of It
The Start of Us
Every Second With You

The Seductive Nights Series

First Night (Julia and Clay, prequel novella)
Night After Night (Julia and Clay, book one)
After This Night (Julia and Clay, book two)
One More Night (Julia and Clay, book three)
Nights With Him (A standalone novel about
    Michelle and Jack)
Forbidden Nights (A standalone novel about
    Nate and Casey)

The Sinful Nights Series

Sweet Sinful Nights
Sinful Desire
Sinful Longing
Sinful Love

The Fighting Fire Series

Burn For Me (Smith and Jamie)
Melt for Him (Megan and Becker)
Consumed By You (Travis and Cara)

The Jewel Series

A two-book series releasing Summer 2016
The Sapphire Affair
The Sapphire Heist

ABOUT

Just call me Mister O. Because YOUR pleasure is my super power.

Making a woman feel 'oh-god-that's-good' is the name of the game, and if a man can't get the job done, he should get the hell out of the bedroom. I'm talking toe-curling, mind-blowing, sheet-grabbing ecstasy. Like I provide every time.

I suppose that makes me a superhero of pleasure, and my mission is to always deliver.

Sure, I've got an addiction to giving, but step right up, and you'll also find a man with a hot exterior, a kickass job, a razor-sharp wit, and a heart of gold. Yeah, life is good…

And then I'm thrown for a loop when a certain woman asks me to teach her everything about how to win a man. The only problem? She's my best friend's sister, but she's far too tempting to resist--especially when I learn that sweet, sexy Harper, has a dirty mind too and wants to put it to good use. What could possibly go wrong as I give the woman I've secretly wanted some no-strings-attached lessons in seduction?

No one will know, even if we send a few dirty sexts. Okay, a few hundred. Or if the zipper on her dress gets stuck. Not on that! Or if she gives me those f*&k-me-eyes on the train in front of her whole family.

The trouble is the more nights I spend with her in bed, the more days I want to spend with her out of bed. And for the first time ever, I'm not only thinking about how to make a woman cry out in pleasure --I'm thinking about how to keep her in my arms for a long time to come.

Looks like the real Adventures of Mister Orgasm have only just begun....

DEDICATION

This book is dedicated to my readers.
You're the reason I write! And, as always,
to my dear friend Cynthia.

PROLOGUE

Ask me my three favorite things and the answers are so easy they roll off my tongue: hitting a homerun for my softball league, drawing a killer cartoon panel, and—oh yeah—making a woman come so hard she sees stars.

Not gonna lie. That last one is my favorite by about a mile. Giving a woman a sheet-grabbing, toe-curling, mind-blowing orgasm is pretty much the Best Thing Ever.

A woman's climax is like summer break, Christmas morning, and a vacation in Fiji all rolled together in one fantastic package of window-shattering bliss. Hell, if we could harness the beauty and energy from women coming, we could probably power cities, stop global warming, and bring about world peace. The female orgasm is basically the manifestation of everything good in the world. Especially when I deliver them, and I've given thousands upon thousands. I'm like a superhero of pleasure, a good-deed doer, the once-upon-a-shy-guy-now-a-stud, and my mission is to dispense as many climaxes to my lovers as possible.

How have I managed to achieve this amazing feat? Simple. I'm both a student and a master of the art of giving Os. I consider myself an expert because—in the interest of full disclosure here—I'm completely, one hundred percent *obsessed* with a woman's enjoyment between the sheets. Getting her off is the name of the game, and if you can't get that job done, you should get the hell out of the bedroom.

But, hey, I'm also humble enough to admit I'm still a learner. Because there's always something new to discover with a woman.

Does she want it soft, hard, fast, light, rough? Does she like it with teeth, toys, my cock, my tongue, my fingers? Does she crave a little something extra, like a feather, a vibrator, or a combination of the above? Every woman is different, and every path to her pleasure is its own erotic journey with so many fantastic stops to make along the way. I take mental notes, study her cues, and always get out and do the fieldwork.

I suppose that makes me the Magellan of the female orgasm. A true explorer, venturing forth, fearless and ready at any moment to map the terrain of her pleasure until she cries out in rapture.

Fine, some might say I have an addiction. But really, is it a bad thing that I love to make the woman I'm with feel good? If that makes me a guy with a one-track mind, then I'm guilty as fucking charged. I'll freely admit that when I meet a woman I'm into, I picture in seconds what she looks like coming, how she sounds, how I want to send her soaring.

The trouble is, there's one woman I just can't go there with, even though lately my brain desperately wants to figure out how to drive her wild. It's been an epic battle, and I've had to keep her in a special drawer, sealed and locked, the key thrown away, because she is the definition of *hands off*.

Which sucks royally because she's about to make things even *harder* with the words that come out of her mouth.

CHAPTER 1

They say men have sex on the brain 99.99 percent of the time. You're not going to catch me trying to dispute that.

Why would I? It's pretty much dead-on accurate, especially when you consider the remaining 0.01 percent of brainpower is tirelessly dedicated to finding the remote.

In my case though—and I suppose, in my defense— sex is part of my job.

And so is schmoozing and signing autographs. Ergo, here I am at An Open Book, a cool bookstore on the Upper West Side. When this signing shindig started a few hours ago, a long line of fans snaked out the door. The event my network set up is almost over, so the line is winding down. The crowd has been fifty-five to forty-five in favor of the fairer sex, which is absolutely nothing I'm going to complain about, especially since my fans were pretty much all dudes several years ago.

Some still are. Like this guy.

"My favorite episode is based on that one," a squeaky-voiced, messy-haired, awkward teenager says, as he points to a panel that features Mister Orgasm rescuing a dozen busty beauties from a remote island where they'd been deprived of sex for far too long. The upshot? Only a cartoonish caped crusader could replenish their depleted stores of pleasure, which had dwindled to terrifyingly low levels.

I shudder at the thought of what those women must have gone through before the hero arrived to save the day.

"Yeah. That one does rock," I say, flashing the kid a quick grin and then nodding seriously. "Mister Orgasm did a great service for the ladies, didn't he?"

"Yes," the kid says, with wide, earnest eyes. "He helped them so much."

It's weird, because he's probably sixteen, and there's a part of me that thinks *why the fuck are you watching my raunchy TV show?* But on the other hand, I get it. When I was his age, I didn't have a clue about girls either. Which probably explains why I started drawing *The Adventures of Mister Orgasm*, the once online cartoon, now late-night television sensation, which includes the storyline about the aforementioned act of good citizenship performed by the titular hero.

Titular.

I said titular.

In my head.

Anyway, that had definitely been a popular episode, and one of the reasons my network packaged up some of my old strips into this graphic novel by yours truly, Nick Hammer. Special edition and all, like the embossed gold stamp on the cover says.

"Can you sign it to Ray?" he asks, and as I raise the black Sharpie, I catch a flash of gold out of the corner of my eye, then a hand in a pocket.

Oh, shit.

I think I know what the woman lined up behind Ray just did.

I finish signing and hand him the book. "Go forth and give pleasure, Ray," I tell him, as if it's a mantra. I knock fists with him, and he stares briefly at his hand afterward, as if he's been blessed by a master.

Of course he has.

"You have my word. I want to be a pleasure purveyor," Ray says solemnly as he clutches the book to his chest, reciting one of Mister Orgasm's famous lines.

Man, someday that dude is going to blow the minds of the ladies. He's got some serious determination. But not yet. Because, ya know, he's sixteen.

I turn my eyes to the next person in line, and I'm practically blindsided by the sheer amount of breast on display. It's pretty much enough to activate a full-on man trance, that glazed-eye, struck-stupid look that only tits can induce in a guy. I'm not immune to it, because . . . tits.

They are one of my favorite playgrounds.

But I've had some serious training in combating the condition. Part of my job is interacting with the public, and I can't just walk around slack-jawed, staring at chests. This woman is going to put my skills to the test though. She's wearing a scoop-neck white T-shirt. That's kryptonite for most men.

She leans forward, making sure I get a front-row seat. I cast my eyes around, hoping Serena, the very pregnant, perennially smiling, but oh-so-savvy PR woman who works with my show at Comedy Nation, will return quickly from yet another bathroom break. She's a pro at knowing when to hold the eager ladies at bay.

Look, I'm not complaining. I do not mind whatsoever that some of the show's viewers get a little frisky at events like this. It's all good. But I've got a feeling this one isn't supposed to be playing.

"Hey there," I say, giving a smile to Bleached Blonde. Interact. Engage. That's part of the job. Be the public face of the hit TV show currently crushing the mother-fucking competition in the eleven p.m. timeslot—and all the programs that run earlier in the night, too. That both thrills the head of the network, and drives him bat-shit crazy, but that's a story for later.

The woman brings her hand to her chest, trying a time-honored tactic to invoke the trance. I remain stoic. "I'm Samantha, and I love your show so much," she coos. "I read the profile of you in *Men's Health* the other week, too. I was so impressed with your devotion to your craft, as well as your body." The profile—'cause it's *Men's Health*—featured a shot of me working out. Then, because she's not subtle, she roams her gray eyes along my ink-covered arms, over my chest, and well, let's just call a spade a spade. She pretty much tries to mate with me via eye contact right here in the bookstore.

"Devotion is my middle name," I say with a smile, and push my glasses higher. She makes me edgy, and it's not the ample cleavage but rather what she did in line a few minutes ago in her pocket.

She bends closer, gliding the book across the table to me. "You can sign right here if you want," Samantha whispers, dragging her finger across her cleavage.

I grab the book with quick hands. "Thanks, but I've found the title page is an equally excellent location."

"You should leave your number on it," she adds, as I sign *Nick Hammer* and hand her the book.

"Funny thing, I don't actually know my number," I say with a harmless shrug. "Who can remember numbers anymore? Even our own?"

Where the hell is Serena? I hope she didn't give birth in the ladies' room.

Samantha giggles, then drags a long, candy pink nail across my signature. "*Hammer*," she says coyly, letting it roll around in her mouth. "Is that your real name, or is it a term of endearment about—"

No, no, *no*.

Abort.

Cannot go there. Will not play the Dirty Synonym game featuring my last name with Samantha, who's about to run those sharp nails down my arm.

"Oh, excuse me. Did you drop something?"

I straighten my shoulders when I hear a familiar voice —deadpan humor and pure innocence at the same time.

The blonde startles. "No," she says with a snarl, snapping at the questioner. "I didn't drop anything."

"Are you sure?" The tone is of complete and utter concern.

I can't help the grin that spreads across my face, because I know the woman behind the voice is up to something sneaky.

Harper Holiday.

Red hair. Blue eyes. Face of a sweet, sexy angel, body of a badass, ninja-warrior princess, and a mouth adept at pitch-perfect delivery of sarcasm. I'd play Dirty Synonyms, Dirty Antonyms . . . Dirty Anything with her.

Harper steps from behind the blonde in line and opens her palm. "Because I'm pretty sure this is your wedding ring," she says, a worried look in those bright blue eyes as she plucks a gold wedding band from her hand and offers it to the hungry blonde.

"That's not mine," the woman says defensively, all that flirty sweetness swiped clean from her voice.

Harper smacks her other hand against her forehead. "Oh, my bad. You put yours in your pocket a few minutes ago. Right there."

She points to the woman's right pocket, and sure enough, there's the outline of what looks to be a wedding band. That's exactly what I'd suspected she'd done in line. Stuffed it away. Probably had forgotten she was wearing it and then tried to hide it at the last minute.

The married woman's face goes pale.

Busted.

"This one," Harper continues, holding up the ring and letting it catch the light from the ceiling, "this is the one I keep handy for situations like this."

Samantha mutters *bitch* under her breath, turns on her heel, and marches away.

"Enjoy the book," Harper calls out, then looks to me, cocks her head, and shoots me an *I-just-saved-your-ass* grin. In her own imitation of the Mister Orgasm groupies, she says, "Nick Hammer. Is that your real name?"

Just like that, I hope Serena stays in the restroom for a lot longer.

CHAPTER 2

My real last name *is* Hammer.

I get asked that question all the time. Everyone thinks it's fake. Like it's a stage name, or pen name, or my stripper name from back in the days when I worked hard for the money.

Just kidding. I was never a stripper.

But I was lucky enough to land a kick-ass last name, and I'm doubly lucky because if I'd been a girl, my parents were going to name me Sunshine. Instead, my mom named her bakery Sunshine and her sons Wyatt and Nick. Our little sister came a few years after the bakery was born, so she dodged the hippy name too, but Josie definitely got the vibe. She's a free spirit.

I point at the ring Harper has in her hand. "Did you jet off to Vegas this weekend and marry Penn? Or wait. Was it Teller?"

"No. Criss Angel," she says, as she stuffs the ring inside a red purse so big it could provide safe harbor for refugees.

"Seriously, though. Why do you carry a wedding band around?"

"I could tell you, but then I'd be breaking Code 563 in the *Magician's Handbook of Secrecy*, which was written to keep mere mortals such as yourself in the dark."

I tap my chest and shake my head. "I beg your pardon. I'm not a mere mortal. 'Fess up."

She cups the side of her mouth and stage whispers, "It's fake. I picked it up so I could do a little sleight-of-hand trick at a party last weekend."

"Did the trick work?"

She nods, her lips curving in a grin. "Like a charm. Turned this into the Green Lantern's ring. The kid was in awe."

"As well he should be. By the way," I say, tipping my chin in the direction of the long-gone lady, "thank you. For a second there I was thinking maybe she had a magic bullet in her pocket."

Her eyes widened. "Has that happened?"

I nod, rolling my eyes. "Once. At a fan meet-and-greet."

"A fan rubbed one out in line?"

"Either that or was just priming the pump for later. But don't worry. I'm pretty psyched that you saved me from the sneak-off-the-wedding-band tactic, too. I think you might be a superhero."

"That's me. I swoop in out of nowhere and rescue unsuspecting men from married women with dangerous husbands who would want to crush the life-force out of wildly popular cartoonists. You'll probably want to take me out for a coffee when I tell you her husband is about ten feet tall, has arms the size of cannons, and wears brass knuckles. Saw him outside the bookstore before I came in."

"Does he lead an underground fight ring, too?"

She nods in mock seriousness. "Yes. He's Vicious. That's his fight name."

"I clearly owe you the coffee. Maybe even a slice of cake, just so you know how much I appreciate you saving me from Vicious."

"Don't tease me. Cake is my religion." She lowers her voice. "I was debating for the longest time whether to use the ring trick or to give her these," she says, dipping her hand into her bag and producing a pair of purple eyeglasses, "and suggesting she wear them to help her eyefuck you better."

I crack up at her choice of words. "Are they specially designed for that? If so, I'd really like to get a pair."

To use on you.

She nods again. "There's a shop in the East Village that sells them. They need to be special ordered, but I can hook you up," she says, then roots around in her bag. It's like Hermione's purse. Yes, I read all of *Harry Potter*. It's only the best story ever told.

She grabs a copy of my collection from inside her bag and sets it on the table. "Can you sign it to Helena?"

I shoot her a look when I see the receipt inside the book. She bought it here. "Harper, you didn't have to come here for me to sign a book. I would have given you one."

She winks. "Good to know I'm on the short-list. For now, I have a client who is secretly in love with you. So I'm giving her this as a gift."

"Tell Helena, Mister Orgasm says hello," I say as I sign it.

When I look up, Harper is wearing the purple glasses.

I blink.

Holy shit. She is red-hot in them. As a guy who wears glasses, I dig a chick in glasses, and I've never seen Harper wear them before. Not gonna lie—the sexy librarian fantasy is strong in this one. This one being me, and I'm thinking pencil skirt, tight white blouse enticingly unbuttoned, and Harper bending over a desk, ready to be spanked for mis-shelving some books.

She ogles me like the woman in line was doing, and whispers in a naughty tone, "Do they work, Nick?"

Absolutely, but you don't even need glasses for me to want to be eye-fucked by you. Also, I'm imagining what you look like in nothing but them.

Wait. Shit. No.

I smack the 99.99 percent of my brain that just thought that. Because Harper is my best friend's sister. And Spencer already promised he would shave off all my hair and dye my eyebrows if I ever touched her. Not that I'm scared of Spencer, I just really like my hair. It's light brown, thick, and—well, I'm just going to be honest here—I could totally do shampoo commercials. There. I said it.

But I also don't plan on acting on any of the damn fantasies I've had about Harper, even if the bent-over-the-kitchen-counter one is particularly potent lately. Though, that's not fair to the up-against-the-wall fantasy, is it?

Note to self: Bring the wall one back into rotation tonight.

But, back to her question about the glasses.

"They work like a charm," I tell her, repeating her words.

She takes them off and glances behind her. A few fans are left, tapping their feet, holding their books. "I've been commandeering your time. I should get out of here."

"Wait. I'm almost done. Want to grab that cup of coffee in fifteen minutes?" I ask, then quickly add, "As payment for your rescue services."

"Hmm. Is there anyplace in this city to get coffee?" She taps her chin, as if truly considering it.

I sigh heavily, playing along. "Good point. It *is* really hard to find coffee. It's not as if it's on every corner or anything."

She nods in understanding. "Usually you have to hunt for it, far and wide. It can take a few hours." She snaps her fingers. "Tell you what. Let me see what I can accomplish with a map. If I can find a cup of coffee within, say, a fifty-foot radius of the store, I'll text you the location."

"Ten-four."

She salutes me and spins on her heel, and I swear I don't watch her too intently as she weaves through the bookstore on her way out. Okay, fine. Maybe I do spend three or four seconds checking out her backside. Five seconds, tops. But, it's a spectacular ass, so it seems a shame not to enjoy the view.

Serena returns, parks herself next to me at the table, and for the next fifteen minutes I focus on my fans, signing and chatting, interacting and engaging.

When the event ends, I check for a text from Harper and am stoked to find one. I tap out a reply then help Serena straighten up. A straight shooter, she started working on my show a couple years ago, before it climbed high in the ratings. "You did good, sweetie. Sorry I was MIA for some of it," she says, twisting her curly black hair into a clip before she stands and scoops the Sharpies into her purse. She pats her belly. "I swear for a few minutes I thought I was going to have the baby in the bookstore bathroom."

"Funny, I'd been worried about the same thing. If you did, you would have named the baby after me, right?"

"No. If I had the baby in the bathroom, I was going to name it Sink," she says, then holds up her finger. "Oh, I almost forgot to tell you." That's how she always prefaces requests from the head of the network. "There's an event Gino wants you to be at on Thursday. It's just a little charity fundraiser schmooze at a bowling alley, but he wants all his home-grown stars there."

"Of course I'll be there," I say, grabbing my jacket. I mean, what other answer is there? Paranoid prick or not, Gino controls the time slots on the network, and he likes me to remember he handpicked my online strip to turn into an animated show a few years back when he was in the development division. I'm grateful as all hell that he gave me a shot, but he's strangely jealous, too, and I suspect it's because he created a show years ago that faded from the limelight quickly, and none of his efforts to craft another one of his own panned out.

"And you know the drill," she says as she zips up her purse and we wander through the shelves, heading for the exit.

I recite the rules. "Gino wants me to be charming, but not so charming that women hit on me instead of him. And I should be awesome at bowling if I'm on his team, and if not, I should throw the game so he wins. Because if I don't play his games, the greater the chance I'll get screwed in negotiations in a couple more weeks, since contract talks are at the end of this month."

She taps her finger to her nose. "Perfecto."

"It's almost as if I'm used to his completely mercurial personality."

She smiles. "That's our boss. You know he was used to being the center of attention 'til you came around. You're the full package, and it drives him crazy. But I really appreciate you doing these public events."

I glance around the bookstore, filled with customers, some of whom just bought my cartoon collection. I've been asked to go bowling with a TV executive, who is a crazy, capricious ass, but who signs my fat paycheck. My show is killing it. I'm raking in the money, and the praise, and I do very well with the ladies. There's something that they like about the scruff, ink, glasses, and hair, and the fact that my once-lanky frame is packed with toned, strong muscles.

Life is good.

"Serena, I assure you, it's not like attending a party is some hardship. The fact that the head of the network has some weird complex about me is the very definition of a first-world problem."

"No," she says sharply as we reach the front door of the bookstore. "You know what a true first-world problem is? The other day I went to Ben & Jerry's and got a pint to take home. I wanted two flavors. Coconut Seven Layer Bar for me, and Mango Sorbet for my hubby. But guess what?"

I hold a hand to my forehead like a fortuneteller. "They didn't have Coconut Seven Layer Bar."

"Worse," she says, slamming her hand onto my chest and practically toppling me into the new release shelves with her exuberance. "They forgot to put a sheet of wax paper between them to separate the flavors. The mango leaked into the coconut," she says with a pout.

I frown. "That's really terrible. I kind of wish I never knew such a horrific thing happened. I'm not sure I can get that image out of my head."

On that note, I say goodbye to Serena and head to Peace of Cake where Harper waves to me from a table in the back. She's reading my book.

Is it wrong that I wish she still had those glasses on?

But glasses or no glasses, she just does it for me.

CHAPTER 3

We share a piece of double chocolate cake.

I know how this looks.

Like a date.

But it's not. It's just that the slices here at this cake/coffee shop are huge. No way can you eat one all by yourself, unless you were born with two dessert compartments. I love dessert, but I only have one.

Besides, it's not like that between us. I've known Harper for what seems like forever, since I've been best friends with Spencer for that long. The three of us went to the same high school, but Harper is three years younger than me, so it's not like I was doing the left-hand shuffle to thoughts of her when I was a senior and she was a freshman. I'd never thought of her that way then.

Besides I'm right handed.

Anyway, now that we're both in our late twenties and living in New York City, we hang out from time to time. Maybe even more so since Spencer got engaged; he's much less available these days. Sometimes Harper and I go to the movies on weekends, and lately, sitting next to her in the theater is the definition of distracting.

Let's just be blunt here: Harper is not cheerleader hot. She's not Victoria's Secret hot.

She's quirky hot. Nerd hot. Video-gamer fantasy hot. She does kickboxing for workouts, she competes hard in our summer softball games, and she knows what house she'd be in at Hogwarts. She's a Hufflepuff, and yes, it turns me on that she didn't pick Ravenclaw or Gryffindor like everyone else usually does, but she chooses the house known for loyalty.

And she's a fucking magician. For a living. The chick pays her own bills performing sleight of hand and slipping the wool over people's eyes.

That's kind of the hottest profession ever—hotter than bartender, than model, than rock star. Maybe not hotter than sexy librarian, though.

I honestly didn't think these thoughts until a few months ago. Until the day last summer when she asked me to help her get even with her brother for something he did to her years ago. To exact her revenge, we pretended we were getting it on at softball practice.

I took off my shirt, she ran her hands down my chest, and the rest is history. The 99.99 percent of my brain started going there with her that day in Central Park.

Look, I'm a guy. It is *that* simple. We're not complicated, and anyone who tries to make us out to be complex is full of shit. That's not to say we aren't capable of advanced feelings, emotions, and all that jazz. But when it comes to women, it doesn't take much for the lightbulb to go on or off.

And the Harper switch went all the way on that day.

I do my best to focus on idle chit-chat with her, rather than cycling through what kind of lingerie she might be wearing, especially since I can see a hint of a black satiny strap at the edge of her V-neck sweater. I force myself not to imagine what the rest of that sexy garment looks like.

Too late. I'm picturing it now, seeing in my mind how the lace hugs her flesh, and that is one fine image. Thank you, brain, for never being afraid to go there. But now I need to zone in on the conversation.

I point at the cake we're working on. "Scale of one to ten. What would you give this cake?"

With her fork poised midair, she stares at the ceiling. "Rapture."

"I don't believe that's on the scale."

"I did say cake was a religion."

"Then I would think second coming would be fitting."

"*Coming.* You said coming," she says with a straight face.

"I say that a lot, actually." I lean back in the chair, keeping it casual.

"I know." She wiggles her eyebrows then whispers, "I was enjoying your book before you arrived. It's so dirty." She says it like this is a secret. Like she just learned for the very first time that my cartoon is a fiesta of naughtiness. "What I really want to know, Nick Hammer," she says, owning my name in a way that the blonde from the bookstore could never even come close to, "is where your inspiration comes from."

You don't even want to know, Harper.

I pretend to study the cake. "I think this cake might be laced with something."

She takes a bite and winks. "Yeah, deliciousness. That's what it's spiked with."

Fuck, see what I mean? She's too much. She makes it really hard not to think about what she'd be like in bed. She operates at this constant state of verbal banter that's flirting, but not quite flirting. The net effect? I'm a cat, and she's working the laser pointer. I'm chasing the red light, but I can't ever catch it. The fact that I'm single doesn't help. I have nothing whatsoever against one-night stands, but I'm less of a hookup guy and more of a serial monogamist, even though I've never fallen in love with anyone I've monogamied serially with, including the last woman, who's in Italy now, working on a book.

Ergo, I'm one hundred percent available, I'm absolutely interested in the woman sitting across from me, but no way can I have her.

I take a drink of my coffee, and she reaches for her hot chocolate. Since I can't spend the entire time staring at her lips on the mug, I look around. The shelves at the counter are full of fantastic-looking cakes, and a chalkboard menu lists mouth-watering flavors alongside the standard coffee options. Peace of Cake is packed. The wooden tables are nearly overflowing with your Upper West Side potpourri of people—moms, dads, and young kids, along with twenty-somethings and couples.

"So how many was it?" Harper nods in the direction of the bookstore.

"How many what? Books sold?"

She shakes her head. "How many times did you get hit on in there?"

I laugh, but don't answer her.

"C'mon," she presses, tapping the table. "A good-looking guy like you. The center of attention. It must have been, what . . . every other fan?"

My ears perk up at her description. Other parts do, too. But see, it's not like she says *good-looking guy* in this come-on way. She says it like it's some known fact. Which is why I can't figure her out. I have no clue if her mind swerved out of Friendshipville and into Naughty Thought Town that day in the park, too. "No, not every other fan," I say.

"But every *other* other fan?" she asks, and I laugh again at her word choice, as if every *other* other is now a thing.

"All I'm going to say is you were an excellent shield when I needed you." I snap my fingers. "Hey, I have an idea. I have this event in a couple days." I give her the details that Serena shared with me and fill her in on my boss's weird jealousy issues. "But Gino still wants me to go, so you should come with me."

"As a shield? So women won't hit on you?" she asks, taking another bite of the cake.

"They generally don't if you're there with a friend."

She gestures with her fork from her to me and back. "Am I supposed to pretend it's a date?" She says this like it's the craziest notion in the world, which tells me I need to stop entertaining any thoughts of Harper Holiday running her hands down my chest ever again. It's not like she needs to know I drew a picture of her O face a few weeks ago. What? Was that so wrong? It's what I do for a living. It's not that weird. Besides, I deleted the file. I was just messing around on the computer, I swear.

"Like Spencer and Charlotte pretended?" she adds, as if I could forget their ruse, especially since it worked out in its own way—their wedding is in two weeks.

"No, that'd be lame if we did the same thing," I say, digging into the chocolate for another bite. "That would be like if a romance writer used the same trope in the very next novel."

That skeptical eyebrow of hers pops back up. "How do you know about tropes?"

"I write a show." *Draw and write*, but you get the idea.

"Yours is an animated spoof of a dirty superhero. And yet you're *that* familiar with tropes in romance novels?"

"I dated a romance writer a few months ago."

"What was that like?"

"Um, it was like dating," I deadpan.

She rolls her eyes. "No. Did she want to practice with you?"

I laugh, loving her boldness in asking. "You mean the scenes, Harper?"

She nods as she takes another drink.

I nod, too. "She did."

"Did you?" she asks, curiosity dripping from her tone as she sets down her mug.

"Yeah."

"Wow. When you read her book was it like seeing your life exposed?"

"That one hasn't come out yet. It's next, I think."

"What happened to her?"

"It ended," I say with a shrug. I'm not upset about it. We had a good time for the few months we were together.

"Why?"

Because it was fun, nothing more. And because J. Cameron—that's her pen name—is obsessed with her work. Fiction is her world. That, and she took off for Italy. "She went to Florence. I think her next book is set there," I tell Harper.

"And I'll be looking forward to reading the one that you"—she sketches air quotes—"*helped* her research."

"Maybe I'll never tell you her pen name."

"I'll get it out of you," she says, as I take a drink of my coffee. "Does she write those cheesy sex scenes where the guy tells the girl he loves her while he's inside her, or right after?"

I nearly spit out my drink from laughing. "Gee. I really don't know how cheesy the scenes get. I don't read romance novels."

"Maybe you should. Some are pretty hot," she says with a knowing glint in her eyes, before she steers back to the matter at hand. "So the event. Let me get this straight. You want me to be your wing-woman to help you with your boss, who's such a douche he can't handle that you're manlier than he is, and because you attract the ladies like a tomcat does the pussycats in heat?"

Ah hell, I wish she wouldn't use that word in such close proximity to the factory of dirty thoughts inside my skull. "I wouldn't say that's true."

Harper points in the direction of the store. "Judging from how badly that woman at the store wanted to *Hop on Pop*, I'm guessing you get hit on all the time," she says, and I would sound like a completely cocky bastard if I told the truth. Yes. It does happen a fuck-ton, but it wasn't always like today. With success comes more interest from women, and more interest not just in me, but in my assets. I'm referring to the green ones, not the ones made of flesh and bone, but they like those, too.

I give a one-shouldered shrug by way of an answer.

She smiles. "I'll go, Nick. And then when I need something, I'll call in a favor from you. Deal?"

"Works for me."

She reaches for the cake, dips her finger in the frosting, and brings it to her mouth, licking it off. Oh God. Oh hell. Why does she torture me like this? Thank fuck I'm sitting down. She does not need to know she is one half of the ingredients in my instant hard-on mix these days—just add an unintentional sexy-vixen comment that I don't know how to read, and it's like a pop-up shop.

"Look! It's Anna the Amazing!"

Harper snaps her head in the direction of the young voice calling out her stage name. She doesn't use her real name with the kids' parties she does. To them, she's Anna the Amazing Magician. She says it's easier to maintain a Facebook profile with her college friends if she doesn't tie her work to it.

A huge smile spreads across her face, and she jumps out of her chair, bends down, and says hello to a girl with wild brown hair and a spray of freckles across her nose. Harper places her index finger on her lips and whispers, "Close your eyes."

The little girl does as asked, and when Harper tells her to open her eyes two seconds later, she removes a carefully folded up dollar bill from behind the kid's ear. Her jaw drops. Spoiler alert: Harper took the bill from her pocket when the girl's eyes were closed. "But wait," Harper says, in her magician's voice, and then her left hand sweeps behind the girl's other ear, and she's got another bill, this one folded like a paper airplane.

Okay, I have no clue how she pulled off that one.

"You're amazing," the kid says in awe then looks up at her dad, and Harper's eyes follow suit. The dad is tall and sturdy, and I have a suspicion that if he's single, which the lack of a ring says he might be, he's scoring regularly. No, I don't find him attractive, because I don't find dudes attractive. You can just tell someone is good-looking when he's a ringer for Chris Hemsworth. Harper stands, and wobbles. She reaches out her hand, steadying herself at our table.

"Haaa . . . huuu . . . hooo . . ."

What the—?

I sit up straighter, my curiosity piqued, as Harper attempts to speak a new language.

Oh wait, she's just failing at saying *hi*.

"Hi, Anna," the guy says, then lowers his voice and whispers like her real name is their special secret, "Harper."

And it sure sounds as if he enjoys saying her name. Shit. The Hemsworth ringer likes her.

Harper opens her mouth again. Something that sounds like *Hiiiyyyyyaaaaa, Simon* comes out of those pretty lips.

"How are you? This place is great, isn't it?" he asks.

I think, but I can't be certain, that she says *yes*. Or it could be *yesh*, given her sudden fit of I-can't-remember-a-fucking-word-of-the-English-language.

"Hayden is so excited for her party in three weeks. She's counting down, and she's still talking about the tricks you did at Carly's fifth birthday last month."

Harper turns her attention back to Hayden. "You had a good time, didn't you? Did you like it when I guessed your secret card? Or maybe when I was able to levitate?" she asks, and her speech has completely returned to normal when she talks to the child.

"I loved the secret card! Yes! I want that at my party!"

"You will get all the good stuff."

Simon glances in my direction then clears his throat. He gives me a quick guy wave, and Harper blushes and says, "Oh, this is my friend, Mister Orgasm."

Silence. It just descends on the whole joint, like someone shattered a glass and we all have to stare at the wreckage on the floor.

It is a certified train wreck watching Harper talk to this guy. It's horrifying and awesome at the same time.

She brings her hand to her mouth then pinches the bridge of her nose as her face turns red. Simon laughs at her faux pas, and Hayden just giggles at the scene, maybe because she finds it funny to see Harper turn the shade of a fire engine. I'm ready to grab a bucket of popcorn and keep watching this show, because it is fascinating that Harper has no clue how to interact with a guy who likes her.

"I mean Nick," she squeaks out. "This is Nick. I saved him from Vicious."

Simon arches a brow. "Vicious?"

I stand up. "Scary dude who heads up an underground fight club. Or maybe it's a biker gang these days. Either way, he was terrifying," I say with a shudder, then extend a hand. "Nick Hammer. Nice to meet you."

"Simon," he says. "And this is my daughter, Hayden."

I say hello to his kid.

Harper hooks her thumb in my direction as she looks at Simon. Speech seems to have returned to nearly normal levels. "He's my brother's best friend. Which means he's totally off-limits."

Ahh . . .

The plot thickens. Harper really likes this guy, since she's letting him know she's available.

"Good to know," Simon says with a smile. "I'll give you a call and maybe we can get together and prep for the party. Talk about the tricks and whatnot."

After an awkward goodbye, Simon takes his daughter to the only free table, on the opposite side of the shop. I stare at Harper pointedly. I can't resist. I have to poke at this. Besides, it'll help me get my mind off the thought of her naked. "You like him, don't you?"

She sighs dejectedly. "Is it that obvious?" she whispers.

"No," I say gently. "I mean, relatively speaking. It's not like you were holding up a sign that said 'I like you so much.'"

She lowers her head. "Ugh. I am such a—"

But she doesn't finish the sentence, because the parade of mortification launches an encore as Harper drops her forehead into her palm, which causes her elbow to slide on the table, which sends her hot chocolate on a fast track for . . .

Me.

And yup.

Three seconds later, my favorite faded gray T-shirt with Hobbes on it is covered in lukewarm milk and the dregs of whipped cream.

"Shoot me now," she groans as she rests her cheek on the table and mimes pulling a trigger.

"Good thing it's laundry day," I say, and I'm thinking *there has got to be a storyline somewhere in this where Mister Orgasm saves the day.*

She lifts her face. "Are you really sure you want me to go anywhere with you?"

I give an exaggerated nod and a tug at my hot-chocolate-stained T-shirt. "You pretty much just sealed the deal on being my sidekick, Princess Awkward."

CHAPTER 4

Harper swings her right arm behind her, arcs it in front, then launches the nine-pound, flaming-pink neon ball. In a glorious straight line, the ball speeds down the lane, which illuminates with flashing silver lights, and I hold my breath until it smacks three pins.

I hate to do this, but I silently send a prayer that the damage ends there.

Only it doesn't. Two more pins wobble and then surrender.

I cross my fingers that the others don't give in.

No such luck. Three more topple then one of those pins clobbers the final pair.

And they all fall down.

Harper thrusts her arms high and punches the air with a fist. Her second strike of the night, along with a spare. Shit, shit, shit. My team is dangerously close to beating Gino's. I sneak a look at him. His arms are crossed, his lips form a ruler-thin line, and his eyes are nearly slits. Perched on the orange plastic chair by the scoring screen, he glares at me briefly, as if it's all my fault for letting her nab a strike. Serena appears, and he smiles brightly as she drops a hand to his shoulder and whispers something to him. Probably reminding him to say cheese for the company photographer, since they're going to post these pics on the Comedy Nation Instagram feed.

I turn my focus back to Harper. Her blue eyes are lit up and sparkling, and she's on some kind of high. She heads toward me at the ball return. It should not surprise me that she can bowl like a champion. I bet she kicks ass at pool, too. Probably nails the bullseye in darts every time. Hell, she can likely change a tire without any help.

Now, there's a helluva hot image.

Ah, fuck.

Bad idea to speculate on her auto-repair skills, because as she struts toward me, I'm mentally drawing a picture of Harper as a hot redheaded mechanic wearing Daisy Dukes and a wife-beater tank stretched over her chest, sexy streaks of grease on her legs. I don't know why, but women are required to wear Daisy Dukes in any chick-auto-mechanic fantasies. It's part of the guy rule book, and you cannot deviate from it. Not that I'd want to. It exists for a reason—it's hot as sin.

"Did you see that?" she asks, beaming as she throws her arms around me to celebrate, and I swat away my out-of-nowhere fantasy so that it's not completely obvious that I'm getting a hard-on for her right now. But really, she'd look so fucking good working on my engine.

The ironic thing is I don't even have a car.

"You didn't tell me you bowled a three hundred," I whisper out of the side of my mouth as I reciprocate, wrapping her in my arms, too. Because . . . well, she started it, and she feels fantastic all snug against me like this.

"Nah, I'm not that good," she says as we separate, snuffing that short-lived moment.

I give her a side-eye stare as she peers into the machine that chugs and cranks up bowling balls from the lanes. "That was your second strike of the night," I remind her. "You're a ringer. You kept that little fact to yourself."

She shrugs playfully. "A girl's gotta have some secrets."

And, hell, do I want to know hers.

"That may be true," I say, then lower my voice even more, though it would be hard for anyone to hear a word above the Go-Go's tune that's blasting on the bowling alley's sound system. "But if you keep killing it, I might as well be a dead man in negotiations."

She claps her hand over her mouth. "Oh, shoot," she whispers through her fingers. "Are we that close to winning? I've been so busy being your Velcro I nearly forgot."

She raises her eyes the slightest bit to a tiny brunette parked next to Gino. Her name is Franci. She works in promotions, and she's wearing a crotch-length skirt, as she usually does. When I first arrived tonight, she sauntered over to me, then quickly turned the other way when she spotted Harper by my side. Now, she's making the moves on Gino, which is perfect, since he'll think he beat me in that regard, too. But little does he know I'm having the last laugh. A few months ago, Franci tried to find me on Tinder. Turns out she found my brother Wyatt instead, since I'm not on Tinder. Wyatt's a carpenter turned big-time contractor, with a business that's growing like crazy, and apparently she was quite pleased with his tools. Or so he told me. I told him that was TMI, but TMI pretty much describes my brother.

As the machine spits up the ball, I grab it for Harper, bring it to my chest, and wrap my hands around it. I drop my voice. "I hate to ask, but I need you to throw the next frame."

Her shoulders sag. "Really?"

"He's going to go crazy if we crush him. He wants his team to win and raise the most money for charity. He wants his picture to be the one they send to all the trade mags."

She sighs heavily. "Throw it like the 1919 World Series?"

I nod. "Do it just like the White Sox did."

She frowns. "This pains me."

"I know. But drinks for life . . . and cake for life, too, 'kay?"

She nods resolutely and reaches for the ball in my arms. For the briefest of moments, her fingers graze the fabric of my shirt, a casual button-down that's untucked and rolled up at the cuffs. Maybe I'm imagining things, but it feels like her fingers linger on my pecs longer than they need to.

I do what any sane man would do—clutch the ball tighter so she'll have to move in closer. She does, and yes, her fingertips are definitely touching me.

Good thing I can hold this ball for a very long time. All night long, if I'm lucky.

"Nick," she whispers in a plea, and it sounds so damn good, the way her voice goes feathery when she says my name. Instantly I hear that inflection, and all that follows it, in my imagination—*more, harder, please, now, yes, yes, yes.* "May I have the ball, please? It's the only way I can fuck up the next turn."

I blink and hand it over to her.

I lean against the ball machine and watch as she heads to her spot, brings the ball to her chest, and pistons her arm behind her. She takes a few fast steps before releasing it. I tense because she looks just as polished as she did when she nailed that strike.

But the girl is good. Her arm swings the slightest bit wider, and the pink orb rolls straight for a second, then veers, and soon acquaints itself with the gutter.

I utter a silent *yes,* even though it's a damn shame to ask her to blow the game. I have no doubt she'd rack up even more points, and look spectacular doing so. She is a sight to behold tonight, in her dark blue skinny jeans, a purple-and-green argyle sweater, and white-and-red bowling shoes. Her hair is pinned up in a twist, all those silky red strands piled high on her head. Her neck is long and elegant, and I've got this feeling her skin tastes spectacular there, and everywhere. I wonder if she'd enjoy soft, lingering kisses along her neck, across the column of her throat, up to her ear. Whether she'd moan, and sigh, and lean into me, her body asking for more.

I decide she'd love it because I'd kiss her so damn well, she'd melt into me. She'd want so much more, and I'd give it to her, making her feel good in every fucking way, driving her wild. I'd lick a path between her tits, down her belly to the button on those jeans. One fast flick, and they'd be undone. I'd have them off her in less than two seconds, my nimble fingers tugging her panties down . . .

She turns and snaps in an *aw shucks* gesture, and I shut down the very vivid, very arousing, very promising fantasy faster than you can clear the history on your Internet browser. She wanders back to me, looking appropriately forlorn. Gino smiles, a slick grin that continues as his team goes on to win, thanks to Harper blowing the final few frames. The photographer he hired snaps a shot of Gino, with his curly hair, dark eyes, and broad frame as he ambles toward me.

"Nice game, Nick," he says, all slick and faux-friendly. "Better luck next time." He punches my shoulder in an *old buddy, old pal* move. "But hey, at least you're good at writing the shows."

"Let's just hope I write better than I bowl," I say, serving it right up to him the way he likes it, with a side dish of suck-up.

He laughs loudly, like a gorilla. Then Gino notices Harper a few feet away, checking her phone in her purse.

"Ah, redheads," he says, as if he's sucking a piece of meat off the bone. "They're fiery and feisty."

Involuntarily, I clench my fists. But before I can say, "Shut up, you ape," Harper spins around and flashes us both her gorgeous smile. It's pure magic. It's what woos the kids and wins the hearts of the parents who book her months out for the parties. It's wide, charismatic, and totally stunning.

"Well, hello there. You played a very good game," Gino says, extending his hand. She shakes it, and I make a mental note to remind her to wash her hands thoroughly when we leave. Maybe even use hand sanitizer a few times. Fuck, the way he grips her hand, we're going to need a full decontamination chamber here.

"Thank you so much. But honestly, you're just so fantastic," she says to him, an adoring look in her eyes. "Quite a tenacious competitor."

I could kiss her for this.

"Oh, you flatter me," he says, waving a hand.

"I assure you, it's not flattery when someone rocks the lanes like you do," she says, then gives a sexy little jut of her shoulder.

And that's the money shot, folks. Gino is eating out of the palm of her hand. He turns to me and hooks his thumb at Harper. "I like her, Hammer. She's a keeper."

"She definitely is," I second.

When we leave, she grabs my arm and squeezes my bicep.

My arms are strong. That's not me being conceited. They really are, courtesy of my devotion to exercise and perhaps my addiction to the benefits it reaps. Her hand curls over my left arm, and yup, the hours at the gym are worth it right now. "Was I obsequious enough?"

"Like you have a master's degree in it."

She wiggles her eyebrows as we pass the vending machine on the way to the shoe counter. She gives another squeeze. "By the way, nice arms."

Then she lets go, and I'm tempted to stop at the machine, buy a crackerjack box, and hunt for a decoder ring at the bottom. Something to decipher what the hell she means with these half-flirting, half-not remarks. Was "nice arms" a compliment, or just a general observation? Did it mean she wanted to run her fingernails along them as I braced myself above her, or that she thought I could be useful for, say, lifting a heavy coffee table in her apartment?

She practically skips ahead of me to the counter. "Don't forget, you owe me a game now, too, Nick Hammer. I want a rematch with you."

"You're on," I say, because at least *rematch* means *more*, and that's what I want most.

She bends to unlace her shoes, and when she stands, she slaps them on the counter. "Oh hey," she says, and her face lights up.

"Harper Holiday!" The guy behind the counter clearly knows her. He's got dark hair, straight teeth, and brown eyes that he can't take off Harper. Christ, is there any man in Manhattan who doesn't want her?

"Hey, Jason, how are you? I haven't seen you since—"

"Senior year," he supplies with a smile, as he takes the shoes.

"This is my friend, Nick," she says and squeezes my arm again. "He went to Carlton Prep, too. But he was a senior when we were freshman."

"Hey, man. I remember you. You were always drawing comics, hunched over a notebook," he says with a grin as he hands me my Chucks.

"That's me," I say, and I hope he leaves it at that. Not that I hated high school. Not by any stretch, 'cause I'm just not a hater. And honestly, being the quiet guy was not the worst fate. I had plenty of friends. But I was completely a cipher when it came to girls.

"Your shit was good," he adds, and I straighten my shoulders and tell him thanks. This guy isn't so bad after all.

"I had no idea you worked here," Harper says.

He holds out his hands and gestures around. "All the time. This is my place. My little patch of land."

"No kidding! You run Neon Lanes?" she asks, sounding thoroughly impressed as she slips on the pair of short boots he's handed her, and I finish lacing my shoes.

"Own and operate." He taps the counter. "I do a little bit of everything. Be sure to say hi next time you're here. And hey, are you on Facebook?"

"I am."

"Look me up. Friend me. Let's catch up," he says.

As we walk away, I stare at her. "You do realize he likes you?"

"What?" she asks, like I've just told her monkeys live on Jupiter.

"Yes. He likes you."

"You're crazy," she says, shaking her head.

"You're a trip, Harper. You have no clue sometimes. It's fucking adorable," I tell her, and then, because we came as friends and we're leaving as friends, but in case any of these other assholes who want her might be watching, I drape an arm around her.

"Seriously, Nick. Why do you say that?"

I tug her closer, and she goes with it, letting me. "Princess Clueless, you're about to get an education in all the things you're oblivious to."

CHAPTER 5

We grab two stools at Speakeasy, a kick-ass spot in Midtown. The bartender, Julia, slides us two coasters and takes our order.

Julia's married to the guy who owns the law firm I use for all my contracts. That's Clay Nichols. He runs the shop, and is pretty much Manhattan's most fearless entertainment lawyer. His cousin Tyler joined him recently. Tyler's a beast, too, and handles the day-to-day for me. He's absolutely the guy I want having to deal with Gino.

Julia pours me an Imperial Stout and then mixes the drink Harper ordered, which is made with tequila and lemon soda.

"And one Long-Distance Lover for your friend, coming right up," she says with a wink to us both, as I give her my credit card.

Julia shakes her head, sliding the plastic back to me. "Your money's no good here, handsome."

"Please. I insist," I say, trying again.

She stares me down. "As if you can pull the whole *I insist* act with me. It's a rule. No client of Nichols and Nichols shall ever pay for his libation. Now, enjoy your drink with your pretty redheaded friend," she says, then hands Harper the cocktail.

"Hope you enjoy it. By the way, love your hair," she says, and it's funny because Julia's redhead comment doesn't bother me—she means it as a compliment, since her hair is the same shade, while Gino meant it in a douchey Neanderthal way. Kind of like how he means everything.

"Thank you," Harper says, running her hand along her locks. She let her hair down when we left the bowling alley. "Same for you."

"It's true what they say. Redheads have more fun. So be sure to have fun," she says, then presses her hand to Harper's arm before she heads off to serve a new group of customers.

Harper looks at me, surprise in her eyes. "She's quite friendly." She brings the drink to her lips, and takes a long sip. Her eyes widen and she points to the glass as she swallows. "She makes good drinks, too. This is amazing."

"She's not an award-winning bartender for nothing. They have the best drinks at Speakeasy. Just don't tell your brother we're here," I joke, since Spencer and Charlotte own three bars in Manhattan.

She pretends to zip her lips. "Our secret is safe with me," she whispers, and as soon as those words ghost past her lips, I find myself wondering if we'll ever have other secrets, like about the things we crave, the things that drive us wild, that turn us on in the dark, and if hers would match mine.

"By the way, did I do okay as your shield tonight?"

"You were the best," I tell her, then I take a long swallow of my drink. Damn, the beers here are spectacular, too.

"What are you going to do the next time, and the next time? The hits come pretty relentlessly from the ladies. It's like rapid-fire interest."

"Hey," I say, stopping her as I place a hand on her knee. "Pot. Kettle."

She arches an eyebrow. "How so?"

"From Simon to Jason, you certainly seem to have the men lining up for you."

She shakes her head and shoots me the universal look for *what have you been smoking?* She follows it with, "What on earth are you talking about?"

I stare at her. "Seriously?"

"Seriously, what?"

I hold up a hand like a stop sign. "You are aware that Jason has a thing for you? Like I told you at the bowling alley. And Simon the Hemsworth-look-alike dad does, too."

She narrows her eyes. "I don't think so."

I nod emphatically. "I *know* so."

She shakes her head, just as certainly. "Nope."

"Oh yes, Princess Denial. Jason likes you. It was obvious."

"No, *this* is obvious," Harper says, holding up her left hand, bending her thumb in half, then pretending to magically remove the tip of her thumb, only so badly it's clear how she does it.

"Wait. So you didn't really pull off your thumb?"

She holds up all ten fingers. "No! Astonishing feat, isn't it? I still have them all."

"And it's equally astonishing that you don't realize Jason 'let me friend you on Facebook' ex-classmate likes you."

She grabs her drink, shrugs, and knocks some back.

It's then that I realize Harper's bafflement over the opposite sex goes both ways. She doesn't know how to act around guys who like her, and she has no idea when they're into her either.

Selfishly, this is kind of an awesome discovery because it means I have carte blanche to continue thinking about her naked, beneath me, over me, coming for me, and she won't have a clue. Considering I think about her naked an inordinate amount of time—like, for instance, two seconds ago my mind wandered to wondering what color her panties were—this is a very good thing.

Especially since the natural next step is to daydream about stripping her of the pale pink panties I've decided she's wearing.

But I care about Harper, and I can tell this little lack of fluency in all things men is going to become a big problem for her at some point. Seeing as I'm all about helping the ladies, I give it to her straight. "First, yes, Jason is into you. Second, Simon is too. And I'm willing to bet my left hand that Simon has already texted you since the other day when you doused me in hot chocolate."

That earns me a small, contrite smile. "Did you get it out of your shirt?"

"Haven't done laundry yet. Ran out of detergent."

"They have stores for that."

"Yes. They do. But don't think you can derail me." I hold up my left hand. "And don't let the fact that I offered my non-drawing hand as stakes make you think I'm not one hundred percent confident that Simon let's-talk-about-the-party texted you. I'm really attached to both hands."

"Fine," she says, with a huff, like it costs her something. "He texted me earlier today."

"I amaze myself. What did he say?"

She reaches into her purse, finds her phone, and shows the text to me.

Hey there. Hope you're having a great week. Would love to get together and talk about the party. Coffee sometime?

"Case. Closed."

"How does that prove anything?"

"Okay. Let me ask you something. Do you regularly need to get together with parents and talk about the parties you're doing?"

"Not that often," she says, answering quickly.

"Could you, for instance, handle the plans for little Hayden's fifth birthday on the phone?"

"Sure."

I slap a palm on the counter. "The guy wants to see you in person because he likes to *see* you." I point to my eyes then to her. "He likes looking at you."

"Ohhhhhhhh," she says as my meaning registers. It's fascinating, like watching a video of one of those baby foals learning to stand for the first time. She brings her fingers to her forehead, and mimes an explosion. "Mind. Blown."

Wait 'til she sees what other mystical insights into the male mind—if you can even call it that—I can perform. "Let's put this to another test. Got Facebook on that phone?"

"Of course."

"Open it up," I say, making a rolling gesture with my hand.

She clicks on the blue icon. "Okay, what am I looking for?"

"New friend request. Jason from the bowling alley. I guarantee it's there."

She scrolls down the screen and blinks in surprise. "Can you do this with lottery numbers, too?"

I stab my finger at the phone, ignoring her cute little snark. "The dude wants to connect with you because . . ." I let my voice trail off and make sure she's looking me in the eyes, as I finish, "he wants to *connect* with you."

"Because I heard the next Powerball is going to be huge—"

I cut her off. "What did you say to Simon when you wrote back?"

She sighs, shakes her head, and screws up the corner of her mouth. She waits a moment before she speaks, like she's trying to figure out what to say, maybe hunting for her next quip. But the words she picks are simple. "That's the thing, Nick."

This time there's no sarcasm, no teasing, nothing unclear in her tone. It's just earnest and nervous. "What's the thing?" I ask gently.

"I don't know what to say to him," she says, with a one-shouldered shrug. "I can stick a pencil in my nose and make it appear to come out of the side of my head much easier than I can figure out what to write."

"Wait. You can stick a pencil in your nose?"

She nods in excitement. "Want to see?"

I kind of do, in a sort of sick-fascination way. But not now. "Another time, unless it's a Blackwing."

"What's that?"

"It's only my favorite type of pencil in the entire world. But let's focus on one thing at a time. Let me walk you through this. You say: *Sure, that sounds great. How about Friday at five p.m.*?"

She shudders. "Too hard."

"To say that?"

She inhales deeply, like she's steeling herself to say something tough. "Okay, look. There's no pretending with you. You've already seen what happens when I like someone. I can't talk. I can't speak. If I can manage words, they're ridiculously inappropriate ones. Even if I texted him, I wouldn't know how to act on Friday at five p.m."

Damn, the way she says that is so sweet and so sad at the same time, and I half feel sorry for her, and half want to tell her she's so fucking cool it doesn't matter. But it *does* matter. Because if she can't get past her inability to speak around guys she likes, life might be lonely.

I move my stool closer. "But you understand women. You knew what that woman was up to at the bookstore."

She rolls her eyes. "Vicious's wife wasn't exactly subtle. But yes, I can understand my native language. It's men that vex me."

"You honestly and truly don't know what to say or do with a guy?" I ask softly.

She levels her gaze at me. "I'm a magician, Nick. I go to kids' parties. I work with moms. I never meet men. Simon is the exception because he's a single dad, and that's rare. I don't know the first thing about the mating and dating rituals of the American male. I'm nearly twenty-six years old, and touching your arms to prank my brother in Central Park last summer was the most action I've gotten in ages."

I want to preen and offer her my arms to touch again, because my ego is keying in on the part about me. Then it hits me. *Most action she's gotten in ages?*

But before she can elaborate on the state of her sexual satisfaction, or current lack thereof, her blue eyes show a hint of sadness, and she looks away.

"It was?" I ask quietly, trying to digest the enormity of that kind of drought. *Sounds like hell.*

She looks back at me and shrugs, almost in defeat. Her expression seems resigned, as if she's accepted the inevitable. "Yep," she says with a rueful smile. "That's the truth, the whole truth, and nothing but the truth."

"You haven't been with anyone, in any way, in a long time?"

"I'm quite close to my iPhone, and I'm kind of amazingly intimate with my pillow. Don't tell anyone. But yes, I've been single in the city since I moved back after college." She sighs deeply, then squares her shoulders. "But it is what it is, Nick. Being a magician is not that conducive to dating. It's a trade-off I have to accept."

"Why does the job hold you back?"

She holds up her fingers and counts off. "First, whenever I do meet new people, usually the first thing they want is for me to show them tricks. They see a magician, not a woman," she says, keeping her chin raised, even though there's an undercurrent to those words. "Second, even though I do a few corporate events from time to time, the vast majority of the people I interact with are moms and kids. And third, the reality of my job is that I spend a lot of time alone. In front of a mirror. Practicing tricks," she says, punctuating each phrase with a pause. "If you want to know why I could barely speak the other day, there you go."

Something clicks. Harper is fantastically sarcastic, something I love, since it's a second language for me. But I bet *this* issue—the solitary nature of her life—is why her sarcasm is so finely tuned. It's a protective armor, shielding her. She uses it regularly, giving it a thorough workout each day to guard a lonesome heart.

"That's kind of a bummer," I say, because it's rough when the job you love hinders you. I'm lucky to be in the entertainment business. I meet women all the time. But if I were spending all my days at home drawing, like I did in high school, I'd probably be better acquainted with the Saturday night TV schedule. As it is, I don't have a clue what's on, and I vastly prefer that my career has a social side to it, since, well, I like people.

"It's fine," she says, waving a hand as if she's making all her solitude disappear in a poof. "I love what I do for a living. If my job makes it harder for me to date, that's just the price I have to pay."

"But why does it have to be that way? Why does one have to exclude the other? I don't think you have to be lonely."

"I didn't say I was lonely," she corrects, but her tone is defensive. Then she brightens her smile. "But hey, I get to have my magic wand in exchange for a meaningful connection with the opposite sex."

"Depends what kind of magic wand you mean," I tease.

She laughs, and stage whispers, "Maybe that is what I meant."

Whoa. Did she make a dirty comment again? And just like that, I'm wondering what exactly she does alone in her apartment late at night. "How many speeds does this magic wand have?"

"Fifty," she says, wiggling her eyebrows. "And there are worse things than coming home and curling up with a deck of cards and a *very powerful* magic wand, right? Especially now that I have the memory of your guns to get me through. And trust me, it's a really good memory."

My throat goes dry. My bones heat up. This girl and her innuendos will kill the last remaining non-sex-focused brain cells. I try to fashion a reply, but my brain is in visual-only mode, picturing Harper and her *very powerful* magic wand.

"I have an idea," she says, in an inviting whisper, and I swear my dick springs to attention faster than it ever fucking has before. She just talked about my arms; clearly she's got big plans for me to end her drought. She wants more than fifty speeds, and I can deliver that, no problem.

Yes, Harper, you can totally ride me, and I will give you ten thousand orgasms before I even have one. Because I am that kind of lover. I am generous and giving, and I would absolutely love to introduce you to my tongue so I can do things to you that will turn your world inside out and leave you begging for more. How's that for an answer?

Evidently, I've momentarily forgotten her off-limits status, because the mere prospect of Harper's idea is already driving me wild with possibilities, and she hasn't even asked yet. But she's going to. She's absolutely going to ask me to give her some much-needed action, and the only response to that is *My place or yours?*

"Go on."

"Well, you know how you kind of owe me?"

Fuck, yeah. I'm more than ready to pay my debts. Let's start payback with you riding my face, shall we?

"I owe you twice, I believe," I say, because I don't want her to forget all that I'm willing to do in this quest. "Once for you saving me from the fan with claws and her fire-breathing dragon of a husband, and again for you making my life easier with my boss tonight."

Nice math, Hammer. You just scored two turns on the merry-go-round of the girl you're lusting after.

"Great then," she says, with a wide smile that spreads across her gorgeous face. "So you're game?"

Bring it on. "Absolutely."

She claps once. "You'll be my tutor and give me lessons in dating?"

CHAPTER 6

Okayyyy. Let's just slam on the brakes while I reroute myself. Because my brain was barreling in one direction, and hers was veering in another. Not gonna lie. I'd been furiously plotting whose home is closer, and whether a cab, Uber, or quick jog—make that sprint—would get us there faster.

Since jetpacks aren't an option.

My phone buzzes. I grab it and open my messages, hoping it'll help me redirect all the blood that's flowing in one direction only.

I'm bored. Charlotte's out with Kristen, and there's nothing good on TV. Up for a drink?

Wow. That worked. Never met a boner killer as effective as a text from the brother of the girl you want to screw. But Spencer doesn't need me to answer right away, so I ignore him, turning the volume off on my phone and sliding it into my pocket.

"You want me to teach you how to date?"

She nods and smiles. "You're good at this. You know women. You can read men. You understand all the things I find completely confounding."

"You want me to be your Cyrano?"

"You don't have to come on dates with me and whisper from the bushes, but considering wanna-see-a-pencil-in-my-nose is my go-to opening line, and that I don't even know what to write back to Simon, I think we can both agree I need a little bit of help," she says, holding up her thumb and forefinger to show a sliver of space as she makes fun of herself.

I glance up at the ceiling, weighing her request. On the one hand, I can't let her fumble through New York City so completely unequipped for conversation. On the other hand, she's Spencer's sister.

"I know it's an odd request," she says, fidgeting with her napkin, her words with a touch of worry to them. "But it shouldn't be too weird, right? Since I know I'm not your type."

Whoa. I frown in confusion. "What?"

"Well, you usually date older women, right?"

And the truth is . . . she's right. Maybe not usually, and certainly not all the time, but J. Cameron was ten years older, and the woman I dated before that was an entertainment executive in her mid-thirties, and as a sophomore in college I went out with a senior. Come to think of it, the woman who took my V-card was five years older than me.

Hello, pattern.

Fine. Evidently, I've been known to appreciate not only women my age, but those who are fine wine, too. Let me just say, though, one of the best ways to learn what women like in bed is to date older women. Those ladies know how to communicate. They teach you, tell you to go faster, harder, slower, softer, there, right, yes, yes, right fucking there.

Maybe Harper's right, but I want to tell her that just because I've dated older women doesn't mean I don't like her. There's no point saying that, though, since she doesn't feel the same. If she did, she'd be tongue-tied and twisted with me like she was with Simon.

And shit. That reality check slams into me like a piano dropped from the sky. Harper may be off-limits, but I still want her to want me. She doesn't though. Instead, she wants me to help her. I straighten my shoulders and focus on that consolation prize.

"And Nick," she continues, softening her voice, stripping away that layer of humor she wields so well, "there's no one else I can turn to. I can't ask one of my girlfriends for help, because they'll all just tell me I'm fine and fabulous. But is this too strange a thing to ask?" Her voice rises, as if she's anxious for my answer. That mix of nerves and hopefulness in her question reinforces my hunch that her request isn't about how to get laid or how to land a hot date. It's about how to connect with another person.

Best friend's sister or not, Harper needs help, and I'm the only one she's comfortable asking. "It's not strange. And my answer is yes. I'll help you figure out how to date."

"Thank you." She drops her hand to my forearm and squeezes. "But you better promise you won't tell Spencer I asked for your help. He'd never let me live this down."

"I promise," I say, and I don't feel bad in the least keeping him in the dark on this matter. No way am I telling him I'm becoming his little sister's love guru.

"Tell me what to say to Simon, then. Can that be my first lesson?" she asks, sitting up straighter, all eager to learn.

I stretch my neck side to side, roll up my sleeves, and slide right into coach mode. Hell, maybe coaching her through adventures with other men will cure me of wanting to get naked with her. Nothing can dampen desire faster than knowing she's into someone else, right? This is going to be just what I need to get her out of my system. A win-win for both of us. "Actually, your first lesson is you need to push him off another week or so. You're not ready to see him yet. He gets you too flustered. You need to learn the ropes with someone else first."

She looks confused. "Okay. But who?"

"Jason. He's into you."

"But I'm not thinking of him that way."

"Even better."

"So I should learn the ropes with him, even if I don't think of him like that?"

I nod. "Sure. You might wind up liking him. You're not Princess Awkward around him. It'll be good training."

She raises an eyebrow. I can't resist. I lean forward, run a finger across it, and brush it back into place. "Don't raise that eyebrow at me. You are in need of some serious training, and Jason is perfect. You like him as a friend, so that's enough for now. I won't let you lead him on too far. I promise, Okay?"

"If you say so."

"I do. Trust me. We're not going to yank him around. We're just going to practice your . . . conversational skills," I say diplomatically.

She laughs and then draws a deep breath. "Let's conversate."

"Do as I say. Open Facebook."

She takes out her phone and taps the app.

"Accept his friend request."

She nods and slides her thumb over the screen. "Done."

"Now, post on his wall."

She draws another breath and gives a crisp nod. "What do I say?"

"So great seeing you tonight. Exclamation point."

She types, posts, and turns the phone to me, like a proud student eager to show her teacher the assignment.

I pat her shoulder. "You did good. Now, if my calculations are correct," I say, pretending to look at a wristwatch, "you'll get a message from him in about twenty minutes."

I leave a twenty on the bar as a tip for Julia, and we head out into a warm October night.

"Nice night. I'll walk you home," I say.

"That sounds perfect."

Twenty minutes later, we round the corner onto her block, and she nearly smacks into a tall dude wearing a Columbia T-shirt and laughing at something his goateed buddy says. I grab her elbow and yank her closer before the guy walks into her.

"Oh, sorry!" The apology comes from the T-shirt guy, who's about my height. "Totally didn't see you. My bad."

"It's all good," Harper says with a quick smile. My arm is around her back still.

The guy swings his eyes to me, furrows his brow, then points at my face. Something like recognition dawns in his expression. "Wait . . . wait . . . you're . . ."

His friend cuts in, a huge fan-boy grin forming. "Mister Orgasm."

"That's me," I say casually.

"Holy shit. Your show rocks," the tall guy says. "I went to a fan meetup you did a couple years ago. Dude, I followed your show back when it was just an online strip."

With my free hand, we knock fists. "Love hearing that."

"I can't believe I just bumped into you walking around the city. I would ask you to sign my T-shirt, but that'd be weird, so let's pretend I didn't say that, but you're awesome," he says, practically bouncing.

"What he said," his friend chimes in.

"He's the best." Harper beams, taking her turn on the compliment train.

"You guys rock. Really appreciate the support. Great meeting you," I say, and we continue on our way.

Once the guys are out of earshot, Harper turns to me, her eyes lit up. "I've just witnessed a Mister Orgasm sighting in the wild, and it was kind of amazing. Does that happen often?"

I shake my head, laughing lightly. "Once or twice a year. I swear it's not that frequent."

She can't stop grinning. "And they love you. They think you're a stud."

"They're obviously right," I deadpan, and she bumps her shoulder into mine. When we reach her building, her phone beeps. She grabs it from her purse, and I say, "I bet that's the Jason reply."

She slides open the screen, clicks on the message from Jason, and shows it to me. *Hey Harper. So great seeing you! Want to get a cup of coffee?*

I mime dunking a basketball. Nothing but net. "It's a gift. Really it is," I say, as we stop near the stoop of her building.

"You're good, Nick. You know just what to do and how to behave. This is why you attract women in droves."

I kind of want to protest. I feel like she has this impression of me that I don't necessarily want her to have, but I'm not sure how to deflect this. "Because I have a gift?"

"That and several other reasons." She waves broadly at my arms. It's October, but it's not chilly tonight so I don't have a jacket on. "First, there are the arms. All that ink and muscle."

She roams her eyes over my biceps. "I mean, your ink is awesome," she says, pointing to the shapes and swirls

I designed myself. The tattoos are abstract lines and curves, but inside them there's a sun, a moon, and stars, because those were the first things I realized I was good at drawing.

"Then, the body. Mr. *Men's Health*-I'm-so-fit," she says in this mocking tone, but it's not me she's making fun of. It's the article.

"You read it?"

"I read everything. I devour information," she says, and we're right back to that place I seem to inhabit with her, where she compliments me, but she could be saying it like I'm a car she's considering buying. *And this one has one hundred seventy horsepower.*

"And then, there's your face, and you have all this awesome scruff on it."

I run a hand over my jaw, and the neat, trim beard that's like an additional sex toy I can bring to the bedroom. "Chicks dig the beard," I say, with a lopsided grin.

"I bet they do," she says under her breath. She doesn't say anything else right away. She presses her teeth into the corner of her lip and then speaks, more softly than before. "Can I feel it?"

FUCK, YES.

CHAPTER 7

She raises her hand and touches my jaw. My breath hitches as she runs her thumb across the light bristles. I'm keenly aware of every second that passes, one ticking into the next as she touches me, stroking my jawline like she's mesmerized by the texture.

"Soft," she whispers, almost in wonder as she stares at my chin. My heart starts hammering, and I fight to stay still. When she says, "But kind of hard, too," I swear, I don't know how I manage not to cup her cheeks, back her up against the stone wall, and just kiss the hell out of her. Kiss, touch, grind, and then some. I want to yank that lush body against mine, let her feel how much she turns me on, and find out if I do the same thing to her. The way her breath barely catches sends my mind spinning and lust spiraling tight in me. I can't help but hope she wants what I do, and it feels like she could, going by the way she touches my face. It truly fucking does, and maybe that's why her name takes shape in my throat like a warning.

So she knows she's playing with fire if she touches me like this again.

Then I remember. This is Harper, and she probably has no idea of the effect she has on me. I've never known someone like her. Here she is saying all these sweet, sexy things, and probably not even realizing what it can do to a man.

Makes it hard to resist, and right now I don't want to. Fuck resistance. Let her play with me for a few minutes. "Anything else you want to feel up?" I ask, hoping she'll take me up on my extremely generous offer to be her test subject. "The arms are available. The chest is on duty, too. Even the hair is fair game." I tip my forehead toward her, inviting.

In a second, her hand is in my hair. She's slow and measured, and takes her time running her fingers through the strands. My mind goes haywire, picturing every other kind of scenario where her hands might thread through my hair, pulling me close. Ones where she kisses me hungrily, consuming my lips with the kind of greedy touch that leads to clothes yanked halfway off in a fevered frenzy. That turns into slammed doors and hot up-against-the-wall sex, her panties falling to her knees. Or to one of my favorites, one of my fallbacks, one of my simplest and yet hottest fantasies—her legs wrapped tight around my head as I taste her on my lips. As I send her soaring with my tongue.

The next day, I'd walk past her, brush a strand of hair away from her ear and whisper *I can still taste you.* She'd shudder, then run her hands through my hair again, needing more.

Like she's doing on the street right now. For a sliver of a second, her hand stops and rests against me. I can feel her soft breath on my face. I meet her eyes, and try to read her, to find that flicker in her blue irises that would match the flame inside me.

"Kiss the girl, Mister Orgasm!"

I jerk my head at the same time Harper does. The two guys are now across the street, cheering me on from the edge of the sidewalk. They probably think we're together.

"Do it!" the other one chimes in. "Like the Kissing Virus episode."

Harper turns back to me, her lips curving up in a playful grin. "He had to kiss her to cure her," she whispers, as if I could forget that little element in the storyline. "Can't disappoint the fans."

I barely have time to register how the hell this is happening, but she's swaying closer. My brain is full of noise and static, and I don't know if this is a double-dog-dare until she mouths, *For the fan-boys right?*

And hell, if the fan-boys make this possible, I should send them a signed collector's edition of every panel. "Let's give them a show," I say, my throat dry as it becomes clear that she's not messing around.

"Hurry! Or the virus will spread!" one of the guys shouts, and Harper shudders, clasping her hand to her chest as she whispers, "You're the only one who can save me."

The very line the damsel in distress uttered in that episode.

She's letting them egg us on. Harper loves games. She loves entertainment; she loves performing. This is the magician in her, taking the trick from its setup through to the payoff.

She runs her thumb along my jawline, and my breath hitches.

There's no time to process, no time to analyze. And since she just had her hands all over me, it's only fair that I get to return the favor.

Possibility hums in me. I slide my right hand into her hair, letting the soft strands fall through my fingers, nice and slow, as I watch her expression flip from that daring playfulness to something entirely new.

Something unguarded.

It's so enticing. That look makes me long for her even more.

Up close, her blue eyes are even brighter, like island waters, and I can smell the hint of something like oranges from her shampoo. It's heady, and my mouth waters, wanting to taste her, inhale her.

I bring my right hand to her chin, gently tipping her face up toward me. My heart rate quickens, and I lick my lips as our gazes lock. Her eyes shimmer with desire that looks so damn authentic. I tug her close, and her lips part, a soft breath escaping as our eyes close. Judging from her reaction, it sure as hell feels like she wants this in a way that goes well beyond the reason we're play acting. But then I stop thinking of reasons at all, as I slant my mouth to hers. The world slows, and I kiss Harper as the pair of fans across the street hoot and holler, shouting "woohoo" and "hell, yeah" and finally a victorious, "She's saved!"

This is the payoff, and what a payoff it is.

I want to high-five them for goading her, or goading me, or whatever happened to make this moment possible.

Because this is exhilarating.

Our lips graze. There's a hint of lip gloss, and the faintest taste of the Long-Distance Lover she drank at the bar. I brush my lips across hers, a barely-there caress that's full of promise, a hint of what it could become if it were real, without the audience.

Whatever this kiss is, it possesses its own pulse, its own frequency, as if the air around us is charged and vibrating with sensual energy.

Or maybe it's just me, because my body is humming. My skin tingles, and this whisper of a kiss lights me up all over, making my mind gallop far beyond the payoff.

"Your lips are so soft," I whisper against her, and she gasps in response, then presses her mouth to me once more, murmuring, "Yours, too."

We've pulled off the ruse with aplomb, but when her lips sweep across mine one more time, it feels way more than necessary for the kiss-the-girl dare to be authentic.

It feels like it's slipped into *more.*

But just as the lingering build becomes almost unbearable and I'm ready to slide my tongue between her lips, the guys shout and clap, beginning a chorus of "Mister O!" that kills the mood.

We snap apart.

Harper blinks, stares down, then slides her gaze back up. The look in her eyes is guilty, like she feels bad that we locked lips. "Well," she says brightly, as if she's trying to smooth over an awkward moment, "good thing Mister O gave the girl the right dosage for the kissing virus."

I clear my throat, trying to make sense of what she just said. Of what just happened. Of how we basically reenacted a scene from my show. How I'm the hero, and she's the girl I rescued from doom.

"I mean, they totally expected you to do that," she adds, like she needs to justify our kiss.

"Yeah, definitely," I say, going along with her, because my brain is swimming in a sea of endorphins, and agreeing is way easier than anything else. I glance across the street and give the duo a quick thumbs up.

"She's all good," I tell them, as Mister O said in the show.

Harper joins in, waving, too. She turns back to me and parks her hand on my shoulder. "Those guys worship you and the ladies' man character you created."

I scrunch my brow, wishing we weren't talking about fictional shit right now, because that felt really fucking real to me. But I have no idea if she liked that kiss as much as I did.

"I'm all about the show," I say, seconding her, as the peanut gallery heads off into the night.

She laughs, then her expression shifts, and it's earnest again, like when she first opened up at the bar. "I really appreciate your help with this whole dating thing," she says, and the kiss has vanished into the night. The trick is over, and the magician and the show creator have left the stage. We're just Harper and Nick now, buddies with a secret project.

"Of course. I'm happy to do it. And, like I told you, Jason is really into you," I say, since it's so much easier for me to make sense of the other dude right now than to sort out the tangled mess in my head.

She shrugs and quirks up the corner of her lips. "Yeah?"

"Absolutely. You should go for it with him," I say, mustering false enthusiasm as I try to return to being her dating tutor, even though I might be a candidate for a split personality study since we just kissed, and now I'm telling her to go all-out for another guy. Maybe I caught some new strain of her *babble-around-someone-I'm-into* virus with that kiss.

"You think so?" she asks, with an inquisitive tilt of her head.

"Definitely. He might be the man of your dreams." Yup. A full-blown case of it.

She shoots me a skeptical look, then shrugs. "Would you meet me after I go out with him, so I can tell you everything while it's fresh in my mind?" she asks, placing her palms together. I'm about to say no, when she adds, "After all, I did 1919 White Sox for you."

"Then you made me look like a rock star in front of my fans just now," I say, still on autopilot. But even though I'm reluctant, I *did* sign up to help her, so this is, evidently, the drill. "Let me know where and when."

"I'll text you," she says, then heads up the steps, and I watch as she unlocks the door to her building, turns around, and waves to me through the glass.

Then she's gone, taking with her the best and strangest first kiss I've ever had.

I return to my home on Seventy-Third, a fourth-floor apartment with exposed brick walls and a huge window sporting a view of the park. As the door shuts behind me with a faint click, I ask myself if it even counts as a first kiss if you don't know if it was real or just a dare?

I don't think it lasted more than fifteen seconds, but those fifteen seconds echo inside me, and I can still feel the imprint of her lips on mine. I can still smell her sweet scent when I breathe in. I can still hear her soft gasp in my ears.

I wish I knew if she was in her apartment, lingering on those fifteen seconds, too.

But I can't know, and I won't know.

I do the one thing that's been a constant my whole life. The one thing that never frustrates me, and that always centers me. I toe off my shoes, flop down on my cushy gray couch by the big bay window, and grab my notebook. I have another episode to work on, and even though I don't do all the writing and animating anymore, the ideas and the storylines are mine.

But as I put the pencil to paper, I find I'm not in the mood to problem-solve for a cartoon hero. Instead, I just draw. Freestyle. Whatever comes to mind.

The trouble is when I finish, it's a caricature of a certain redhead in Daisy Dukes and high heels, working under the hood of a car. I give the drawing the evil eye, and toss it on the coffee table. Me and my fucking imagination, getting away from me once again.

A text arrives from her a minute later, and I wish I didn't feel a spark of possibility when I see her name.

The spark is doused coldly as I read the message.

Coffee with Jason Saturday afternoon. Meet afterward?

It's official. It was a kiss on a dare, and it absolutely doesn't count. In fact, it's as if it never happened, so I file it away in the *not-gonna-happen-again* drawer, then I tell her yes. After that, I finally write back to Spencer, making plans to see him this weekend. Perfect. That'll knock his sister right out of my solar system.

CHAPTER 8

"What if a Great Dane mated with a chipmunk?"

I roll my eyes at the question my brother poses the next morning as we crunch across a pile of fallen leaves on the path in Central Park. Autumn has coasted into New York City, and the colors are gorgeous. For a moment, I study a cranberry-red leaf that has drifted to the ground, picturing how I'd use that color in an animation. This is something I've always done; it's second nature for me to think about color, shades, and all the permutations they can take.

"Would the Great Dane have a fluffy tail, or would the chipmunk have crazy long legs?" Wyatt continues.

"Dude, you know that's not how this works," I say to my brother as the Min Pin mix I'm walking tugs on the end of the leash in hot pursuit of a squirrel.

"Or a squirrel and a Min Pin," Wyatt suggests, waving an arm at the critter.

"Again, you're getting away from the focus of the dog mash-ups game," I remind him as the long-haired, white-and-brown teacup Chihuahua he's walking tries to chase the tail of my dog. Well, not *my* dog, but the one I'm walking for a local animal rescue, Little Friends, that specializes in finding homes for small apartment-friendly dogs. We both volunteer there.

"Iguana and a terrier," he suggests, trying once more, then his furry friend balances on her two front legs, lifts her rear, legs and all, and pees on the grass.

"Handstand piss!" my brother shouts, doing a little victory shuffle by the tree.

I high-five him with my non-leash hand, because that is a serious win in our *other* dog game—dog bingo. We're multitaskers. We can play two games at once. "Ten points. Nice work," I say, but I'm competitive as hell with my little brother, and even though we're almost done with the walk, I've still got a chance to beat him. "But not if a fire truck drives by and mine howls."

He shoots me a doubtful look as we make our way out of the park. "Yeah, don't bank on that. That's both the unicorn and the pot of gold at the end of the rainbow in dog bingo."

"Someday I'll get it, though," I say, since dogs howling, especially tiny dogs like these two, is kind of fucking adorable, and that's why it's fifty points on our scorecard of random, unplanned canine activities. That's our version of car bingo, which we've played since we were kids. Points are also awarded to dog yoga poses, in honor of our dad, who's the most laidback guy you'll ever meet. I credit that to him being a yoga teacher, and to my mom keeping him well fed with her cupcakes. And no, I mean cupcakes *literally,* because I'm not even going there or thinking about that.

Ever.

Anyway, Wyatt and I both love dogs. We grew up with a bunch of small ones, as well as a little sister, Josie. Dogs kept us from killing each other. I love my brother like crazy, but he's also a total pain in the ass. Younger brothers are like that, even though he's only younger by five minutes.

"Corgi Mastiff pair-up. Who was on top?"

"Mastiff," I answer immediately, as we return to our *other* dog game. Because who's on top is the point of Dog Mash-ups.

"Ouch."

"Yeah, imagine how the Corgi felt. Greyhound Basset?"

"Greyhound. And now their puppies try to run with those short little legs and their toes turned out," he says, as we leave the park and make our way uptown to where Little Friends shares space with a doggy day-care.

"Hey, you know the chick who runs the little dog center?" he asks, shifting gears.

"Penny, you mean?"

He nods. "She asked if I would help fix up a section of the rescue."

Before I can respond, I spot a woman across the street with a long mane of red hair blowing in the breeze, walking into my building. Her hair is like the color of that leaf—red with a golden tint.

"Whoa," Wyatt says, stopping in his tracks at the crosswalk and leaving the Penny conversation in the dust. His teacup buddy pulls up short. "Who's the sexy little snake charmer heading into your building?"

I smack him on the back of his head. "Seriously. That's not cool, man."

"Ouch," he says, rubbing his skull as a bus rumbles by.

I shoot him a steely glare. "That did not hurt. Don't even pretend."

He matches my evil eye. "It was a legit question. Since when am I not allowed to—?"

He cuts himself off, and his lips form an oval. "Oh. Oh. Oh. Oh." He repeats the sound as if it's the refrain to a rap song. He punches me in the arm. "You have a thing for Little Red Riding Hood."

Shit. This is my brother. My unfiltered, does-not-know-the-meaning-of-TMI, fraternal twin brother. I push my glasses up higher on my nose, and glance at the crosswalk sign. The little man is now green.

"You like her," he continues as we cross Central Park West.

"No." I shake my head, keeping all lingering images of the kiss that didn't count at bay. "She's a friend, so it's rude to talk that way."

"What way?" he asks, challenging.

"I know what you were going to say, Woodrow," I say using the middle name that he loathes. "That you wanted to *tap that*."

He gets in my face as we walk, mocking me. "Aww . . . and look at you going all protective. That's adorable." He snaps his gaze to my building when we reach the sidewalk. "Wait."

I follow his eyes to see Harper turn around and head out of my building, grabbing at her phone, a big grocery bag on her arm.

"Randall Hammer," he says, throwing my middle name back at me, since I hate mine, too. "Does Spencer know you're hot for his sister?"

Fuck my life. She's half a block away now. Her eyes light up when she sees me, and she drops her phone in her purse then waves. All I can think is now would be an excellent time for a cop car or fire truck to roar by, sirens blaring. Wyatt can have all the points he wants and then some if his dog howls.

"I'm not hot for her. She's a friend. Besides, the chipmunk was on top of the Great Dane," I say to distract him. Sometimes, you just have to throw a dog a bone.

That cracks him up and earns me a temporary reprieve as Harper arrives and greets my brother first. "Hey, Wyatt. Haven't seen you in a while. How's everything?" she asks, and he moves in for a hug. With his hand still gripping the dog's leash he wraps his arms around Harper and then wiggles his eyebrows at me and mouths, *Charming my snake.*

He's such a little shit.

"Do you have a dog now?" she asks once she separates from him, and I swear I breathe easier now that my brother's arms are no longer around her.

"Does it make you want me?" he tosses back at her.

Harper laughs, shaking her head in amusement. "I see you still haven't had the surgery yet."

He smirks. "The one to install that filter between my brain and my mouth?"

She nods. "That one."

He shakes his head vigorously. "Nope. But the surgeon has an opening next week."

"Excellent. I'll come visit you in the hospital." She gestures to the dogs. "What's the story here?"

"They're with Little Friends rescue," I say.

My brother chimes back in, resting his elbow on my shoulder, acting all casual and cool. "Did you know Nick and I walk dogs from the rescue two days a week?"

Her eyes sparkle at both of us, but she shifts her gaze to meet mine. "That's really sweet."

My heart flips, and I'm right back to last night outside her building.

The didn't-happen kiss, you dumbass.

"It was my idea. I'm the sweet brother," Wyatt says, turning on his sparkling smile.

"Hey," I say, butting in. "Didn't you say you had to talk to Penny about hammering her? Oh, sorry. I meant hammering some nails in her building."

He rolls his eyes at me. "Ha ha ha." He reaches for the leash I'm holding. "Give me your little dude. I'll take them back," he says. The rescue isn't far from here. I bend down and give one dog a scratch on the chin, then the other.

As I stand, Wyatt bows to both of us and bids a dramatic adieu. "I'll let you two get back to your reindeer games."

I want to whack him, but that's par for the course.

When Wyatt leaves, I turn to the star of my dirty dreams. Her lips are curved in a grin, and she seems pleasantly surprised. "I didn't know you did that with the dogs."

"I like dogs. I like helping out, too." And this ease of conversation reminds me that the kiss didn't happen for her either, so we are all good.

"I like that. No, I *love* that," she says, and her expression is soft, free of the usual undercurrent of sarcasm. The way she says it is disarming and makes me feel warm all over, not just hot for her. "I help out at the New York ASPCA. I do some fundraising for them."

"You do? I had no idea."

"Yeah. I help organize some of the 5Ks to raise money for shelter pets, spread the word on social media, help set up the events . . . Someday, I'll get a dog. For now, I do what I can."

"That's awesome," I say, enjoying learning this new detail about her. I've been friends with her for so long, but not best friends, so uncovering these pieces of her is a whole new experience. "What kind of dog do you want?"

"The kind that laughs at all my jokes," she says, and I laugh.

"Sounds perfect. I'd like that kind of mutt, too."

She clears her throat and holds up the canvas grocery bag. "You might be wondering why I'm here."

"The thought did cross my mind. But then I figured you were bringing me groceries. Please tell me there's a pint of mint chocolate chip ice cream and two spoons in there."

A too-big pout forms on her face. "Damn it. I really fucked up. But I know what to get you next time. For now, I have this offering of detergent. I was just going to leave it with the doorman," she says, glancing in the direction of my building.

But she *didn't* leave it with the doorman. She's still carrying it, and she was hunting for her phone a minute ago, like she was trying to call me. Maybe to tell me she was here? Hell, maybe she wanted an excuse to see me.

Before my thoughts careen out of control, I give myself a mental eye-roll.

Yeah, right. If the chick were into you, she'd be speaking in tongues and babbling.

She's not. In fact, she's cool, confident Harper. Ergo, I'm reading something into nothing.

I take the bag and thank her. "You really didn't have to. I was going to pick some up today after work."

"But this way I can convert you to my brand. It's cruelty-free. No animal testing."

"Ah, that's awesome."

"Want to know what else is awesome? It smells really good."

I groan. "Am I going to smell like lavender or something girly?"

"I don't think so. I use it. Want to sniff me?"

I freeze. A million dirty thoughts dance in my head. I would fucking love to sniff her, to inhale her scent, to run my nose along her neck, down her breasts, across her belly. Then I decide, *fuck it.* This chick asked me to teach her about dating. She needs to know that the things that come out of her mouth are sometimes insanely naughty. I park a hand on her shoulder. "You are aware that sounded ridiculously filthy? Tell me you know that. I need to understand how far back your training must go."

She rolls her eyes. "C'mon, I wasn't trying to be dirty. Just sniff. It's like springtime. It smells really good," she says, and tugs at her own shirt, a turquoise V-neck underneath a light jacket.

Like I'm saying no to that. I lean forward and bring my nose to the fabric. She smells amazingly good, and I'm temptingly close to her breasts. Closer than I've ever been. So close that if, say, the person walking behind me conveniently bumped me, I could have my face in Harper's chest. My mouth waters, and my pulse thunders, and I've never prayed so hard to be bumped into in my life.

But it doesn't happen, and obviously I can't spend the entire day hanging out here sniffing her clothes. It's probably grounds for insanity, so I raise my face.

"Doesn't it smell nice?"

I meet her gaze. I have no witty comeback. No snappy retort. "Yes."

For some reason that earns me a smile. Only this one seems different than the one she flashed Gino last night or the one she gave my brother. One that seems to last longer than a friendly smile should. It appears to linger, and it reminds me of last night and how our kiss seemed more than friendly, too.

"But I already knew you smelled nice," I add, my lips twitching up. Maybe I'm letting her know I'm cool with everything. Maybe I'm flirting.

Her eyes widen, and she nibbles on the corner of her lips. "And now your clothes can smell that good, and you should do your laundry today so I can sniff you when I see you tomorrow."

Once she leaves I find a missed call from her marked five minutes ago. Like I had hoped. I fight like hell not to read anything into it, reminding myself that tomorrow she has her starter date with another guy.

And that guy isn't me.

Hopefully she won't be sniffing Jason. I really hope he doesn't smell her either, because I don't want anyone else to know that her detergent is a massive turn-on.

CHAPTER 9

After an all-day brainstorm meeting with the show's writers, I return home, gather my laundry, and grab my new detergent from the canvas bag. My hand scrapes across cardboard at the bottom. I peer into the bag and find a stowaway. The detergent isn't riding solo. It has company.

I pull out a slim box of Blackwing pencils.

A black satiny bow with pink polka dots hugs the middle of the box. This is the girliest bow I've ever seen, but it's completely adorable because it's from her. Tucked under the ribbon is a white piece of paper, folded in quarters. I open it.

Nick,

Did you know the slogan for these pencils is "Half the Pressure, Twice the Speed"? I suspect there's a great dirty joke in there, but I think we'd need more pressure, right? In any case, I wanted to say thank you in advance for all your help. And nothing says thank you like a box of pencils. Just don't put any in your nose. Well, until

you learn how to do so properly. Then, by all means, go crazy.

xoxo
Harper

Damn her. I grin ear to ear. I love these pencils. They are just the motherfucking bomb.

I grab a sheet of paper and sketch out a simple dog, laughing, as if he's chuckling at a joke his master told. I snap a photo and send it to her. I keep the bow, placing it in a kitchen drawer. I don't know why. It's too small to be of any use in the bedroom. But I save it anyway.

I pull on a pair of basketball shorts, drop my laundry bag and the new detergent with the doorman to send out for cleaning, and head to the gym a few blocks away, where I log several sweaty miles on the treadmill and do a long round of weights. An hour and a half later, I open the door to my apartment as my phone buzzes with a reply from her, under the new nickname I gave her in my contacts.

Princess: I see you're enjoying your new pencils. Meanwhile, I'm enjoying a pint of mint chocolate chip. It tastes sooooo good.

I stop in my tracks. Not because the text is dirty, but because I'm picturing her eating ice cream and imagining how her mouth tastes.

Cone or spoon? I need the full licking visual.

Her reply comes quickly.

Princess: I'm licking a spoon right now.

Mint chocolate chip tastes good licked off other things, too.

Princess: Is this a lesson now in how to eat ice cream?

Actually, this is your first lesson in dating. Starting tonight. How to send a flirty text . . . Mint chocolate chip ice cream tastes so good licked off someone you like . . .

She doesn't respond right away, so I leave the phone on the kitchen counter, but I can't stop thinking about her and ice cream and how the cool of the mint and the sweetness of the chocolate would mingle on her tongue. How she'd taste different than she did after Speakeasy, but still just as alluring. How I could drive her wild with a kiss that didn't stop, that made her knees weak and her panties damp. One that turned her on so much that she'd break the kiss to lick her way down my chest, to the waistband of my shorts, yanking them off. She'd raise that sexy eyebrow, lick her lips, then get them intimately acquainted with my dick.

In case there was any question, yes, I'm hard as fuck right now.

Actually, if we're going to get technical, I'm pretty sure this is the textbook definition of pitching a tent. My dick aches for attention. I'm so wound up from wanting this girl I can't have, and this boner isn't going to fade gently into the night.

I strip out of my gym clothes and head straight for my shower, turning the water as hot as I can handle. Considering I think even her eyebrows are sexy, I clearly need to get this girl out of my system. An unapologetic, no-holds-barred shower jerk will do the job.

The power spray setting works best for that. I adjust the mode selector, and water pours down, wetting my hair, sliding down my chest, running over the ink on my arms.

Since I'm not going to have Harper for real, maybe I won't be so fucking aroused around her all the time if I give her a thorough workout in my mind. She's been in the shower with me many times, and she gives great head in here. With her banging little body and smart, sexy mouth, she's played a starring role in a handful of shower jerks during the last few months. Maybe more than a handful. Like ten helping handfuls. Or ten times that.

But who's counting when your hand is full?

Not me, that's for damn sure.

As steam fills the bathroom, I wrap my hand around my hard-on in a nice, long, lingering tug.

I let out a breath.

A reel of images flashes in front of me, and this is so easy, since I see the world in pictures. The hottest ones snap before my eyes as my fist curls tighter.

Her crawling across my bed on her hands and knees, wearing nothing but those fuck-me glasses.

Her unbuttoning her shirt, spreading it open, revealing her luscious tits to me. Tits I'd love to fuck.

My blood runs hot, and a shudder races through me as that particular picture fights its way to the front of the line. I stroke up and down my shaft as I thrust between those delicious breasts. She'd push the soft flesh together with her hands, creating a warm valley for my dick. Her tongue would dart out, licking the head on each stroke.

I draw a shaky breath as my hand slides along my length, imagining Harper's mouth on me instead. Tonight I'd like her on her knees, the red lips that say those dirty things wrapped around my dick while she sucks, licks, and takes me deep.

I groan, and the sound is swallowed by the relentless pounding of the hot water on the tiles. I stroke harder and faster, desire flaring in my muscles, skating over my skin as I see her in all her naked beauty, pleasuring me. Then, out of nowhere, the images flip.

I no longer picture her servicing me.

What gets me off more than anything is the prospect of her coming. The sounds she'd make. The way her lips would part in an *O*. How her back would arch. Fuck, I'd love nothing more than to get out of the shower, walk into the living room, and find her naked on my couch, legs spread, one hand between them, the other playing with her tits.

My spine tingles as the image intensifies, grows sharper, and feels more real. The muscles in my legs tighten, and I let the fantasy play out. Hell, do I ever want to discover her masturbating, to walk in on her pleasuring herself when she's so damn close to the edge.

She moans and writhes as her fingers fly across her wet pussy, over the delicious rise of her clit. She's worked up and desperate, clawing for release.

Her eyes snap open. She doesn't even have to beg me to finish her off. Those blue eyes, hazy with lust, tell me how much she needs my mouth.

I slide my hands up her thighs and spread her legs wide. I bury my face in her sweet wetness, and holy fuck. The start of an orgasm barrels into me as I taste her. It races through me as I devour her. It wracks my body as I make her cry out and come so fucking hard on my face.

I'm right there with her, my fist flying, a wild groan ripped from my throat as I finish.

Panting, I stand there for a few minutes, the hot water raining over my back as my shoulders rise and fall from the intensity of that Harper-fueled orgasm.

A little while later, I'm freshly showered, clean as a whistle, and naked in bed.

I park my hands behind my head, a satisfied man. Yup, I came, I saw, I conquered my lust. Mission accomplished. Harper Holiday has disappeared from the 99.99 percent of my brain devoted to sex, and now I can focus on helping her tomorrow without even a single stray dirty thought getting in the way.

Clearly, I don't want to fuck her anymore.

Nope. Not a bit. Not even when my phone buzzes. Not even when I open the text from her. Not even when I see the picture she sent—a super close-up selfie of her licking ice cream off a spoon.

I close the screen, and I swear I don't dream about licking a mint chocolate chip ice cream cone all night long.

CHAPTER 10

The next afternoon, I sit in a coffee shop, earbuds in, listening to music and working on the next storyline of *The Adventures of Mister Orgasm* after yesterday's massive brainstorm fest with the writing staff. In this episode, our hero has to break into a three-hundred-year-old spooky house to rescue a woman who's being haunted by the Ghost of Orgasms Past.

Something about the animations the head writer sent me feels off, but I can't put my finger on it. I shut my laptop, slide it into my messenger bag, and grab a notebook. I need to figure out what's wrong, and sometimes I do that best by just drawing what I see playing out in my mind.

I loop my arm around the sheet of paper, and soon enough I like the way this concept is taking shape. It's still got the dirty humor the show needs, and I know this sounds weird, but it has heart, too. That's key. At the end of every episode, Mister Orgasm is ultimately a good guy who helps the world.

Look, I know who I am. I don't harbor any illusions. I'm not curing cancer or saving the whales, but I take some pride in the fact that when people watch my show, they laugh. Sometimes they even laugh so hard they pee.

Yes, I've received fan letters to that effect. Some viewers get frisky with each other after watching. Maybe they're laughing and maybe they're fucking and maybe they're peeing, but I hope the thing people aren't doing is fighting. *The Adventures of Mister Orgasm* is not violent, and ultimately the hero uses both his skills and his brain to save the day, but never his fists.

That's why I draw a bubble near the hero's mouth and write the words, "I'm a lover not a fighter."

I keep drawing, moving on to other images swirling around in the corners of my mind. Random things—a ninja banana, a dog walking on its front legs, a trio of puppets presenting a naughty puppet show. Maybe I can work that into an episode. Everyone likes dirty puppets. With the pencil flying over the paper, I sketch out the story in their puppet show, about a hot mechanic who's washing her car under the sun, her wife beater clinging to her sweaty chest. She sweeps her red hair off her face, and pulls it back in a bow—

Shit. Shit. *Shit*.

Out of the corner of my eye, I glimpse the door opening. Harper crosses the distance, and I scramble, folding the paper into quarters, or eighths, or sixty-fourths so she won't recognize that I drew her.

And drew her like *this*. Because she's crazy sexy even in a sketch.

As I jam the page into my pocket, I silently curse myself. My mind is like a fucking loose canon with this chick, firing without warning, even though I distinctly recall giving her the heave-ho from my mental real estate last night. Why the fuck is she invading my drawings again?

She arches an eyebrow when she reaches me, and I yank the earbuds out in time to hear her ask, "State secrets?"

I shake my head. "Nope. Just a storyline for the show," I say, in my practiced cool and casual tone.

"Ah, well it's best to keep that away from me, since I have a reputation for revealing all of Mister Orgasm's secrets if I can get my greedy little hands on them." She darts out her fingers, pretending to grab my shoulder, then my forearm.

Holy shit, she has fast hands.

Well, duh. She earns a living with them.

My eyes widen as she makes a move for the jeans pocket. But it was a fake play. She laughs and holds up her palms in surrender. "I was just teasing. I would *never* try to sneak a peek at your show ideas," she says, grabbing the seat across for me at the spot we picked for her date download. "But I do want to watch when it's on. I've seen every episode."

I tilt my head. "You have?"

She nods and smacks her lips. "Seen every episode, loved every episode."

Warmth spreads in my chest, and it has nothing to do with desire for her this time but everything to do with pride for a job well done. "That's awesome. I love hearing that."

She moves her chair closer, and I steel myself to hear all the details of how Jason is wooing her. Instead, she points to the sketchpad. "What was the first comic you loved?"

I answer immediately. "*Get Fuzzy.* I love that strip. That cat killed me."

"I love that one, too." She flashes a smile. "What else?" she asks, parking her elbow on the table, resting her chin in her palm, and just looking relaxed and happy as we chat. "In all the years I've known you, I've never seen you read a comic book like *Superman* or *Spider-man*. You're all about the cartoons and comic strips instead, right?"

I nod. "Superheroes weren't my thing. But I was always into the drawing and the comedy. These days it's *Family Guy* and *American Dad* for humor. And when I was younger, I devoured every *Far Side* and *Calvin and Hobbes*."

"Is that why you have a tiger on your chest? For Hobbes?"

I cock my head, curious. "How did you know about the tiger?"

"I might have noticed it," she says, with a cute little shrug of her shoulder. She grabs her phone, clicks open her gallery, and scrolls through some photos. She holds up the screen and shows me one from the summer in Central Park. I remember her snapping pics of me that day when we pranked her brother.

"I zoomed in on it that night," she says, then stops, shakes her head, and tries to laugh it off. "That sounds really pervy doesn't it?"

I'm so damn tempted to say, *you don't know what pervy is 'til you hear about the things you do in my shower. You have no idea how flexible you are some nights. You have no clue how dirty you get in my head when you bend over the edge of my bed and beckon me to your perfect naked body.*

Still, I can't resist the volley. "It only sounds pervy in the best possible way."

A splash of red races across her cheeks, but she doesn't hide her face or look away. Instead, she says, "I was curious, so I looked closer. That's when I noticed the ink on your chest."

Fighting back a grin has never been harder in my life —because she saved my picture. Her admission flips a switch in me, and the light blinks now with possibility. "Hobbes is kind of my inspiration," I say, but now I'm the curious one. She has no visible ink, but what if she had a tattoo someplace hidden? Someplace intimate? "Do you have any ink?"

She shakes her head, and her eyes widen with worry. "I'd love one, but no way."

"Why do you say it like that?"

"You're going to laugh, but I'm a complete pansy when it comes to needles." She shudders. "I'm terrified of them. I hated shots when I was a kid, and I really have to grin and bear it when I donate blood every eight weeks."

"You hate needles, and you still give blood?"

"Until they can find another way to get it out of me, I just sit back and think about the Oreos I'll get at the end," she says. I'm impressed she does that regularly, especially when she's afraid of it. "But you know what I'm not afraid of?"

I take the bait. "What?"

"Pens. Want to draw Bucky the cat on me?"

I wiggle an eyebrow. "On your chest? Right now? Yeah, just take off your shirt."

She flashes me a saucy grin. "How about my arm instead?"

"That works, too."

I pull her chair closer as she pushes up the sleeve on a soft red-and-blue plaid shirt and extends her arm. Our knees nearly touch when I hold her forearm as a canvas in the coffee shop. An espresso machine hisses from the counter, and "No One's Gonna Love You" by Band of Horses plays overhead.

"I love this song," she says softly.

"Me, too."

I lower my gaze to her arm, starting with the cat's body. She speaks first, asking a question. "What would you do if you couldn't draw?"

I stop, shudder, and meet her eyes. I press my finger to her lips. "Shh. Never say something that awful again."

"No, I mean it," she says, insistent, as I return to her arm.

"I don't know, Harper. That sounds like the definition of hell. I'd rather die." I begin to sketch the tail. "What about you? What would you do if you didn't know magic?"

I look up briefly. She screws up her lips. "The same," she says with a nod, and I love that we don't have to explain more about why we feel this way. We're in sync when it comes to the fire in the belly that drives us both.

"How did you know you wanted to be a magician?" I ask while I add in messy bursts of hair on the cat's belly as she answers.

"I just knew, from the time I got a Christmas gift with a magic set in it when I was five. I learned every trick in every book I could get my hands on from the library and bookstore," she says, and I move to the cat's face. "I made my mom and dad take me to every magic show I learned about. I studied acting and public speaking in college so I could be comfortable on stage. I honestly can't imagine not doing magic tricks. Which sounds silly, because it's one of the weirdest professions to have. I can't tell you how many people say, 'You're really a magician?'"

"No one believes you do magic for a living?" I ask as I draw whiskers.

"Anyone I meet for the first time doubts it. I constantly have to prove it, and like I told you before, people are always asking me to show them tricks. Like Jason," she says, almost as an afterthought.

I stop for a second. I'd nearly forgot she'd gone on a date, and that I'm supposed to help her analyze it or something. This is the first it's come up. "Did you show him a card trick?"

"Yes. And he wanted to know how it was done, but of course I couldn't tell him."

"Because of the code? Code 563 in the *Magician's Handbook of Secrecy*, I believe," I tease, remembering what she said at the bookstore.

She laughs and shifts the slightest bit in her chair, her knees now touching mine. "Yes. That code. I mean, there's not an *official* code, but it's an unspoken rule." She adopts a serious voice, like that of a teacher. "The secret of a trick or illusion should never be revealed, unless to a student of magic who also takes this same oath." Her voice becomes normal again, though still earnest. "You just can't do it. It's completely frowned upon in the magic community. It goes against the whole point of what we do, which is to make people suspend disbelief."

I add up all the times she's ever told me how she'd pulled off a trick. The number is officially zero. I let this roll around a bit longer—keeping secrets is who she is. But she keeps them because she has to, not because she's a sneaky person.

"That's part of it, too," I say absently as I work on a very surly cat's mouth.

"Part of what?"

"The trade-off. When you said your job was a trade-off. It limits your ability to meet people, but on top of that, you also have to constantly keep up a mask."

"Some days it's all an illusion," she says in a quiet voice, with a soft sigh. She snaps out of it in a nanosecond. "What are you afraid of?"

I look up. "Not needles."

"What then? Spiders? Open spaces? That the Blackwing pencil company will go out of business?"

I point my finger at her, and wink. "That one."

"For real, Nick," she presses, using that voice of hers that is vulnerable, free of snark, and just works its way into me. That voice says she wants to know me more.

I stop drawing, and focus on her, laying bare my deepest fear. "That it will all fall to pieces—the job, the show, the success. I've been really lucky. Most cartoonists barely make a living, and I've landed an awesome gig. The stars all aligned. But success can be so fleeting. It could all go away tomorrow in the blink of an eye."

"Do you really believe that?"

"I have to believe that. It keeps me on my toes. Keeps me focused on doing the best show I can. That's why I just roll with Gino's bullshit. Because I want all this to continue," I say, tapping the drawing on her arm. "I want to keep doing this for as long as I possibly can."

"You love it," she says, and it's such a simple statement, and an obvious one, and yet it resonates inside me.

"I love it more than showers. And I really fucking love showers," I say, completely serious. In this moment, I don't mean *shower* as a euphemism. I mean it for the complete and utter awesomeness of turning the water on high after a good, hard workout, or shortly after you wake up, or following a long, sweaty afternoon in bed with the woman of your dreams.

She cracks up. "That's amazing. I really love showers, too."

Lest I loll around in the shower zone too long, I school my thoughts, return to the design, and force myself to be her tutor. "How was it? Your date."

"It was fine. He was nice, and we talked."

"What did you talk about? As your coach, it's important for me to know these details," I say.

"Bowling. College. Work."

"Sounds like what we just talked about. Minus the bowling."

"No," she says, her tone firm. "We talk about stuff that's deeper, don't you think?"

I meet her eyes, try to read her expression. But this is a woman who's had to perfect the art of not revealing. I can't tell what she's thinking, feeling, or wanting, and it's starting to drive me crazy because her words seem weightier than usual. "Do we?"

She doesn't look away. Her blue eyes stay fixed on me, and she answers simply. "Yes. Didn't we *just* do that?"

And she's right. We did. I nod. "Do you like him?"

"He asked me to go out next week. For dinner."

My muscles tighten, and I grip her arm harder. "What did you say?"

"I said yes. Isn't that what I'm supposed to say? You told me to try with him, coach. So I can learn how to date and not be a complete buffoon."

I laugh at her choice of words. "I'd hardly call you a buffoon."

She squares her shoulders, taking a beat. "What were your dates like with the romance novelist? Can you tell me so I know I'm not totally flailing around?"

I shake my head. "We're not talking about me right now, Princess Not-a-Buffoon. We're talking about you. Are you starting to like him? You didn't answer the question, and it would help me prep you for your dinner if I knew the answer," I ask again.

She quirks her lips, considering. "I don't get that crazy fluttery feeling in my chest when I look at him or talk to him. I suppose I probably should if I like him?" She makes it a question, her gaze locking on mine.

My own crazy, fluttering chest gives me the answer. "It's not a bad start." Then, because apparently I'm a glutton for punishment, I press on. "Do you feel that way when you're with Simon?"

Her eyes widen, and she shrugs.

"That's not an answer," I say gruffly. Evidently, I really like abuse.

"I haven't spent any more time with him. You gave me orders not to see him," she says, tossing the ball back in my court. "Though, I *did* talk to him on the phone earlier this week."

My pen stops. A bolt of red-hot jealousy slams into me. I'm so damn glad I'm looking down, because I don't want her to see my face, or that it drives me crazy that she's into him. "Yeah?" I ask, in my best cool and casual tone as I return to the blue lines on her skin. "How was that?"

"Fine. We just talked about Hayden's party in a couple weeks."

"And you were able to speak?"

"Ha ha ha. Yes, I retained the power of *oral* communication," she says, and I groan at the innuendo she served up. "Besides, the phone is easy for me. Especially texting."

"Good to know," I say, as I finish the ink on her arm.

I move my palm a few inches up her skin, raising her forearm to show her my work. As my fingers skim across her flesh, I swear for a second that her breath catches. The smallest sound floats to my ears, almost like a little gasp, and it sounds fantastic. It trips me back in time to our kiss. To the faint murmur that escaped her lips when I brushed them with mine. I want to press the button on her that controls that noise, that turns it up, that makes it music in my ears. Our eyes meet, and I'm not awash in crazy, dirty thoughts. I'm thinking about how pretty she is, how much more I want to know her, and how I don't want this time with her to end. I can listen to her talk about cartoons and dreams, work and passion—all these deeper things, and all the simpler things, too—for as long as she wants to share them with me.

Talking to her is so easy. So enjoyable. It's like breathing. My heart pounds as I try to memorize the expression in her eyes, the tiny spark dancing across all that sapphire blue, that makes me believe she *has* to feel the same way.

Her lips part the slightest bit, and that small shift is the *very* detail I'd draw in the picture of a girl who was starting to like a guy.

My pulse races as she holds my gaze captive. There are no fans egging us on. There's no trick we're trying to pull off. We might be surrounded by people, but this is a coffee shop full of white noise. Right now, it's only Harper and me, and her shoulders dip forward, as if there's a magnetic pull between us.

She leans into me, swaying closer, like she's keen to finish what we started on the street. If she is, I want it all, but it has to come from her so I know this isn't just another illusion. Every inch, every bend, every second until our lips meet has to start with her. I need to know whether this is all in my mind, or if this crackling electricity between us truly is as two-way as I want it to be.

A cup clangs from somewhere behind the counter, and the sound of it hitting the floor breaks the spell. I straighten, she flinches, and we both look away. When I dare to return my focus to her, she's staring down at her arm, so there's no chance I can find an answer. It slips through my fingers like smoke.

"I love it," she says in a soft voice. "How long will it last?"

"'Til you shower."

"But I *love* showers."

"It won't last long then. So unless you plan on letting yourself get pretty dirty tonight, it'll be gone tomorrow."

"Now who's the one saying ridiculously filthy things?"

I smirk. "Touché."

"Can I ask you a serious question?"

"Of course."

"Do you think Jason is going to want to, you know"—she raises her eyebrows and croons like Marvin Gaye—*"get it on*?"

"Maybe. Second date protocol suggests he might try to kiss you," I say, trying to stay focused on the question and not my own reaction to it, which is that Jason is a *lucky fucking bastard*. "First date is to see if you actually want a second date. So you passed that test. Second date is to see if there's any real chemistry, and so you graduate to dinner and probably a test kiss. And third date is . . ." I let my voice fade, and she raises an eyebrow.

She whispers, all conspiratorial, "Wait. Don't tell me. Let me guess. Third date is for . . ." She slows, licks her lips, then inches the slightest bit closer so it's like she's imprinting her words on the air as she holds my gaze captive and purrs, "Hot, dirty sex."

All the blood rushes to my dick.

There's no space between us for other people. Her words are between her and me. My brain stops working, lust spins wildly through me, and I say the first thing that comes to mind. "No," I say, taking my time, too, because this is my territory. I know dirty words and deeds inside and out, and if Harper wants to go toe-to-toe, I'm in it to heat her up. "It's for hot, dirty sex that lasts all night long."

Now she's caught off-guard. She blinks, swallows, and exhales hard.

I'm tense, wishing she'd start speaking in tongues like she did with Simon. Something to give me the confirmation that she's into me, too. Instead, she bites her lip, then says, "I bet that's the best kind to have."

"It absolutely is, princess." Her eyes darken when I say that last word, my voice sliding into the tone I'd use with her in bed.

Dirty. Rough. Hungry.

That's the problem.

If I keep lingering in this zone, I'll be participating in way more one-man shows than are good for my ego.

And I really need to get her out of my head, especially since I'm seeing her brother tomorrow.

CHAPTER 11

"Bond. James Bond."

Spencer adjusts his cuffs, then eyes himself approvingly. He glances over at me as I finish off my bow tie.

"Can't help myself," he adds. "It's a requirement. You can't wear a tux and not say it. Because I do look like Bond."

I laugh and shake my head. "You and every guy in the world thinks that about himself."

We're at the tuxedo shop the next day for the last fitting for his wedding, making sure the measurements are right. The petite black-haired woman, who runs the shop that's open even on a Sunday, fiddles with the lapels on my jacket and says, "You look good. You're all set."

I tip my head to Spencer as I begin to undo the bow tie. "Got anything that'll improve his situation? A paper bag, maybe?"

She smiles then turns to the groom to work on final adjustments. I change back into my own clothes, and when I rejoin them, Spencer tilts his head toward me and sniffs the air. "Why do you smell like my sister's laundry detergent?"

It's like a car slamming on the brakes. Everything in my head screeches, and I'm caught red-fucking-handed.

My brain sputters, and tons of excuses scurry toward my tongue. Then I tell myself to chill. Tons of people use the same soap, and just because she gave me detergent doesn't mean I'm wearing a billboard that says *I want to bang your sister.*

I just feel like I am. As if every little thing—even the most innocuous—reveals my hand. I've got to get my shit together especially since I have a dinner with Spencer, Charlotte, and Harper in a few days.

I slide on a poker face. "What are you talking about?" I ask, giving him a look as if he's the crazy one.

He leans closer, arches an eyebrow, and sniffs again. "Hmm."

"Dude," I say, stepping away. That one word conveys everything: *this is a no-fly zone.* But inside, I panic because how good is this guy's nose that he can tell I'm using the same laundry detergent as his sister?

"Also, nice cat," Spencer tosses out.

My pulse pounds in my neck. "What cat?"

"On Harper's arm," he adds. "She was with Charlotte this morning, picking up the bridesmaid dresses."

Oh. Right.

The evidence in ink. On Harper's arm.

Note to self: Find out why the hell Harper didn't shower today.

"Yeah? Charlotte liked my Bucky the cat?"

Spencer cracks up. "Absolutely. If the TV business doesn't work out, you should start aping other cartoonist's work for a living."

I roll my eyes.

His expression shifts to serious. "What's the deal though? Harper told Charlotte you were hanging out more. That you had coffee yesterday, and she gave you detergent since she spilled something on you?"

"Hot chocolate. Everywhere. Like it was a new design," I say quickly, since that's the truth. Besides, there's nothing wrong with us getting a drink now and then. And then, like a frying pan to Woody Woodpecker's head, it hits me why Harper told Charlotte the simple truth. The fact that we're hanging out isn't something Harper has to hide.

I'm the one with the big secret—that I'm completely fucking tempted by my best friend's sister in every way.

Unrequited lust sucks balls. Don't let anyone tell you otherwise.

The tux lady pats Spencer's shoulder. "You're all set now," she says to him.

He thanks her then eyes me in the mirror. "You're just hanging out with her, right?"

My chest pinches even as I answer honestly with a nonchalant, "Yeah."

"Good." He sounds relieved, and part of me wants to ask why the hell I'm not good enough for her. He claps me on the back. "Because Charlotte wants you to meet her sister at the wedding. Natalie's single, and a babe."

"Oh," I say, surprised, because that was not the answer I'd expected at all. I try to play it cool. "I never pegged you as a matchmaker."

He shakes his head. "Not my idea. My bride's. And what she wants, I want."

"Sure. Happy to meet her." Maybe Natalie and I will hit it off, and she'll get my mind off the one person I need to stop thinking about.

"Wedding hookups are awesome, right?"

"They're the best," I say.

"And if there were anything more than hanging out going on with you and my sister, you know what I'd do to you."

I run a hand through my hair. "You do realize neither I, nor my hair, are the least bit afraid of you. You're like the definition of not scary, right?"

Spencer laughs. "I can be terrifying. Just ask my sister."

But I don't really want to talk to Harper about her brother. When I take out my phone later that day to text her, I find she's already sent me a note.

CHAPTER 12

I must have missed her text when it came through earlier.

Princess: Hey. Charlotte knows you smell like springtime, and it's my doing. She saw my Bucky tattoo. I could have passed it off as my initiation to a new badass feline aficionado gang, but instead I fessed up. But I didn't let on that you're like my love doctor or something. And that you're writing me prescriptions for the good stuff.

I laugh at her ability to poke fun at herself. As I kick back on my couch, I respond.

That's not the important issue. What I want to know is —have you now given up showers in protest of something?

Her reply arrives quickly.

Princess: So . . . don't laugh. But I really liked the drawing, so I didn't wash my left forearm this morn-

ing. Picture that. I had my arm poking out the shower door so I wouldn't erase it.

I push my head back into the couch pillow. Yeah, I'm picturing that perfectly. Almost like I've imagined it a million times before. Hot water streaming down her hair, droplets slipping over her tits then sliding down her belly and between her legs.

Yup. Got that image one hundred percent clear. But a picture always helps.

I can't resist, even though I know there's no chance she'll ever send me a naughty photo. In fact, I'm not even sure she's going to reply, since my phone is silent for several minutes, long enough for me to grab the paper and hunt for the Sunday crossword puzzle. This is the only reason I get the paper. The puzzle will take me all week, but I can almost always finish it.

As I find the section, my phone buzzes.

With an image.

Oh shit. There is a god. Wait. Make that a goddess.

Harper stands in her bathtub fully clothed, lifting her face to the showerhead that's not on, snapping an image of herself reenacting her shower from this morning. This is hot, and my dick is going to thank me later for this photo when I can really spend time with it. She's not even undressed, but she's wearing a V-neck shirt that gives me a fantastic glimpse of cleavage. I want to bite that swell of her breast, draw her nipple between my teeth, then suck hard—make her moan, and writhe, and whisper my name. As I drink in the rest of the picture and how her neck is stretched long and inviting, I know I want to spend a lot of time there, too. I bet she'd like neck kisses. I'm certain she'd like my mouth all over her skin. I could do things to this girl to drive her out of her mind with pleasure.

And I really fucking want to.

I open the message, and write back.

Hard to see. I think I'd have a better idea if you turned on the water.

Well, she does have a white T-shirt on. I mean, c'mon. A man has to try.

A note from her pops up.

Princess: Seriously, though. I just told Charlotte you and I have been hanging out. Did she say anything to Spencer?

And I deflate.

Yes, but there's nothing to worry about, and pretty soon he moved to the next topic—he wants to set me up with someone at the wedding.

My phone goes quiet, and I hear nothing from her. Not a peep for several hours. Maybe she's jealous. That would be kind of cool if she was. I work my way through the puzzle, taking breaks to talk to my attorney, Tyler, work out at the gym, and make dinner. As I eat, I draw, returning to the naughty puppet cartoons I sketched out yesterday, and the story of their crazy-hot, redhead mechanic who's flirting with a guy who just dropped off his car for a lube job.

"Wait. I meant brake job," he says, embarrassed.

She juts out a hip, her perky breasts making his eyes pop out. "But the lube job will feel so much better on the drive shaft."

What can I say? I like crude humor. I close my sketchbook and return to the puzzle. About the time evening slides into Manhattan, my phone buzzes once more as I'm filling in the squares for a twelve-letter word for "special liking" with "predilection."

Princess: Hi . . . so . . . I want to ask you a question . . . about dating. Since you're the love doctor.

Go for it. I'm an open book.

Princess: It's about the first, second, third date protocol you talked about.

Yup. I'm well versed. Ready to answer. Fire away.

Princess: Did you kiss the romance novelist on your second date?

This is the second time she's asked, and she really seems to want to know what I've done. From my spot on the couch, I contemplate how to answer. The phone bleats again.

Princess: BTW, I was at a party all day. Incidentally, I KILLED it with the six-year-old crowd.

Which means she's not pissed that Spencer wants to set me up with someone. She was just busy. Dammit. I drag a hand through my hair, wishing she was jealous. Then I scold myself, because my mission is to be her coach.

Yes. And the first date, too.

I move to another clue, and in seconds she responds.

Princess: That's so unfair! You're applying different rules to me. Anyway, what else did you do on your dates with her?

Um . . . we didn't really date that much. We met, we kissed, we screwed. We screwed again, and again. She asked me to tie her to the handle of the refrigerator and do it standing up, so she could test that bit of mild bondage for a scene in her book. I obliged. She wanted me to fuck her on her desk to make sure she knew how all the parts would align. I did my service. She insisted we get it on by the window, too, so she could press her hands on the glass of her Park Avenue penthouse and have me fuck her hard from behind.

I suspect that chapter in her novel was quite accurate as well. The relationship was great and completely absurd at the same time.

As I begin to respond, another note arrives.

Princess: I'm just trying to figure all this out. That's why I'm asking.

Quickly, Harper and I fall into a rhythm, and the texts fly fast and furious.

They weren't entirely traditional dates in the drinks, dinner, and a movie sense.

Princess: Gee. I wonder what that means. You spent a lot of time in your birthday suit?

That's one way of putting it.

Princess: What sort of things did you two do? Is that too forward to ask? I'm curious. I'm honestly curious. Okay, maybe I'm nosey too. :)

I stare at the screen, contemplating the depths of Harper's curiosity. I wish I could grasp why she's asking —if this is part of her effort to understand the modern man, or if there is any undercurrent. But I've got to accept that I just don't know. And fuck, if sex is on her mind, then at least we have that in common right now. Welcome to my wavelength. Let's spend some time together.

You really want to know? You want to go there?

   Princess: Yeah, I think I do. You said you're an open book. I kind of want to know.

Kind of? Just kind of?

   Princess: Fine. I REALLY want to know. I really, really, really want to know. Believe me now?

Almost . . .

   Princess: I want to understand the protocol. The dirty details . . .

Fine. She wants the nitty-gritty. This is my specialty. This I can do. I'm not the shy, quiet guy she knew in high school. I've studied women. I've learned what they like.

I start to type, to tell her about the fridge, the desk, the window. To say my ex liked to be tied up with rope, scarves, and one time with her pug's leash. But when I stare at those words, I *can't* send that to Harper. I can't tell Harper what an ex of mine liked in bed. It's wrong to J, wrong to me, and wrong to Harper. But I don't want to lose this moment, with all its possibilities, so I say something else.

Oh, Miss Princess Curious . . . sex is my favorite topic in the entire universe . . . but what if we tried rephrasing that? I'm happy to answer the question more generally. Like, if you were to say, 'what sort of things do you like,' I'd answer that.

Princess: WHAT SORT OF THINGS DO YOU LIKE?

Now we're getting somewhere. And I'm getting horny just thinking about the answer. Make that hornier.

Picture a menu at a restaurant. One of those diners that has everything. Breakfast, lunch, dinner, dessert, drinks, à la carte, sides, entrees. I'm looking at it. I'm ordering one of everything. I LIKE EVERYTHING.

Princess: Really? EVERYTHING? That's pretty broad. Everything???

If we were having this conversation in person, I'd run my finger across that eyebrow of yours because I know it's arched skeptically.

Princess: It might be. But 'everything' encompasses far too many things. You must have a favorite thing. Do you have a favorite position? A preference? A predilection?

A slow smile spreads across my face as I read that last word.

Predilection was one of the answers to the Sunday crossword puzzle.

Princess: You do the Sunday crossword puzzle?

I try. It's a predilection of mine.

> *Princess: I'm impressed. I want to see a finished copy. Do you do the crossword naked?*

To answer your veiled question, I'm wearing jeans, boxers, and a T-shirt right now.

> *Princess: What kind of boxers? Do you smell like springtime?*

Black boxer briefs. Yes, I do. Want to sniff me?

> *Princess: I bet you smell yummy. Now tell me more about your predilections. Do you like hot cops? Sexy librarians? Catwoman? Schoolgirls? Dominatrix?*

I laugh at the last one, and though hot cop would ab-solutely work for me, there's no question as to my answer.

Sexy librarian.

> *Princess: Do you like doggy style? Woman on top? Man on top? Bent over the bed? (You said I could ask anything! I'm asking!)*

Holy fucking turn-on of all turn-ons. Just seeing those words from her heats my skin all over. An intense, aching want spreads to every corner of my body as Harper asks me about sex. She wasn't kidding at all when she said texting was easier for her. Her message becomes an image in my mind. I'm seeing her before me on all fours on my couch, ass raised. I run a hand down her back, spread her open, and sink into her. Then, I pic-ture her riding me, those luscious tits bouncing as her hips move in wild circles. I switch positions, and now I fuck her hard and fast, her legs hooked on my shoulders. Then, she's bent over the end of the couch, and my fist is around her hair, pulling, yanking.

I don't just like all of that. I love all of that. But you forgot a few. 69 rocks. Woman sitting on my face is fantastic. Up against the wall is terrific.

Princess: You really do like to sample the whole menu.

I can't think of anything better than an all-you-can-eat buffet.

Princess: But you really don't have a preference among those?

How about I just list some of my favorite things to do?

Princess: Tell me.

My fingers hover on the keypad. I'm dying to tell her everything, to lay it all out for her, but if I do, we're leveling up. We're moving from practical texting, to flirty texting, to full-on dirty texting.

Yeah, when I think about it like that, it just makes me type faster and hit send with a flourish.

Kissing. Licking. Touching. Tasting. Kissing. Feeling. Fingering. Biting. Fucking. Eating. Spanking. Kissing. Caressing. Pinching. Nibbling. Fucking. And kissing. Always kissing.

She doesn't answer right away. As I wait, clutching the phone in my hand, my dick on high alert, my skin sizzling, I'm keenly aware of how much I want to do all those things to her. I run my palm over my jeans and against my straining erection as I stare at the screen and wonder if her hand is slipping between her legs. Gliding inside her panties. If her back is bowed and her lips are parted. If her fingers are flying so fucking fast that she's making herself come before she writes back.

I write one more note, because I can't help myself with her. And because I want to put this picture in her mind.

Actually, my favorite thing to do is to make a woman come so hard she loses her mind with pleasure.

My phone rattles.

Princess: That's. So. Hot.

It feels even better.

Princess: I can only imagine.

Imagine . . .

Her reply is enough to fuel a million fantasies.

Princess: I am. Right now.

Screw fantasy. Reality rocks. Because I'll bet a million bucks she's on her bed, her phone in one hand, the other hand down her panties.

This time, I know I played a role in getting her there. What I'm also far too certain of is if she wants me the same way, I'm not sure I could turn her down.

CHAPTER 13

I can slice and dice it a million ways, but there's no denying I sexted Harper. Or that she sexted me back.

And it doesn't seem to be stopping.

The next morning as I ride the subway to the Comedy Nation building in Times Square for a promo meeting, I click on the thread, and tap out a new message.

Enough about me. What do you like? Do you have a favorite thing?

I leave the question open-ended, so she can answer however she wants. With a noun. A verb. A position. Hell, she can even mention her favorite food group if that's easier. She's one of the boldest, most confident people I know—except when it comes to love, sex, and romance. I wouldn't call her shy in those areas, especially not after last night. But she's more like someone who has laced up ice skates for the first time, wobbly as she tries to move on sharp blades.

Princess: I've never been one to play favorites . . . until I have a favorite to play with.

So you don't?

> *Princess: It's not that I don't. More that I don't know yet.*

Interesting. That tells me her experience in the bedroom might parallel her dating experience. The train bends around a curve in the tunnel as I write back.

All right. Let's figure it out. Tell me what you like in a guy.

> *Princess: I like abs. Firm, toned abs.*

I glance down at my belly. Check.

What else?

> *Princess: I like strong arms.*

Oh yeah. Got your number there. Before I can ask anything else, my phone dings again.

> *Princess: I like black boxer briefs.*

I crease my brow as the train stops at the next station. Well, that's interesting. Pretty sure that's exactly what I told her last night I had on. I exit onto the platform, joining the crowds of New York pushing their way up the steps to work, bent over their phones.

I like your answers. What else do you like?

> *Princess: Smart guys.*

I grip the phone tighter as I head up to Forty-Second Street, resisting the impulse to make a comment about smart guys in glasses. Because, ya know, it's not the glasses that make the guy smart. It's what's inside the brain. But society has decided glasses are a symbol for intelligence, so if she wants to see me as a smart symbol, fine. I mean, sex symbol. Either one is good with me.

More. Tell me more.

> *Princess: I like soft lips and hungry kisses. Lots of kisses.*

A bolt of heat courses through my body as I flash back to last night's messages. To my long note about fucking, and kissing, and more kissing. Maybe I'm reading into this, but it's like she's giving some of that back to me. Like she wants the exact same thing—the next chapter in that kiss that started outside her home. So I reply.

What kind of kisses?

> *Princess: Kisses that make me melt.*

That's the best kind.

I don't want to stop this conversation. I'm greedy for more of her words, so I keep up the volley.

And so are kisses that go on and on.

> *Princess: And kisses that stop time.*

That turn you on.

Princess: That turn to more. That start soft and slow, and then you can feel them in your whole body. All over your skin. Deep in your bones.

My throat is dry, and my mind is immersed in the memory of those fifteen seconds and the possibility of what might have happened had the seconds stretched into minutes. Maybe just one more note . . .

That take your breath away.

Princess: And drive you wild.

Metal connects with my thighs, and a loud oomph escapes my lips. I just walked into a trash can. I put the phone in my pocket and try not to think about kisses that make her melt, since I'd rather not get to know any more trash cans in this city.

* * *

Not only do we not stop, we speed up. We change lanes. We take turns. We veer off course. And we text and sext and write more.

The next night, I crack open a beer and settle in at the standing desk where I do most of my computer animations. I take a drink, spend some time with my drawing tablet, then write to her.

So, we've got arms, abs, briefs, brains, and lips. Anything else you like?

I swear I can feel her smile in the one-word reply that lands immediately.

Princess: Eyes :)

Though it might be the emoticon that's giving me the warm-fuzzy. Or maybe just her when she adds another message.

> **Princess: I want to look into someone's eyes and feel like he knows me, gets me, understands me. I want him to see my quirks and accept them, not try to change them. I want to know what that's like.**

Damn, her words are intense and so . . . naked. Something about this small screen makes her open up and reveal parts of herself to me. The sides she doesn't show anyone. Except, she showed them to me at Speakeasy, and then at the coffee shop, and now it's like an unveiling. The pieces of Harper she hides inside her top hat, or behind the red scarf, or just beyond a witty joke or quip. Most of the time she's all *now you see it, now you don't.* But this is a whole new part of her. Take away voice, face, and body language. Lean only on words and she . . . blooms.

I step away from the desk, pace across my apartment to the kitchen, then restlessly head to the bay window, staring out on the night sky of New York with the skyscrapers and neon gazing at me. I don't want to say the wrong thing, and I don't want to send her racing back to Veiled Harper land, so as I pick up my phone I choose a safe response, but one that acknowledges all her quirks.

You deserve all of that. I want you to have that.

> **Princess: I want it, too.**

And quirks should never be changed. Keep all your quirks, Harper. I like them.

> **Princess: Same for you, Nick. I like yours, too.**

* * *

I'm addicted to my phone. That's something I've always tried to avoid, but I never know if she's going to send me something that turns me on.

Except pretty much all her messages do, so I'm living in a state of suspended desire.

It's fantastic and terrible at the same time. It feels amazing and also completely foolish. But this dizzy, heady sensation of wanting? It's in charge right now, and it leads me on. I'd like to think this newfound infatuation with her texts is good for my show. Because this next episode is coming together like a dream, and after I leave a meeting with the head animator the next day, I make my way to the elevator so I can take off uptown to meet Tyler at Nichols & Nichols.

"Mister Hammer."

The voice curdles my stomach.

"Hey, Gino."

The network head strides up to me and straightens the jacket on his pin-striped suit. "Been thinking about *The Adventures of Mister Orgasm*," he says, wiggling his eyebrows. "I like to think I have several things in common with the hero."

I stifle a cringe and just suck it down, so hard I might choke on it. "That so?"

He tugs at his tie. "I'm a bit of a ladies' man myself."

"I bet you are, sir."

"And you know, I *did* create a show myself back in the day."

Of course, he has to mention his brief flirtation with the other side. "I heard it was fantastic," I lie.

He waves his I'm-so-humble wave. "It was a damn fine show. But here's the thing. It wasn't quite as racy as yours. Which got me to thinking," he says, as he furrows his brow. His eyebrows are like two caterpillars river-dancing. "What if *The Adventures of Mister Orgasm* were more, say, family-friendly? I wonder if we could go broader, make it less naughty, and find an even bigger audience?" he says, giving me whiplash with his Mister Orgasm meets *The Brady Bunch* ideas. "Think about it."

He slaps my back and takes off, and I scratch my head as I leave to see my attorney. The Uber I ordered waits by the curb so I slide in, say hello to the driver, and return to my new favorite thing—my text messages. It's like hitting the jackpot, because there's a note waiting for me.

Princess: I thought of some other things I like.

Tell. Me. Now.

Princess: Pretty, lacy lingerie.

Dragging my hand over my face, I sink down in the leather seat. Like that will hide this problem. I breathe out hard. Like that will make this steel rod in my pants fucking disappear before I walk into my attorney's office. There are certain words that flip a switch on a hard-on, and she just used one of them. *Lingerie.*

What kind? What color? What style?

Princess: White. Black. Purple. With a little bow. On the rear. Picture a lacy panty, with a pretty little ribbon on the butt that can be untied.

I raise my face, and stare out the window. Maybe there's a store somewhere with a tub full of ice. Maybe I can just go sit in it for a couple of hours to make this lust dissipate. *Bows on panties that can be untied?* C'mon. No man is strong enough to withstand those words.

Especially not a man who was sent a black satin bow with pink polka dots. A scorching heat wave crashes into me as I mouth *holy shit*. When Harper sent me the pencils tied with ribbon, it was like she left me a little hint before I even knew what it was. A clue to all her desires, to her secret fantasies. It's like a woman undressing as she walks down the hallway, glancing back at you, her eyes saying *follow this trail*.

And I will follow.

Like a black satin bow with pink polka dots?

Princess: Yes. Did you like it?

I'm not sure I'll ever look at it the same way again.

Princess: Did you enjoy untying it?

Jesus fucking Christ. I tug at my shirt. No way can I make it through this meeting. But there's no way I can stop.

I did. I love untying little bows. In fact, 'untied' is my new favorite word.

Princess: I like dirty words, too. That's another thing I like.

Have I told you I'm a human thesaurus for dirty words?

Princess: You don't have to tell me. I figured that out on my own.

Then you know me so well.

Princess: Sometimes I do. Sometimes I don't. I also like letting go. And I like when a guy is just so consumed with making you feel good that you want to do the same to him.

I pinch the bridge of my nose as the car swings up the avenue. I swear Harper can read my mind. I lick my lips and tighten my grip on the phone.

Do you watch porn?

Princess: Does Tumblr count?

Yes. What do you watch or like to look at?

Princess: That's hard to describe.

No. It's not. Try.

Princess: You just want me to tell you what type of gifs or photos I like?

Yes. That would be awesome. In fact, it would make my day. It would make my day fucking amazing.

Her answer will have to wait, because I've arrived at the offices of Nichols & Nichols, where a well-coiffed young blonde receptionist rises from behind a sleek desk and greets me by name.

"Good to see you, Mister Hammer," she says with a crisp, bright smile. "I'll let Tyler know you're here."

"Thanks, Lily."

Before I can even grab a seat on a plush cranberry-red couch in the lobby, the head of the firm opens the glass door. "Nick Hammer," he says in his deep voice as he walks over and claps me on the back. I stand. The man is pure class. Clay Nichols wears a dark suit, a crisp white shirt, and a purple silk tie. "Tyler told me you were coming by. Couldn't miss the chance to say hello and congratulate you on all your success."

"And you as well. Love the new digs. And tell your wife she does not have to give me free liquor."

He laughs and shakes his head. "Let me give you a piece of advice. The wife takes orders from exactly no one."

He guides me down the hall to Tyler's office.

"My favorite client!" Tyler says as he greets me. I met Tyler back in the day when I was at RISD studying animation, and he was a history major at Brown. He's risen up quickly in entertainment law, and it's not only because he has a mentor in Clay. He's just really fucking good.

"I bet you say that to all your clients."

He shoots me a grin. "Only the ones who make me laugh."

"Then I've got a funny story for you," I say. Both men take seats on the couch. I grab the comfy chair, lean forward, take a breath, and give this the pregnant pause of ridiculousness it deserves. "Gino wants me to make the show more wholesome."

Tyler raises an eyebrow. The guy is the spitting image of his cousin—dark hair, brown eyes, square jawline. If I didn't know better, I'd think he was his younger brother. He's suited up, too. "That's insane. You don't ask Seth MacFarlane to make *American Dad* less fucked up," Tyler says, stretching his long legs in front of him.

"Look, I'm not a prima donna. I'm all about giving the viewers what they want. But I just can't wrap my head around what he wants from me."

"Leave it to us. It's our job to figure out what he wants, and if that aligns with what you want," Tyler says, and for the next thirty minutes we dive into their plan for how they want to handle the renegotiation at the end of this month, less than two weeks away. It all sounds reasonable to me, and frankly, that's why I work with these guys. When we're done, I ask what they're up to tonight.

Clay goes first. "I have a date with my two favorite girls. My wife and daughter are meeting me at the playground in a few hours. This man," he says, patting his cousin's shoulder. "He's trying to win back an old flame."

Clay gives me a quick download on Tyler's romantic situation, and it's a tough one.

"Ouch," I say, shuddering and then meeting my lawyer's eyes. "Good luck with that, buddy. Negotiating with Gino might be more fun."

Tyler laughs and shakes his head. "Believe you me, I know. What would Mister Orgasm do to win her back?"

I stroke my stubbled jaw. "Aside from sending in your place a rich, hot, successful, well-endowed cartoonist to win her over?"

Tyler narrows his dark eyes and shoots me a look.

I flash him a smile. "He'd probably just let her know how much she means to him, then make her feel like a queen."

"Truer words," Clay says, then I say good-bye, leave their office, and head into the crisp air of a late fall afternoon in New York City.

But as I slide into the next train downtown, I'm not thinking about Tyler's woman anymore. I'm thinking about the text Harper just sent me. Actually, *thinking* is the wrong word. *Feeling* is the only one that fits. As I open her new message and scroll through the pictures, I hit one thousand degrees Fahrenheit in seconds.

I sink onto the train's plastic seat, and my eyes are hostage to these images. Someone says, "excuse me," as he walks past, and I barely pay attention. I *can't* look anyplace else. Not possible. Not feasible. There's nothing else in the universe but these photos, and I can't wipe the naughty grin off my face.

I'm cooked, roasted, and fried to a crisp. I'm seared all the way through. This text is the mother lode of Harper's fantasies.

They say a picture is worth a thousand words, but maybe that should be revised. A photo is worth a thousand heartbeats, because that's what mine skipped looking at this insanely sexy series she sent me.

The first shot is of a woman in black panties, which are tied with a tiny pink polka dot bow at the top of her ass. Her legs are smooth and sculpted. In the next one, a woman wears stockings with a vintage ruffled thing on the top of the thighs, and she's bending, unsnapping a garter belt, her rear in view. I rub my hand across the back of my neck, and breathe out hard as the train rattles underground.

It only gets hotter from there, and I'm already an inferno, baking in public transportation, surrounded by guys in suits and moms with toddlers, by hipsters and tourists, by anyone and everyone, and I don't care.

Because these photos are all I see. The shot that follows has a woman on her back, spread out across the bed, naked, her lips in an *O*, while the guy she's with devours her pussy with his mouth. His hands are curled around her ass, squeezing it, as he buries his face between her legs. She is in some kind of wild bliss.

But the next woman is in unholy heaven. She stands in nothing but heels, bent over a kitchen counter, and her lover kneels, spreading her cheeks open and licking her pussy, his fingers digging into the flesh of her rear as he laps her up.

I close the text and shut my eyes, soaking in what Harper has just told me without words.

In these pictures, I've just learned she has a total ass fixation.

This might be a new dividing line in my life. There's no way I can go back to not knowing this insanely arousing penchant of hers. I can't return to a time in my life when I didn't think about what it would be like to do this to her. To this woman who's bold enough to tell me she doesn't know what men want and also bold enough to show me what *she* wants.

And what I want. Truly. Madly. Deeply.

I barely know how I'm going to make it through dinner with Harper and her brother tomorrow.

Then, my heart sinks as the train arrives at my stop with a jolt. She's seeing Jason this week. And she hasn't asked me one question, or told me a single thing about how she's feeling about him, if she's starting to like him, or whether she's sending him photos, too.

Or if I'm just the warm-up act to the date she really wants.

On that note, my fingers curl around the screen, and I nearly crush it.

CHAPTER 14

Harper is late, and I'm not pissed.

I'm not irritated.

I'm not annoyed.

I'm just enjoying this India Pale Ale at Spencer and Charlotte's favorite pub in the Village, not far from their home, and listening to Charlotte chatter about their wedding.

"And the florist, get this, his name is Bud Rose," she says, her eyes all lit up and lively.

"And do his roses bud?" I ask, since I can't resist.

"I'm not even having roses. I was going to have cornflower bouquets," she says, then places a hand on Spencer's arm. She tilts her head to look at him. "Did I ever tell you that, Snuffaluffagus?"

Every now and then they call each other that, and I've never asked why, nor do I want to know.

"No, you didn't tell me. Tell me now," Spencer says, his eyes totally fixed on her. Damn, he is hooked, lined, and sinkered with Charlotte. But then, he's marrying her, so that's how it should be.

"In medieval days, it was believed that a girl who placed a cornflower beneath her skirt could have any bachelor she desired," she says, with a glint in her eyes just for Spencer. "And I got the one I desired."

"Yes, you did," he says, then moves in to kiss her.

The kiss goes on much longer than it should. I look at my watch; I check out the black-and-white photographs of old trucks on country roads on the walls; I study the menu. When I'm done their lips are still fused, and show no signs of separating.

"It's started already?"

I straighten at the sound of Harper's voice. She's here finally, pulling out the chair next to me. This is the first time I've seen her in days, and she looks . . . edible. She's wearing a red sweater with tiny black buttons down the front, and some kind of lacy black camisole thing under it. Her hair is down, long and silky, falling over her shoulders.

I haven't talked to her since I sent my response to those photos yesterday. I told her my phone had exploded from the hotness, and that was the last I'd heard from her. I'd forced myself to go cold turkey after that.

I can't keep rappelling down the cliff face of this untamed desire for her. I've got to reel it back in, stuff it into a trunk, lock it up, and then toss the motherfucker to the bottom of the ocean. That's the only way I can make it through this dinner and the wedding events this weekend, let alone help her learn the ways of being single in the city without wanting to simultaneously jump on her and throttle every guy she likes.

I swallow and shrug casually. "Yeah, by all accounts it'll be this way for the next"—I pause to stare at the ceiling—"five to ten years."

She smiles back at me, and at last her brother and his fiancée break their lip-lock.

"Please, don't stop on account of us," Harper says. "I've got a lot of catching up to do with Nick, so you two should continue competing for the Newlywed Smooch of the Year award."

"Hey! We've got two more nights 'til we're newly-weds," Spencer points out, then he stands up and hugs his sister and in a softer voice says, "So good to see you."

In the span of those five words, my chest pinches, and a knot of guilt burrows inside of me. Sure, technically I have the moral high ground, since I've never *officially* touched his sister. I've never crossed a real line. But the guy loves her like crazy, and I can't be encouraging her to send me photos of stockings, and bows begging to be untied, and . . . *stop*. I just have to stop. Even if those bows can bring a grown man to his knees.

After Harper hugs Charlotte, she gives me the briefest friendly embrace. I catch the faint whiff of oranges in her hair, and the scent of citrus is a new form of torture because it stirs up the memory of that fifteen-second kiss outside her apartment. I've got to stay strong. Must fight off this lust. It's pinning me to the ground, wrestling me, trying to make me succumb. I hate to do this, I truly fucking do, but I call up the image of Gino tracking me down in the hall, and yep, that solves the problem.

It's like Lust Be Gone spray.

Harper settles back in the chair next to me. "Sorry I'm late," she says to everyone. "I had a dinner tomorrow night that I rescheduled to drinks tonight, so I had to squeeze it in before this."

I grit my teeth.

Fucking Jason.

But wait. I remind myself that I don't care about Jason. He's in the trunk at the bottom of the ocean.

I don't ask why she moved the dinner to drinks. I don't ask how it went. I'm not going to ask at all if she kissed him.

Because I. Don't. Care.

"How was it?" Charlotte asks sweetly.

I want to reach across the table and stuff the question back into her mouth. She doesn't care, either. No one cares.

"It was fine," Harper answers with a sweet smile, and the waitress arrives, inquiring if she wants a drink.

After Harper orders a glass of wine, the women return to discussing wedding flowers, and Spencer and I get caught up in a debate about beer. Misplaced desire, the trunk in the ocean, and bows on panties have all vacated the premises.

Sometime after dinner arrives, Charlotte gets that excited look in her eyes, waves her hands, and points at me. "Oh my God, I saw that J's book just came out this week. I have it on my Kindle."

Harper's eyes widen, and she looks at me. "J?"

Shit. I had no clue that book was coming out now. How the hell do women know these things?

Charlotte nods at Harper and explains helpfully. "J. Cameron. She writes these crazy-hot romance novels. She and Nick used to be together."

"I would hardly say we were together." I try to downplay it.

Spencer fake-coughs. "If by hardly together, you mean you were her muse and inspiration, then sure." He stops to draw air quotes. "'Hardly together' works."

"You were *J. Cameron's* muse?" Harper asks, latching onto the name I've never revealed to her before. Her books are wildly popular.

I shake my head. "No. I was *not* her muse."

Spencer guffaws under his breath. "Yeah right."

Charlotte takes over the reins. "She's so talented and so gorgeous. But you're definitely not still with her, right?"

"No. It's over. It's been over for months," I say, suddenly feeling backed into a corner.

"Good," Charlotte says, smiling conspiratorially. "Because I can't wait to introduce you officially to my sister this weekend. She's going to adore you. How could she not? You're so handsome, Nick. Isn't he handsome, Spencer?" she asks, nudging Spencer.

He gags. "If by handsome you mean—"

Charlotte darts out her arm and covers his mouth with her hand. "Natalie will like Nick, don't you think, Harper?"

Spencer pretends to chew on Charlotte's palm.

"Sure," Harper says, nonchalant.

"How could she not? He's kind of insanely hot, isn't he?" Charlotte asks, staring at Harper and waiting for an answer.

Harper parts her lips to speak, when Spencer bites down on Charlotte's hand.

"Ouch!" She swats his shoulder and giggles, and the two of them kiss once more.

Harper never answers.

I don't hear from her after dinner, either. Nor do I write to her.

CHAPTER 15

On Friday afternoon I pack a bag and head to Grand Central to meet my parents, as well as Wyatt and Josie and Harper, so we can all catch a train to New Haven for the wedding. A new strain of guilt rushes through me as I walk through the terminal—guilt over ignoring Harper's efforts to figure out men, because of my own jealousy. I've dropped the ball on her project, and I feel like a complete jerk for doing so. After I drew on her arm, everything became all about me, and my ravenous appetite to learn all her likes and dislikes.

I'm not sure I'll be able to chat with her on the train, so I tap out a quick text as I near the big gold clock inside the station.

How was the date with Jason? Any questions? Anything I can help you with?

Her reply is immediate.

Princess: You were wrong about the second date.

My jaw clenches as I head onto the platform, and I'm tempted to ask *how wrong?* I push my bag higher on my shoulder, and step onto the silver train bound for the next state, scanning the crowd for my family. My phone dings, and I dread whatever's coming next. She's going to tell me her second date was amazing, and that she's got it bad for him now.

Princess: *He didn't even try to kiss me.*

A weight lifts from my shoulders. I'm pretty sure I might even be able to fly right now. I look up from my phone as a skinny man pushes past me, and I spot my parents. My mom waves from a pair of seats. My dad is next to her, with Wyatt a few rows away since it's hard to grab seats together on a Friday. Josie is here, too, her pink-streaked hair twisted on top of her head and held in place with what looks like a chopstick. She beams when she sees me. I give my mom and sister each a kiss on the cheek and say hi to my dad then turn abruptly when Harper says *hey*. She's across from them, and she pats the seat next to her. I toss my bag in the overhead and take the seat. "He didn't even try?" I repeat in a low whisper, so only she can hear.

She shakes her head, a bright smile on her face. "Nope. He's very sweet. But I'm glad he didn't. I didn't want to kiss him."

I can't help it. That just makes me . . . happy. Then I'm ridiculously happy when she adds, "And I told him that while I enjoyed chatting with him, I didn't see it going further."

"You said that?" I ask, fighting back a grin, even though I like that she was direct and honest with him, and I love that he's out of the picture.

"I did," she says. "I still don't get that crazy fluttering feeling in my chest with him, and I don't think I will. Best not to lead him on, right?"

I nod as my thoughts slip-slide in a thousand directions. I want to say so much, but I narrow in on my role with her. "So how am I supposed to help you figure out how to date?"

She shrugs. "I don't know. I don't want to talk about other guys right now."

"What do you want to talk about?" I ask in a low voice, my heart racing, my skin heating up just from being near her.

She holds up her phone and taps on the screen. "This," she says, pointing to our thread of messages.

"What about that?"

"Didn't you like the pictures I sent you?" she whispers.

My jaw drops. "Are you kidding me? I loved them."

"You hardly said anything," she says, and there's the tiniest bit of hurt in her voice. "You only sent one reply."

Oh shit. I fucked up. She opened up to me with the photos, and I shut her down because of my stupid jealousy. Those pictures should have been the start of a new hot text conversation, not the end. "I'm sorry," I say, speaking honestly. "I should have written again." I drop my voice further. "But they sent all the blood rushing everyplace else but my brain."

That makes her smile. "I just wanted to hear back. To know you wanted more."

I raise my face, meeting her eyes. They look the way they did when I showed her the drawing on her arm in the coffee shop. Hungry, ready, wanting. The same as mine, I'm sure, so I say the next thing—the thing that sets me on fire. "I want so much more."

She licks her lips, and they start to form what sounds like a feathery *me, too*, but it's cut off abruptly when Josie pops out of her seat, nudges my elbow, and tells me to switch with her. "You've monopolized Harper long enough. My turn," she says, with a smile that shows off her dimples. Josie is close in age to Harper, and they spend the whole ride to Connecticut catching up.

Wyatt becomes my traveling companion for the next two hours. When we reach the hotel, we all check in together, Harper going right after me, and then we scatter to hotel rooms on different floors.

At the rehearsal dinner, Harper is consumed with family and is then commandeered by her friend Jen for a drink. I play pool with my brother, and proceed to clobber him, and that victory marks the end and highlight of my night.

* * *

"I now pronounce you husband and wife. You may kiss the bride."

I smile for the happy couple from my spot near the groom, and Harper beams from across from me. Her dress is sleek, simple, and royal blue. It lands at her calves and shows off her shoulders and makes her hair look fucking amazing. Those red locks are piled high on her head, and loose tendrils fall by her face.

As the newlyweds walk down the aisle and through the guests in the huge room overlooking the hotel grounds, Charlotte's sister wipes a tear from her eye and clutches her bouquet. I talked to Natalie at the rehearsal dinner last night, and she's whip-smart and fun. She's blonde, like Charlotte, with big blue eyes and legs that go on forever.

I guess I should get to know her more, but after the bride and groom kiss, we're all pulled into various wedding photos and festivities, so there's no time to talk. Later on, the dancing begins, and once Spencer and Charlotte have their first dance, the DJ spins some faster tunes. Harper and her friend Jen take to the floor while Wyatt and I watch from the open bar, and then Natalie joins the women. A slow song comes on, and the women separate. Natalie weaves her way to my brother and me.

Wyatt taps his chest. "She wants me."

Harper and Jen head for the ladies' room, and I can't resist the chance to beat Wyatt, so I speak first. "Want to dance, Natalie?"

"Sounds great."

I offer her my hand and lead her out on the dance floor, then proceed to slow dance in the most chaste way possible, with as much distance between us as I can manage.

"I hear my sister wanted to set us up," Natalie says with a quirk in her lips.

"Yes, she did."

"She's got hearts in her eyes these days," Natalie adds, but there isn't any flirting in her tone, just amusement. I should be disappointed. I'm not.

"No surprise there," I say as we move in a small circle, my hands on her waist, hers on my shoulders, our bodies many inches apart. I wonder if she feels it, too—this lack of attraction. It's not because she isn't pretty. It's not because she isn't smart. It's just one of those things—the spark is either there, or it isn't. Natalie and I don't spark.

She parts her lips to say something, when I feel a tap on my shoulder.

"May I cut in?"

Like someone grabbed the remote and changed the channel mid-scene, my pulse speeds up.

"Be my guest," Natalie says with a smile, and then Harper's in my arms, and without a second thought, there's barely any distance between us. My fingers curl over her hip bones, and her hands wrap around my shoulders. Everything sparks. She's so much closer than Natalie was. A few more centimeters and our chests would touch. A little more and we'd be dancing cheek to cheek. More than that and we'd be arrested for public indecency.

"Is this the obligatory best man/bridesmaid dance?" I ask playfully.

"Wouldn't a maid of honor/best man dance be more obligatory?"

We sway, moving the slightest bit. "You stopped that from happening," I say, nodding in the direction of Natalie's exit. "Did you sense I needed you to perform your patented swoop in and save?"

She laughs lightly. "She didn't seem your type," she whispers. "Too young."

"Why do you keep saying—?"

But she shushes me and tips her head to the right. Wyatt is already dancing with Natalie. "Maybe I just felt bad for your brother. I could tell he had eyes for her, and I'd feel terrible if you beat him out. Poor Wyatt. Always second best to his big brother."

I laugh and shake my head. "We've never fought over girls. Everything else, though."

She shrugs, and as her shoulder juts up, I wrap my fingers more tightly over her hip, brushing against the bone. Her breath catches, and these are the moments that turn my world with her into a bumper-car ride. I don't ever know if we're coming or going. We smash into each other, then we bounce apart, and then we're right back like this. Bows, skipped breaths, and glossy eyes. That's how hers look right now. This very second they shine with desire, as if she's showing me how she pulls off a trick. As if she's revealing her truth.

"Besides," she says, low and soft, "maybe I felt territorial."

My lips curve up in a grin, and my heart pounds wildly. *Territorial* is my new favorite word.

"Did you?" I ask as we turn in a lazy circle. Somewhere nearby is my best friend, and I don't care.

Because this woman is in my arms. She is all I see, all I hear, all I smell. The need to be closer to her consumes me, blotting out everything else—most of all, the reason to stay away.

Her hand moves closer to my neck, and she fiddles with the collar on my shirt. "Your tux looks good," she says, breathless, and as much as I like that, I also hear what she doesn't say. *You look good.*

There's a difference between the two. A big difference.

Spots of light play over the hardwood floor as the song slides to the end. "So does your dress," I say, as I roam my eyes over her clothes then back up to her face. Then I show her how it's done. She asked me to teach her. This I can do honestly—compliment her the way she should be complimented. With my eyes locked on hers, I say, "And you look gorgeous, Harper."

Her chest rises and falls against my own, and I stare at her mouth as her lips part, as if she's taking her time to say something. Then she does, and the words topple out in a nervous mess, but still they're fucking perfect, as she says, "You look so hot."

That's all I can take. The sliver of space between us is thick with lust. It's strung tight with desire, and I'm confident for the first time it's not a one-way street. Her eyes are clear and focused on me, only me, and even if she's not good at reading men, she has to know what's happening with us. I'm done fighting this.

This is all I can take.

I burn for her. Everywhere. My hands, my chest, my skin. I want this girl so much. My fingers inch across her collarbone, and I run them over a loose curl of her hair. I move closer, dip my head toward her ear. "Do you want to get out of here?"

A fork clinks on a glass. Spencer's father clears his throat. "Thank you all for coming."

As if we've been electrocuted, we wrench apart, and it's painful. Completely, utterly painful, especially since I'm not sure this erection is ever going away. But as I zero in on the face of the father of the woman I want underneath me . . . yep . . . done . . . gone.

Instant boner killer.

Whew.

He toasts, and then I toast, and then the bride and groom share the cake my mom made, and at some point, my phone buzzes lightly in my pocket.

I slip away from the crowd to look at her one-word reply, zoning in only on three beautiful letters.

Yes.

CHAPTER 16

I pace in the brightly lit hall outside the reception, waiting for her to slip out, too. But two, three, four minutes after her text, and there's still no sign of the girl in the blue dress.

I weigh my options. Head back into the reception to look for her like Captain Obvious. Send her a text asking what's up like a Pushy Dick. Or make my way to the bar like Cool and Casual Guy.

Before I settle on the no-brainer of Scotch, the text message light blinks.

Princess: Trapped by a very tipsy Jen. Give me a few minutes. Meet me in a dark stairwell? Vending machine on second floor? Library? Underneath a tree on the grounds?

I smile. So very Harper.
And I'm going to be so very me, now.

Room 302.

Once I'm inside my room, my bow tie is undone, along with the top two buttons on my shirt. I toss my jacket on the bed, kick off my shoes, and flop down on the mattress.

I grab the remote.

No time like the present to find out what's on the tube on a Saturday night.

Clicking through the hotel menu, I learn that not only can I watch a ton of reruns, a plethora of cooking shows, and a host of filthy movies, I can also order my continental breakfast for tomorrow, plan a spa day, or take a tour of the hotel grounds on the interactive map.

Wow. That sounds immensely fascinating. Not sure I can contain my excitement at the mere suggestion of a TV-screen tour of the hotel.

I manage, though, stabbing the *off* button then checking my phone.

That killed ten minutes, but there's still no text from Harper.

Flicking through some apps, I manage to carve another five minutes out of my night before I peek again at the texts.

That's when I see the *unsent* status on my last note. Oh shit. I sit up, scrambling to resend the note that didn't go through for whatever reason.

But before I can even click, there's a knock on my door. When I cross the few feet to open it, I find Harper in her blue dress, her hair half-down, and one hand behind her back.

She wastes no time.

"My zipper is stuck. And you never told me where you wanted to meet, but I remembered your floor from when we checked in, and I knocked on a few doors, taking a chance, and someone down the hall asked if I had the chocolate-covered strawberries they ordered, and obviously I don't, but they sounded really good, and well, here I am, thinking about strawberries and hunting for your room while my zipper is stuck."

A grin tugs at my mouth at everything she just said, but I key in on the last one. "Your zipper's stuck?"

She turns around and shows me, and it's a tangled, mangled mess, caught in the red strands of her hair. I grab her arm, pull her into my room, and guide her to the edge of the bed. Sitting her down, I appraise the zipper. "Your hair is in the zipper."

"I know," she says with a huff. Then softer, "Can you fix it?"

"Yes."

She breathes a sigh of relief.

"What did you do to make this happen?" I push some of the loose hair off her back. The dress has two slim straps, and her shoulders are exposed. Her skin is pale, and I want to kiss it.

"I was in my room," she says as I start working on the zipper, gently tugging a few strands from the teeth.

"I thought Jen corralled you?"

"She did, but then I escaped, and I didn't hear back from you right away, so I went to my room to change into something else and let my hair down, and when I started to take off the dress, my hair got stuck and this happened."

"My message didn't go through. But I had texted you my room number," I say, as I free more pieces of her hair.

"You did?" she asks, and I can hear a smile in her voice.

"Yes. When you sent me your list of meeting places."

"I found you anyway. I wanted to find you," she says, and I freeze, my hands stilling on her zipper.

Find me.

That's what I've wanted from her—for the lightbulb to go off, and for Harper to see I'm the one she wants.

"You're a good detective. I'll get you those chocolate-covered strawberries if you want," I tease.

"I don't want that right now. I want something else."

"What do you want?" I ask as I resume my work, practically holding my breath with the hope that she wants the same thing I do.

"I want the night with you not to end."

CHAPTER 17

She came looking for me . . . and her hair is stuck in her zipper. I've got to focus on part two of that first. I wiggle the zipper one way, then the other, then back again, until at last, her hair is free and the zipper is undone.

I don't unzip it. Not yet. Instead, I sweep all her hair off her back. "Your zipper is fixed," I tell her, as I press my fingertips against her bare shoulder.

"Your hands," she murmurs. "You have good hands. You know what to do with them."

"I do know what to do with them, and what I *want* to do with them," I say, as my fingers travel to the edge of her shoulder. Even this small touch turns me on like crazy. "And I want to touch you so fucking much."

"Oh God, please touch me." The words spill out of her in a breathless rush.

Everywhere there are sparks. Just everywhere—lighting up my skin, spreading inside me like wildfire. I run my left hand down her arm. The little hairs on her arms stand on end as I trace her soft skin, my fingers heading for her wrist. I lay my hand on top of hers, and she opens her fingers. I slide mine between hers, and she gasps.

That sound ignites me, makes me want to never stop touching her.

I clasp her hand, and it feels erotic and romantic at the same time, and I've never in my life enjoyed holding hands this much. It's as if every cell of hers reaches for me, and every nerve inside me blazes for her. I have never felt so sure that a feeling is mutual before. Never.

She wraps her fingers tightly around me, and I'm pretty much done. I brush my lips against the back of her neck, and my mind goes hazy with desire.

"*Oh,*" she says, a gentle moan.

She tastes so fucking good. With my free hand, I thread my fingers in her soft, silky hair and skim my nose across her neck, inhaling her, letting her scent wash over me, like the best drug. She doesn't smell like springtime; she reminds me of honey, and oranges, and all my fantasies. I nip her neck, flicking my tongue over her flesh. The need to kiss her everywhere builds.

Her shoulders rise and fall, her breathing grows fast, and her fingers grip me harder. I layer kisses all over the back of her neck, drawing out moans, and gasps, and sighs that drive me crazy. They tell me how much she's into this. How much more she wants.

I've been dying to kiss her lips, to feel her body mold to me. Now, here she is, alone in my hotel room, and she came for me, and that staggers me. It's everything I wanted and refused to believe would happen.

"*Harper.*"

"Yes?" It sounds like she's dreaming.

"What would you do if I kissed you right now?"

I ask not because I'm unsure, not because I'm worried she doesn't want it, but because she likes to talk about kissing, I've learned.

She's feathery soft as she answers me, "I would probably melt."

Or maybe I will.

I let go of her hand and turn her face to me. My eyes hook into hers, so open, so vulnerable, so damn ready. I run my thumb along her cheek, and she shivers. Her lips part, and I want to crush her mouth to mine this second, but I want to draw out the anticipation even more. Because in her eyes I see so much want, so much desire, so much of everything I've craved from this girl, everything I've seen flashes of in the last few weeks. I want her to feel *all* of it. To experience every second of this moment before I kiss her.

But I can't wait any longer.

I press my lips to hers, and the temperature in me soars. I kiss her soft and tender as I touch her face, my fingers exploring her. It's such a rush to kiss her in private with no one watching, to have her permission behind closed doors. It's a privilege to know this part of her, this side she so rarely shows. The side of her where she lets me in, where she lets go.

We fit so extraordinarily well, our lips eager and greedy. She's so soft and so hungry at the same time. Soon, this pace isn't enough, and I slide my tongue between her lips. She opens for me, and it's electric. Her tongue meeting mine. Our breath mingling. We both moan at the same instant, because this is so fucking intense. So damn good. I kiss her harder, deeper, wetter. I suck that sexy bottom lip of hers between mine, and her hands shoot up and thread through my hair. She's not a hot mess at all. She's just hot and fevered, bursting with need. She's rough, too, as she curls her fingers around the back of my head and clutches me closer, like she can't get enough of kissing me.

I can't get enough of her, either.

Kissing has never been like this. It's never been this good, this intense. I'm drunk on her, intoxicated on her taste, her tongue, her mouth, her sweetness.

Harper fucking loves being kissed. And she's right. She does melt. She melts into me, and that's where I want her, so far gone. Her warm, pliant body is like water in my arms, moving with me, gliding against my chest, pressing against every inch of my hard body. I can only imagine what it will be like to have my lips all over her, to explore every inch of her, to drive her wild with my tongue.

She moans, and I swallow that sound. She wriggles even closer, her breasts pushing against my chest, and her hands play with the hair on the back of my neck. At one point she kisses me so hard, she pushes my glasses against my nose.

"Ow," I say softly, breaking the kiss.

"Sorry," she says.

I separate from her, set my glasses on the nightstand, and return my attentions to Harper, running my fingers down her arms, making her shiver.

"I hardly ever see you without your glasses," she says softly as she studies me.

"Do I look like a different guy?"

She shakes her head, then takes my face in her hands, running her fingers over my beard. "No. You look like you, and you look so good. And I love kissing you." Her voice is stripped bare and full of a beautiful lust that heats my skin all over, that burns in my bones.

Her lips fuse to mine and that frenzied pace returns. This kiss ignites, picking up speed, racing to a whole other level. She makes the sexiest sounds as she moans and murmurs, completely consumed with the way we kiss. Her noises make me want her even more, and I didn't think it was possible to crave a person this much.

But I do. I just fucking do.

Her fingers brush across my stubble as we devour each other. I bring my hands to her hips, shifting her so she's on me, straddling me. I'm so lit up with her. I can feel her everywhere, and I want to do everything with her.

I'm pretty sure she wants the same because she pushes against my hard-on, grinding into me through all these goddamn clothes we're both wearing. Too many stupid layers. I don't know where we're going tonight, how far or how fast, but I can't even think. I want to be in the moment with her. Every moment, including this one, where my hands find their way to the hem of her dress, and I slide them under the fabric.

I break the kiss. "Stockings," I say, like a man hypnotized.

"You like stockings."

"I do, and you're killing me." My fingers travel up the back of her legs, and she rocks against me.

I grow even harder as she thrusts. Then harder still as I reach the top of the stockings. They're thigh-highs, and I want to look at them, gawk at them, stare at them. But I'm not moving her off me. No chance of that. Not when she breathes this rapidly, each one coming faster than the next. Not as she grinds against my dick. And not as I move my hands to her delicious ass, sliding them over the sheer lacy fabric.

She cries out, and her face falls into my neck. She buries it there, moaning as I squeeze those luscious cheeks.

"Oh God," she whispers, her voice strained as she rocks into me, her breathing wildly erratic.

"So you like this," I ask rhetorically as I grip her ass. I can tell she likes it. I can tell she loves it.

"So much." Her voice breaks, her pitch rises, and this moment crystallizes to its pure, wicked possibilities.

I grab her skirt in the front, gather the material in a flash, and yank it up to her waist. She still straddles me, still riding, still thrusting against me. My hands return to her ass again as if I'm steering her, moving her sweet hot body against the outline of my rock-hard cock. It's just Harper in her wet panties, rubbing on me.

"Ride me, princess," I whisper harshly in her ear. "Ride me like that 'til you come."

I'm rewarded with another *oh God*, as she moves faster, rocks harder, picks up the pace. She grabs my face, grips my jaw, and holds me as she dry-humps me. Every single thing about her turns me on—her need, her want, her wild lust, her sounds, and this ass. It's spectacular—firm and so damn soft at the same time. I grip the flesh hard, how she likes it, and she lets out a sexy squeak.

"I fucking adore your ass," I say roughly.

She moans something unintelligible.

I dig my fingers inside the lace on her rear, guiding her moves, making her ride my erection faster and wilder. "You're so close, aren't you?"

"Yes," she cries out. "Oh God, Nick. Oh my God."

Those are the last words I can make out. The rest is just noise—pure, carnal sound as she rides me to the edge, and then trembles, shaking as she comes on me. So hard. She comes so fucking hard on me, clothes on, the friction itself all she needed to get there. I lace my fingers in her hair, pride surging through my entire being as I take in the flush in her cheeks, the shuddering in her shoulders. I want to remember every detail of what it feels like to make her shatter this first time.

Truth be told, I kind of want to draw a picture of her, too. Because she looks amazingly beautiful like this.

"I want to make you come again. I want to hear you go wild, and make you fall apart," I tell her as she breathes hard, panting in my arms.

She runs her fingers over my face and brushes her lips on mine. "I want it all."

After she comes down from her high, she blinks. Her blue eyes register surprise, as if it's just dawned on her what she did—dry-humped me. Which is completely awesome in my book, but in hers, I have no idea. I tense, waiting for Harper to slip into that armor she wears so well.

Instead, she loops her arms around my neck. Okay, that's much better. Then she says, "There's something I want to tell you."

CHAPTER 18

I've never been a huge fan of those words, so it's time for me to don my own trusty shield. I unsheathe the sword of humor and brandish it. "You want to strip me naked and have your wicked way with me?"

She smiles and nods. "I do."

Well, I'll just keep up this tactic. Since that particular weapon, if you know what I mean, is all the way up. "Great. Start here," I say, pointing to my belt.

She laughs and then grips my shoulders, lowering her voice as if she's about to admit a secret. "But seriously. I have a confession. As soon as I learned her name, I read J. Cameron's newest book."

Sighing, I run a hand through my hair, unsure why we're back on this topic. "You did?"

Her eyes dance with naughty delight. "It's so delicious. It's so hot. And it made me curious," she continues, and maybe I don't mind her bringing up the ex at all right now. Not if those books get her turned on rather than ticked off. Hell, maybe I should gift her some.

"What did it make you curious about?"

Harper sits up straighter on me, as if she's about to make a Big Pronouncement. "I know this may shock you, given how utterly cool you've seen I can be, what with getting my hair caught in a zipper and speaking in tongues," she says, then stage whispers, "but I've never been tied to a fridge. Or done it on a desk."

"And do you want that?"

"That's the thing," she says, an excited undercurrent to her words. "I only know what I like to look at. What I like to read about. I have an idea of what I might like. But . . ." She lets her voice trail off.

"But what?" I ask, because I'm dying to know what comes after that.

She takes a breath, purses her lips together, then speaks. "I was a virgin until I was twenty. I've only had sex with two guys, and none of it was very memorable. None of it was on a counter, or the dryer, or even in a hotel bed," she says, patting the mattress.

Maybe it's the dark of the night, maybe it's her, maybe it's just that the only thing better than having hot sex with the woman you want is *talking* about hot sex with the woman you want. Or, just possibly, it's that she's opening up to me for real now. Perhaps that's why I open up to her.

"I was twenty the first time I had sex," I say, serving up a detail I don't share with many people, because it's personal.

Instantly, her eyes widen. "Are you serious?"

"No, I'm lying," I say sarcastically.

She pushes my shoulders, nearly toppling me on the bed. "Stop it. I want to know the truth."

"I was a sophomore in college when I finally ditched the V-card."

"You were a late bloomer," she says softly, something like wonder in her voice.

"Girls were a complete mystery to me before then. I didn't know how to act around them, or what to say. Sort of how you feel sometimes, too." I realize that maybe

Harper and I aren't that different. I just got over my awkwardness around the opposite sex well before she did.

She gives me a sweet smile. "I guess we do have that in common. Among many other things," she says, and my chest heats up as she inches closer. "Was she a sophomore, too?"

I shake my head and laugh. "No. She was a grad student. She was the teaching assistant in my animation class."

Her eyes turn into moons. "Did she teach you everything you know?"

I reflect on her question, and the answer is a big no. But she started my education in women. She was instrumental in showing me the ropes, and telling me every little thing that drove her crazy. I was a good student. I followed her directions, and it was the best damn class I ever took. Any guy who thinks he automatically knows how to please a woman is a conceited ass. Every woman is one of a kind. Every woman has her own titillations and turn-ons. From my teaching assistant, I learned the foundation—how to listen to a woman's cues, how to give her what she needs, how to make her want more and more.

I don't say that to Harper. I liked the conversation better when it was about us. "How would you feel if we stopped talking about other women?" I ask, echoing her sentiment from the train on the ride here. "I'd rather talk about what we just did, and what other things I can do to you."

She swallows and takes a breath. "When I said touching your arms in Central Park was the most action I'd gotten in ages, I meant it. I haven't done *that* much. But I want to, Nick. I really want to," she says, her voice impossibly soft. "I just feel like I don't know what I'm doing."

I tuck my finger under her chin and lift her eyes to mine. "You were amazing, Harper. You rode me like a champion equestrian. I loved every second of it. Wait. I loved every millisecond of it." I shake my head. "Make that every nanosecond."

She grins, then erases the smile from her face just as quickly. "Riding you was easy. But beyond that, I want to know what feels good to you, and what you want. And I want to know what I like. I can tell you what I *think* I like. My God, I love looking at dirty pictures, and sexy pictures, and naughty gifs, so I think I have a good idea."

"So you're *not* curled up at night with your deck of cards after all," I say, fixing on a look of overdone surprise as I touch her fingers. "You're saying you've done a lot of one-handed computer work?"

That naughty grin returns in force, shining at full wattage. "My web history is an homage to the hottest Tumblr feeds around," she confesses.

"I'm going to need to see that. As part of this whole dating lessons thing. I need to know exactly what you've been looking at. And to look at it with you."

"That's what I'm getting at." She stops to take a breath, then holds her chin high. "That's why I kept asking you what you liked, and now I want to ask you something else, since you seemed to like what we just did."

And it clicks. It goes off like a starting gun. "*Teach you.* You want me to teach you," I say, my voice raspy, full of want.

Her eyes twinkle with naughtiness. "I do."

Her words echo back to another *I do*, one I heard earlier in the day. We're at her brother's wedding, and I'm messing around with my *best friend's sister*. For the briefest of moments, a streak of guilt flashes like a warning sign on the highway. *Danger ahead*. But hell, it's too fucking hard to think of anyone except her when she's with me. Truth be told, it's not easy the rest of the time either. It's like my desire for Harper hogs the remote control and flicks all the channels back to her.

Besides, Spencer takes off for Hawaii tomorrow, and what he doesn't know won't hurt him. Especially since Harper and I won't hurt each other. We know the score, and everyone in our game wins.

I shake off any doubts.

I drag my hand down her chest, palming one perfect tit. "You want to kick our lessons up a notch and learn what feels good to you."

"Yes," she says, mirroring me as her fingers play along the front of my shirt. Damn, that feels fantastic. "And what feels good to you."

"Let me think about it." I sigh heavily and stare at the ceiling then back at her. "I thought about it long and hard—"

"Long and hard. It felt that way to me when I was riding you like a rodeo star."

I give her an appreciative nod. "Oh, it is long and hard. Especially around you and that dirty little mouth of yours," I say, running my finger across her lips.

She nips my finger. "I have a dirty mind, too. I just want to put it to use now. In every way."

"You came to the right man," I tell her. "And you came with the right man. And you will again, and again, and again."

She shivers, then starts to unbutton my shirt. "But I want you to come, too."

"Don't worry about me. And yes, obviously, I'll teach you anything." I can't say anything but yes to this girl. It's like an affliction, the amount of craving I have for Harper. Any doctor would tell you the only path to recovery is to take a full dose of medicine. In my case, that's *her*. Maybe I'll take several doses, just to be safe.

A few lessons and I'll be cured, ready to return to us being buddies.

"I'll teach you anything you want to know. Under one condition," I say, arching a brow.

Her eyes widen. "What would that be?"

I clear my throat and adopt a teacherly tone. "I'm going to need your full commitment to the lesson plan for the next week," I say, laying it on thick with the seriousness. "Can you agree to that, Miss Harper?"

She nods earnestly, sliding into her role in this impromptu game. "I'm a very good student. What else do you need . . . *Professor Hammer*?"

I smile approvingly when she bestows a nickname on me. "Proper focus. Diligent homework. Thorough preparation. And the willingness to be spanked if you deviate from the lesson plan."

She moves in closer, loops her arms around me, and says in a deliciously naughty good-girl voice, "You can spank me even if I don't deviate from the lesson plan."

Oh holy hell. Harper Holiday is going to be a star pupil in my school of hot, filthy sex. "I'm giving you an A+ so far," I say in my studious voice. "And I fully expect you to earn gold stars in my intensive course for the next week."

She pulls back and speaks as herself. "But it'll only take a week?"

I nibble on her neck. "When the cat's away . . ." I whisper, hoping my meaning is clear. I speak in my own voice, so we're both on the same page. "It's just easier for us to do this for the next week, right?"

"Of course," she says quickly. "Makes perfect sense, Professor Hammer. Does this mean you'll hammer me?"

She laughs, and I crack up, too, because at last the innuendo of my surname is being used with the right woman. "That's a guarantee. In fact, I think we should start your coursework right now, and I have a very particular lesson in mind."

"What is it?" she asks, a little breathless, a lot eager.

I lean in close to her and rub my beard against her cheek. "I want to strip you naked so I can taste every inch of your skin. I want to spread your legs, and make you come on my lips," I say, as I bring her hand to my jaw and finish the thought, "and all over my face."

She gasps, and her thighs clench against my legs. "*Now*," she says, like a desperate order.

My fingers return to the zipper on her back. A new round of lust pounds through me as I slide it down, undressing her for the first time. But I only get a few inches when a loud trill sounds from the bed.

"Shoot," she mutters and reaches for her phone on the mattress. "Let me just see who that is at two in the morning."

She slides her thumb across the screen, falls to the bed, and throws her arm on her forehead, muttering, "Jen."

She thrusts the phone at me. A text message flashes.

Everyon left. I thin I'm gonna b sick. Wrshping porcelain g d. H l p

I roll to my side, frustration thick in my veins. "Go take care of your friend," I say, even though I'm thinking Jen is winning the gold medal for cock-blocking. "But tomorrow, Harper? Your first lesson is turning off your phone. Then you're getting a full serving of multiple orgasms. Is that clear?"

Harper grabs the collar of my shirt, pulls me close, and says, "Yes." Then she gives me the hottest good night kiss ever.

I jerk off when she leaves.

Obviously.

CHAPTER 19

On the train the next afternoon, she steals glances at me.

Family surrounds us. My parents, Harper's parents, her very hungover, cock-blocking friend Jen, and my siblings are spread out in the first few rows of the car.

Harper sits by the window, next to my sister, and I'm in the seat that directly faces her. It kills me to be this close. I spread the Sunday paper over my lap, grateful that the crossword puzzle serves twin purposes today. Distraction and cover-up. I fill in a clue and then sneak a peek at the hot redhead I intend to fuck in so many ways.

Her head is bent over her e-reader, and she nibbles the corner of her lips as we roll along the Connecticut coast. A swath of hair falls over her forehead, obscuring the side of her face. Briefly, she looks up at me, and her eyes are hazy with lust.

Her gaze sends a charge through me, and I adjust the paper more over my thighs.

I don't dare text her now, because I don't know who'd peer over her shoulder and see my words. Probably Wyatt, and I might as well hire a skywriter if that happened.

My sister types on her phone, and Wyatt leans over the armrest, chatting with my dad across the aisle. My mom talks to Harper's mom in the row behind us, discussing when the first Holiday grandchild will be born. As soon as those words land on my ears, I tune them out and put in earbuds. I toggle through my music, hunting for something to occupy me for the next hour as the train roars along the coastline, headed for New York.

When Band of Horses appears on my scroll of songs, I stop, remembering when Harper said she loved the song in the coffee shop. Casting my eyes around, I confirm everyone is busy, so I raise my phone, briefly flashing the screen at her.

I'm rewarded with a sweet smile, as she mouths, *Love that band*.

She returns to her book, and I lift my pencil, ready to tackle more clues. Out of the corner of my eye, I notice her slide her thumb across the screen. Then she brings her finger to her mouth and runs it absently across her bottom lip.

Desire slams into me, full-force, unabated. I would do just about anything to grab her hand, tug her into the train restroom, and kiss the fuck out of her. Because I know what she's doing. She's remembering how I touched her, how I kissed her, how she let go with me last night.

She's lingering on the memories, and I wonder if she's even fully aware. Her eyes are on the screen, but she shifts in her seat like she's turned on.

This train is a straitjacket. All I want is to touch her, talk to her.

She raises her face once more and locks eyes with me. I mouth, *Are you wet?*

She doesn't answer with words. She simply nods once. As she returns her gaze to the screen, a little grin forms on her lips. An *I-know-what-we-did-last-night-and-I-loved-it* grin.

Briefly, she draws her eyes back up to meet mine, maybe to gauge my reaction. After a quick scan to make sure no one's looking, I lick my lips once, enough to let her know where my mind is, too.

Her shoulders tremble, and she blinks, then she seems to force her focus back to her book.

That silent exchange is enough for any ounce of concentration left in me to disintegrate. I can't even pretend to return to the crossword puzzle. Not when all I can think about is how she tastes. I close my eyes, listen to music, and let the scene unfold on the movie screen of my eyelids. This is the best X-rated show I've ever been to.

One interminable hour of a constant hard-on later, the train rattles into Grand Central and comes to a stop. It takes longer than I want to get out of here because we're all together, tumbling onto the platform, wandering through the terminal, hunting for late Sunday afternoon cabs and cars. The crew splits up with some heading downtown, some to the Upper East Side, and some to the West Side, like Harper, Josie, and me.

I let my sister sit in the middle of the cab, where she conducts a post-wedding recap on her favorite moments. We shoot across town, the traffic mercifully light, then up Central Park West. I get out first, give my sister money for the cab, then say good-bye in a light, easy tone. No lingering, burning stares at the woman I want. Nothing to reveal my hand.

As I head into my building, I take out my phone to text her. But it's too soon, since Josie lives five blocks away and they'll still be in the car. I drop off my bag, take a piss, wash my hands, and grab some condoms. I bet Harper doesn't stock them.

I check the time.

Josie should be gone by now, and Harper will be alone. Ordinarily, I wouldn't think twice about sending her a text. But with so many people around who know us both, we need to be careful.

Twenty minutes 'til that show that you like is on.

Snagging my keys, I head for the door. But I stop when my hand wraps around the doorknob. I inhale sharply as I make a critical change in the batting lineup. This pains me. Truly it does. But I'm a patient man. I remove the condoms from my pocket and toss them on the kitchen counter, benching the possibility of sex as I leave them behind.

She wants lessons in seduction. One of the most important ones is how to wait for it. Besides, there are so many other ways to make her come.

I arrive at her building, and she buzzes me in. When I reach her door and knock, she opens it, and I'm pretty sure I growl—low and guttural like an animal—because of how she looks. Her face is flushed, her cheeks are red, her hair falls wildly, and she's changed into shorts and a white T-shirt.

"Hi," she says.

I don't look around. I don't take in the decor of her tiny apartment. I roam my eyes over her, but it's not the new outfit that gives her away. It's the rosy glow on her cheeks. I shut the door behind me, bring my nose to her chest, and drag it along her flesh up to her ear, whispering harshly, "Did you just masturbate while waiting for me to get here?"

I wrench back, and the answer is evident in her eyes. They have that caught-red-handed look, and oh what I wouldn't give to have walked in on her a few minutes ago.

She swallows and nods. "Are you mad at me?"

I shake my head and grasp her wrists, pinning them at her sides, crowding her against the wall by her door. My body is pressed to hers. "Do I feel mad?"

"You feel hard."

I push against her, and a jagged moan falls from her lips as she feels my erection. "I would never be mad at you for coming. But tell me something—why couldn't you wait?" There's no anger in my tone, only a pulsing curiosity. I want to hear her answer. I grind my pelvis against her.

Her eyes flutter closed as she moans. "I was so turned on on the train. It was all I could think about."

I dip my head to her chest, letting go of one wrist to tug at her shirt. I brush my lips against the swell of her breast then nip her soft flesh. "What did you think about when you were getting off?"

"*You.*"

The way she says that one word unleashes a current of desire under my skin. "What did I do to you?"

"It was what I did to you."

That stops me. I raise my face. "What did you do to me?"

In a flash, her hand darts out, and she presses it against my hard-on, palming my dick through my jeans. I hiss. Fuck, that feels good.

"Got down on my knees and took you in my mouth," she answers, and my dick is practically ready to smack me upside the head for ditching the protection. What was I thinking, wanting to be patient? I want to be inside her for the rest of the night. I want to go through one, two, three condoms or more. She is so fucking hot, and my mind is swimming in a sea of lust.

"Is that something you want to do? Something you want me to include in our lesson plan?" I bring my hands to her sexy little shorts and pop open the button, then tug down the zipper.

Her hips wriggle. "Yes. So much. I want to give it to you exactly how you want it. I want to do all my homework."

I've never looked forward to an assignment so much. Because *with her tongue* is exactly how I want a blow job.

But not now.

I meet her gaze and arch an eyebrow. "Good to know. Now you have to wait for it. Because I told you I was taking care of you first, and I'm not changing my mind, princess, just because you're so fucking wound up for me."

"I'm so wound up," she says, clasping my face, running her hands over my beard like she did that night on the street outside her home. I wonder briefly if she was touching me then in an exploration, like she is now, with fire in her fingertips, with lust thrumming in her body, with this same dose of raging hormones that I feel.

"Have you ever come more than once?"

"In a day?"

I roll my eyes, laughing briefly. "No. I'm going to presume those busy fingers have polished the pearl more than once in a day. Let's say, in a thirty-minute timespan. As in, one right after the other?"

She shakes her head. "I don't think I can."

"First time for everything."

I yank her shorts to her knees, and they fall to the floor. She steps out of them, and I inch back to look at her. I drag a hand over my jaw. She's so stunning. Her legs are long and toned. Her panties are black lace with a tiny pink bow on the front. It's dainty and sexy at the same time. And it's for me.

My temperature shoots through the roof.

"So you were so worked up you couldn't wait," I say, as if I'm musing on the topic. I drag my hand down her belly then under her shirt. My fingers trace her soft stomach.

She trembles as I touch her. "I was so wet, Nick."

I hum and breathe out hard. "I bet you're still wet. I bet you're even wetter now that I'm here. Is that right?"

She swallows and nods. "Find out," she says, rocking her hips into me, rubbing against me.

Goddamn, this woman is a livewire. She's crackling everywhere. This is how I want her. Ready to shatter. My fingers turn south, and I toy with the little bow. Her eyes blaze with desire, a hot, wild neediness. I dip a finger inside the waistband, brushing over the curls of hair on her mound. She gasps as I slide my fingers between her legs.

Lust slams into me from all corners, as if it's invading my every cell. Because she is so fucking wet. So slick. "Look at you. Look at how wet you get, even after you come," I say as I glide my fingers through heaven.

As I stroke her slippery sweetness, she grabs at my arms, curling her fingers around my biceps. Her breath paints my cheek. Her wetness coats my fingers as I glide them over her pussy lips then up to the soft rise of her clit. When I touch her there, her moan is desperate.

"Did it feel like this when you fucked yourself a few minutes ago?"

She shakes her head.

I rub faster over her swollen clit. "Like that?"

She rocks against my hand. "No. Not even close."

My fingers explore her more, sliding over her silky heat. The fact that she's this turned on drives me wild. "How long did it take you? When you sucked my cock a few minutes ago?"

"Not long," she pants, her nails digging into my arms, her body rocking into me.

My God, I haven't even pushed a finger into her, and she's flying to the edge. Her legs are shaking, her breath is coming fast, and her eyes squeeze shut.

With one more stroke through all that heat, I push in, and she cries out "Oh God" as she dips down onto my fingers.

"And what about this?" I add another finger and crook it just right, hitting the spot that could send her soaring. "Did it feel like this when you fucked your hand?"

"No, God no, not even close."

She tightens around my fingers.

"Go wild on me, Harper. Fuck *my* hand now."

She moans, gripping my biceps, riding my fingers, fucking me in a mad, fevered frenzy. She clenches around me, so tight, so hot, so fucking good. Then she screams, a wild, gorgeous sound that makes me want to push down my jeans and bury my cock inside her right this second. My dick throbs, begging to be freed from the jail I've locked him in.

But the lack of condoms means I can keep doing my favorite thing—focus on her—and I'm not even remotely close to done. When her panting slows and her moans soften to murmurs, she opens her eyes. I crush my mouth to hers, kissing her lips for the first time today. She tastes as good as she did last night. Maybe even better.

She breaks the kiss. "My God, Nick. What did you do to me?"

Her voice is a little hoarse, a lot breathy. Her eyes shine with the afterglow. This is what I've always wanted to see. I saw it last night for the first time, and I love the way she looks when I make her come—blissed out and beautiful.

I gently remove my fingers, bring them to my mouth, and taste her. Salty and sweet, and so fucking good. "You wanted to learn what you liked. I showed you that you like it a lot when I reach your G-spot, princess," I whisper, then slide my hands to her bare ass. I'm rewarded with more sweet murmurs as I lift her up. "Wrap your legs around me."

She does, locking them around my ass. "Are you going to fuck me like this?"

"I have other plans for you."

Her apartment is tiny, and I carry her to her nearby couch, setting her down gently on the purple surface. She sinks into the cushions, her body looking relaxed and warm, probably from having come so hard. The rich shade of purple frames her face. Deep red and sparkly silver pillows cover her sofa. All these colors seem perfect for her. They match her personality—bright and vibrant.

But it's not her personality I'm thinking about this second as I kneel on the floor between her legs, placing a hand on each of her knees.

"You know that menu of things I like, Harper?"

"The all-you-can-eat buffet?"

I nod. "I still like everything, but if I had to choose . . ."

CHAPTER 20

"Take off your shirt," I tell her.

She shakes her head, darts forward, and tugs at my shirt. In a flash, she pulls it over my head. Her eagerness to strip me sends a hot charge down my chest, on a beeline for my cock. She tosses the shirt on the floor, and I set my glasses on the corner table.

"You're so hot, Nick," she says, then smiles guiltily. "I said that last night. I must sound like a broken record."

"Say it again. I love hearing it from you."

She leans forward and places her hands on my chest. I shudder, and my eyes close. I want to savor this moment when she touches my naked chest for the first time. My breathing intensifies as her nails trace over my pecs, along the outline of the tiger.

"I love looking at you," she whispers. "When I checked out your tattoo on my phone, I wanted to touch it."

My eyes snap open at this admission that she was attracted to me over the summer. "You did? Back then?"

She nods, dragging her nails down my chest to my abs. "Is this okay?" she asks, her eyes meeting mine, her question reminding me of the score. We might have a connection, but I'm here because she wants to learn what she likes, and what guys like.

"Yes," I say, as her fingers trace lines between the grooves of my abs. "You're doing great."

"I remember lying back on this couch that night and opening my pictures, zooming in on that one. I ran my finger over the screen, thinking about how I'd touched you briefly in the park, just for fun. I loved the way you felt, even for those few seconds. All I wanted was to touch you again. To know if you'd like . . . this," she says, running her hands across my waist now. Pure pleasure floods my brain.

"I do like it." I want to exist in this moment for a little while longer as her soft, talented fingers explore my body. I want to be her playground. But the more she touches me, the more vulnerable I become, and the more I can see myself feeling something deeper for her.

I reach for her shirt and pull it over her head.

My dick practically begs for freedom now, mad as hell and banging on the jail bars. Her breasts are one layer of black satin away from me. She unhooks her bra, and I stare, a groan rumbling up my chest. Her breasts are sublime. They're not big. They're not small. They're just perfect. Creamy skin and rosy nipples, tipped up and calling for my mouth. I dip my head to her chest, and suck on each delicious peak as my hands travel to her thighs.

"I'm going to spend a lot of time getting to know these beauties, but right now, I need my mouth between your legs." My fingers roam up her thighs to her wet, hot center.

"Nick," she starts, nerves racing back into her voice. "I've never come like that before."

Those are my favorite words to hear. Little excites me more than the uncharted terrain of a woman's orgasm, especially this woman. The chance to be the first to taste that sweet moment of shattering is like a winning lottery ticket. Out of nowhere, a possessiveness curls through me, and I want to be the only one to know this part of her. I want her pleasure to belong to me, and only me.

"Well, that's about to change, isn't it?"

She smiles, and it's a wicked sort of grin, full of carnal delight. "This is what I thought about the first night we sexted," she says, and I burn up all over, the red-hot memory slamming back into me as she confirms what I suspected she was up to.

"You have no idea how many times I've gotten off to eating your pussy." I brush my fingertips along her thighs. "But there's one thing I need you to do as I go down on you."

"What do you want me to do?" she asks, breathless, as if she's eager for my direction.

"When you really like something I do, when it drives you crazy and makes you want to beg for it, you need to tell me, okay?" She nods. "I know you love to say dirty things, and I want to hear them all. The more you give in to your own turn-ons, the more you'll enjoy every single second of what I'm going to do to you, and the harder you'll come."

She nods several times now. "Coming hard sounds pretty damn good."

"Oh, believe me, it will be so fucking good for both of us. Let me give you some suggestions. Off the top of my head," I say drily, and she giggles, "you can say things like, *that feels so good*, or *I'm going to fuck your face, Nick*, or *I'm going to come so fucking hard all over your face*."

Her eyes light up, twinkling with pure naughtiness. I brush a kiss along the inside of a thigh.

She quivers. I like that response.

I kiss a path up her leg, the intoxicating scent of her arousal growing stronger. I rub my face against her, letting her feel the bristles on her smooth skin.

"That," she moans, low and long. "I like that."

I grin as I slide my hands under her ass, cupping those luscious cheeks.

"That, too," she says on a quick gasp.

I squeeze her rear. "Then tell me if you like *this*," I say, and I just can't wait any more. I kiss her pussy, and she bucks against me.

"Oh God, yes!"

Best answer ever.

I flick my tongue against her, then lick a long, delicious line down her pink flesh then back up, drawing her clit between my lips and sucking. She groans. "I like everything. Your tongue, your face, your lips," she whispers in a broken pant. "So much."

And so do I. I'm turned on beyond anything I've ever experienced as I kiss her sweet, hot center. I swear I'm drinking her, lapping her wetness, and she's all over me. She's the most intoxicating thing I've ever had, and she gets me even higher as her fingers slide into my hair. She curls them tightly around my head, holding on.

She floods my tongue, and lust pounds mercilessly in my body as I eat her. Her taste is addictive. She's better, so much infinitely better than she was in my dirty dreams. She's all real, all wet, all heat as she rocks against my face. She grips me tighter, thrusts harder, and I lick, suck, kiss, and devour her delicious pussy.

I can tell she's almost there. I can tell by the way her legs fall open. By how much wetter she gets with each stroke of my tongue. By those wild sounds falling from her mouth. It takes all of my strength to pull away for a second to remind her. "Tell me. Tell me what you like," I growl, then return to her.

That's when she lets go. She clutches my hair, wraps her legs tightly around my neck, and fucks, and fucks, and fucks. "I'm going to fuck your face," she cries out. As soon as those filthy words fall from her lips, she's there. "Oh God, I'm going to come so hard on you."

And she does, on my lips, my tongue, my mouth, my jaw. My face is just buried in her as she pulses around me, so wet, so crazed, and, I hope, so fucking satisfied.

That about describes me to a T, too. So fucking satisfied, especially as I watch her come down from her high. Her lips part, her breath is fast, and she drags one hand through her hair, the other over those gorgeous tits. This is an image I could jack off to over and over—Harper, high on my mouth, not an ounce of self-consciousness as she touches herself while floating down.

Come to think of it, I take a mental snapshot. I'm totally going to draw this image later. Don't judge. I've only been obsessed with capturing a woman's O face since, well, forever. And hers is like the holy grail.

So I decide to make it a double. Without giving her a chance to protest—not that she would—my lips are on her again, and just like that, she's moaning, groaning, and writhing into me once more, flying into another orgasm in mere minutes. Judging from her wild sounds and her crazed cries, this one was just as good as the last. When I look up at her, she seems lost in a world of bliss.

Excellent.

I press my lips to her thigh, giving her a soft, gentle kiss, then I toe off my shoes and join her on the couch, lifting her feet onto it so we're lying down, tangled up together. I pull her close to me, my arm wrapped around her as she breathes hard. "I think I'm going to call you Princess Come-A-Lot now. That work for you?"

She flashes me a woozy smile. "As long as you keep earning the right to call me that."

I pretend to doff a top hat. "I am dedicated to your service." Tugging her closer, I kiss her temple. "Wait. You don't mind that I kissed you after I did that? I'm kind of covered in you right now."

A light laugh falls from her lips. "I pretty much gripped your face and locked your head in a vise until I came all over your beard, and you think *I* mind that you're kissing me?"

"When you put it like that . . ."

She shifts in my arms, then her eyes darken. "Kiss me again," she whispers, low and dirty.

I oblige, all too happy to have my lips anywhere on her. I groan as she takes control of the kiss, her lips hunting me, her tongue searching my mouth. She is ravenous, and she kisses me like I'm her dinner, and holy fuck, it makes me delirious. Her hands are on my shoulders, and she pins me, pressing her deliciously naked body to my side. Her skin is so warm, and her lips are so greedy. Her hand slinks down my chest, her nails running through the hair on my pecs, and in seconds her hand is on my jeans, unbuttoning, unzipping, and scooting them down.

I'm helpless to resist. Not that I want to, mind you. Not the fuck at all. I just can't. Because this girl is steering the ship. She shoves my jeans to my knees then off. In a heartbeat she breaks the kiss and stares at me stretched out on her couch.

"Why didn't you tell me?" she asks, her tone an accusation.

"What?" I ask, confused. "Tell you what?"

She curls her soft fingers around my hard shaft, and I hiss out a breath. "Fuck," I groan, as she touches my dick.

"That you were packing this kind of heat," she says, grinning like the very naughty girl she is.

What can I say? I've never had any complaints about the size of the machinery; I'm just glad Harper likes what's under the hood. "Whew. I thought you were . . . I don't know . . . pissed about something."

She shakes her head in an exaggerated fashion as she strokes me. "Not pissed. Try *excited about something*." She runs her hand up and down my cock. "Excited about riding you."

A shudder wracks my body, and I grab her face, thread my hand in her hair. "You don't need lessons in anything. You say these wildly dirty things that turn me on." I tip my forehead to my cock, thick in her hand. "Feel that. Do you feel how hard I get when you say that stuff?"

She shoots me a sexy smile. "All these things I want to do are in my head. Now I want to try them out. With you."

"We can try anything you want, but I didn't bring condoms tonight."

She pouts but then picks up the pace, curling her hand tighter. "Tell me how you like it."

"A hand job?"

"Sure."

"Haven't had one in ages. But it helps if you get it wet."

She lets go of me for a second and dips her fingers between her legs. Holy fuck. She's lubing me up with . . . herself. I push my head back against the couch pillow, blown away by this girl. Returning her hand to my erection, she spreads some of her wetness on me. "Like that?" she asks, breathy and sexy.

"Yeah, that'll do just fine," I say, as I thrust up into her palm. I can't even remember the last time I had a hand job. At a certain point in life you just graduate to fucking and sucking. But the way she grips my dick—twisting her wrist, sliding up and down my shaft—sends hot sparks through me and makes me wonder if I've been missing out.

On hand jobs . . .

Or maybe I've just been missing out on her. Because the way she looks at me, her eyes roaming between my face and my dick, as if she's appraising her work and checking for a reaction, makes me want to let go with her, too. To give in to whatever she wants to do right now. Let her touch me anytime, anywhere.

"Tell me how you like blow jobs so I can give you what I was fantasizing about," she says as she sits up, nudges my thighs, and then kneels between my legs. She doesn't let go of my cock the whole time, and I'm really fucking thankful for her commitment to the task at hand.

I groan as her thumb catches a bead of liquid from the head of my dick, then spreads that over me, mixing her arousal with mine. It's so hot what she's doing. Makes thinking hard. "I like a lot of tongue," I say, trying to collect my thoughts. "I like it when you wrap your lips nice and tight, but lick as you move up and down."

"Mmm. That sounds delicious," she whispers on an upstroke, her eyes blazing with desire as she watches me.

"I like a lot of suction, if you can."

She draws an excited breath. "And deep? Do you like it deep?"

Electricity radiates in my body with that word. *Deep.* "Fuck, yeah. I want to hit the back of your throat," I groan.

Her hand keeps busy, moving faster now, like a tight, hot tunnel. I thrust up into her fist, gritting my teeth as desire climbs inside me.

"And what about this?" she asks, then brings her other hand to my balls and cups, playing with them.

"Love that," I grit out. "Love it when you lick them, too."

Her hand flies faster, head to base and back. "But you don't like hand jobs?"

"Now I do. I really fucking do," I say, groaning as I fuck her hand. I might have to reconsider my position on mouths being better, because Harper's hand is blowing my mind. But when my eyes land on those red, naughty lips of hers, I'm sure what I want. "Know what makes a hand job really great?"

"What?" she asks, her voice so damn eager.

I grab the back of her head, meet her gaze, and tell her. "When you put your mouth on it."

In an instant, her lips wrap around the head of my dick, and I moan. A long, hungry moan that feels like it lasts forever. She follows my instructions, making her lips tight, and flattening her tongue. She takes me deep in one swift motion. Pleasure crackles all through my body, barreling down my spine, racing through my veins, and lighting me up everywhere.

It's like a sneak attack. An ambush orgasm. I don't even have time to give her a heads up. I just come hard in her throat in mere seconds.

"Fuck, Harper," I grunt, and she sucks me tight until she swallows it all. She gives me a long, lingering lick, then lets go with her mouth. But bless her wicked heart, she keeps her hand on my dick, and gives one last stroke, making my whole body jerk as I groan once more. She grins, looking like the cat who ate the canary's whole clan.

I drag a hand through my hair, words coming out choppy as my body hums with the aftereffects of the best hand job with a blow job finish I've ever had. "Or . . . yeah . . . that works, too. That's another way I like blow jobs," I deadpan.

She clears her throat. "Does that mean I can call you Prince Come Quickly?"

I smack her ass, chuckling. "I won't be earning that title again. Besides, you got me all worked up with those magic hands of yours."

She makes an *abracadabra* gesture.

We both laugh even harder, and she snuggles against me. Damn, this feels pretty fantastic, too, Harper curled up by my side. We stay like that for a few minutes. When her stomach growls, I brush a hand across her soft belly. "Let me take you out to eat."

She says yes, and dinner out with Harper seems a perfect way to top a damn near perfect evening.

CHAPTER 21

"We did the order all wrong." Harper shakes her head and sighs heavily.

"The food order?" I ask as the waitress walks away, her notepad in hand. We're at an Italian restaurant a few blocks from my house. It's busy, even on a Sunday night, as waiters scurry by, arms laden with plates of pasta.

"No. The activity schedule," Harper says, running her foot up my leg. She's flirty, and I'd be lying if I said I didn't enjoy this affectionate side of her. She's across from me at a table for two. The restaurant is dimly lit, with candles perched on red and white checkered table-cloths.

"Ah. You mean we had dessert before dinner?"

"Yes."

"We're unconventional. Mixing it up," I say, as Harper reaches for a slice of bread from the basket. Loose strands from her high ponytail frame her cheeks. After we cleaned up, she changed once more, pulling on a tight green sweater and jeans, along with short high-heeled boots. As we walked here, the struggle not to check out her ass the entire time was real. Sorry to report I received an F on that test.

Wait. Not sorry at all. The view was worth it.

She gives a one-shouldered shrug. "I like this reverse schedule, too. I liked everything today," she says softly. "But seriously . . ." She lets her voice trail off. "Did you like it?"

I scoff. "That doesn't even begin to cover it. I *loved* every second of every single thing we did."

She lights up, her blue eyes sparkling now. "I want it to be good for you, too, because for me, it was amazing."

"It was the same way for me," I say, and I'm tempted to slide my hand across the table and hold hers. But something stops me. Maybe because that seems like way too much of a couple thing. She wants to be temporary lovers, teacher and student, and all I want is to simply get her out of the starring role she's been playing in all my solo flights. A few more nights and I'll definitely be able to relegate Harper Holiday to a supporting part, then absolutely downgrade her to an occasional cameo, and bam, before I know it she'll stop occupying so much precious real estate in the dirty-thoughts lobe of my brain. Which, obviously, is the biggest one. For now, I zoom in on our lessons. "Let's recap today's classwork. We tackled dirty talk. Turns out you're a natural."

She wriggles her shoulders proudly, brings her index finger to her tongue, and pretends to wet the air, letting it sizzle.

I point at her. "You also learned that you can, indeed, have multiple orgasms, one right after the other."

"I had four in an hour," she says with a big grin.

"Show off," I tease, then stop. "Wait. One was solo."

"I'm still counting it, since looking at you on the train was my foreplay."

And like that, I'm ready to go again. She is a sexy little cupcake, and I want to bite into her. "And you also learned that the G-spot isn't a myth."

"Oh, I believe in it big time. I'll be building a shrine to it, in fact," she says, ripping off a corner of the bread and popping it in her mouth. When she finishes, she lowers her voice. "Want to know one more thing I learned about what I like?"

"I do," I say, and my muscles tense, not from worry, but anticipation. I want to know her. What she likes. What she dislikes. What makes her feel good.

Her eyes lock on mine. "Seeing you undress for me," she says, and her voice slides into that vulnerable tone she uses every now and then. The faintest of smiles tugs at her lips and pulls at my heart. We're talking about sex, but we're also not. She's saying something else it seems, something about what it means to open up to someone, to let him in. Or maybe I just want to think that. I half wish I had that Harper decoder ring and could translate what she just said into what some part of me wishes it meant. But I'm not sure how to get in touch with that part. For so long, I've been primarily focused on one thing with women—driving them wild. With Harper I want that in spades, but I want something else, too.

More.

Even though I know I can't have that with her, and there's no point in dwelling on it.

I grab a piece of bread, instead, and bite into it to keep from saying anything too revealing in response. The waitress arrives with a glass of wine for her and a beer for me, bringing to an end the serious moment.

The rest of the meal is easy. We talk about work and movies, agreeing that *The Usual Suspects* has the best twist, then books, and which *Harry Potter* spell we'd most want to do. We both choose the ability to apparate. "Instant transportation. No more airplanes, no more cars, no more waiting," I say, pressing my index finger to the table for emphasis. "We could just go to Fiji right now."

"Next stop, Bora Bora."

We even chat about the crossword puzzle, and she's surprised when I tell her I finish it nearly every week.

"Every week?" she asks, arching an eyebrow.

"When you signed up to ride this ride, did you think you were only getting beauty here?" I gesture to myself then tap my temple. "There's brains, too."

"The Sunday crossword is just really hard."

I shrug. "I like puzzles." *Like you. You're a mystery to me sometimes.*

"Me too," she adds, and sometimes we have so much in common it scares me.

* * *

We stroll along Central Park after dinner. The evening air is cool, and a flurry of golden brown leaves skip past our feet in the night breeze.

"I love fall in New York City," she muses, glancing up at the trees, their branches bursting with color, canopying us as I walk her home. "It's my favorite season."

"Why?"

"I love fall clothes and scarves," she says, her boots clicking against the sidewalk. "Fall colors, too—all the orange, and red, and gold. And the air is crisp, but not cold. And mostly, it just seems like the season Manhattan was designed for."

"How so?"

"It's romantic. It's as if . . ." She pauses as if she's taking time with her thoughts. She slows her pace and looks at me. "It's as if Manhattan and fall have chemistry. Know what I mean?"

"Like they're meant to be?"

"Yes. Exactly. New York was made for autumn," she

says, as a tall brunette and an even taller blond dude walk toward us, his arm draped around her shoulder. Harper and I move slightly to the right, and her eyes linger on them for a moment.

"And autumn was made for New York," I add, then I go for it. I wrap my arm around her shoulder. "Are you cold?"

She shakes her head. "Not anymore."

Silence falls between us for the next block. It's weird, because we're usually so chatty. But it's nice like this, walking through the city, New York unfolding before us in all its autumn splendor, elegant buildings on our left, a jewel of a park on our right.

"Now it feels like a date," she says under her breath, and my heart speeds up, pounding against my chest. Because I really like dating her. More than I should.

But as I flip her words in my mind, I wonder if I've overstepped with her, and crossed a line she doesn't want crossed. "Is that okay?"

"Of course," she says, as if she's saying *duh*. "This is still lessons in dating, right? I mean, just because we added sex to the mix doesn't mean we're leaving the dating lessons in the dust, right?"

My heart skids, slamming cruelly against my rib cage. I tell it to shut the fuck up, because I can't keep letting it get out of line and wanting more. "Sure," I say gruffly, but now I wonder if that dinner was a mock date. Is she practicing dating with me now, too? Sex is one thing, but trial dates gnaw at me. I don't know why. They just do.

"I thought I was pretty impressive at dinner with you tonight. I didn't spill any red sauce on myself. I didn't tell any embarrassing stories, and I spoke in complete and intelligible sentences the entire time," she says, poking fun at herself.

I manage a small laugh, trying to let go of whatever weirdness is ping-ponging inside my head. "You were pretty damn impressive."

"You know what this means, then?" she asks, a know-ing grin on her face.

"Nope."

"C'mon. Try," she says, elbowing my ribs.

I draw a blank. "No clue. Coming up empty."

"But I thought you liked puzzles," she says, with a quirk in her lips.

"I do, but I can't solve this," I admit, my tone clipped. I don't know how to play her game.

She tsks me. "It means," she says, stopping, stepping closer, and grabbing the neck of my shirt, "that last night in your hotel was our first date, and this is our second date. And you know what third date protocol is."

Schwing!

The decoder ring worked! I get it. She's donned her Princess of Innuendo cape tonight, and she wants to fuck tomorrow. And that's what I'm going to focus on. Not this dating shit that's vexing me. Besides, there's no need to be pissy when I'm going to have her coming all over my cock in less than twenty-four hours.

Ah, there. I feel so much better with that image front and center in my head. Thank you very much, brain.

I loop an arm around her waist. "I do, indeed, know what third date protocol is, and I intend to give you the full and proper treatment."

Then, because I want to give her a taste of what to-morrow will be like, and maybe, too, because I want to remind her that I can wind her up in a second, I kiss the hell out of her on the streets of Manhattan, yanking her close to me. She grinds her pelvis against my growing hard-on, and I'm about to whisper dirty things in her ear about how wet she's getting. But I don't want to end the kiss yet. I don't want to stop at all, and she doesn't seem to either.

Until a bus rumbles by, spewing out a thick plume of exhaust that ruins the moment.

Her phone buzzes as we separate, and she grabs it from her purse.

Her mouth forms a surprised *O* as she scans her screen. "It's Simon."

I clench my fists and look away. My jaw is set hard, and I *hate* the reminder right now. He's the guy she's really into. Fuck, he's the one I'm training her for, right? For a moment, I wish that he doesn't really like her, that he'll let her down, that he'll hurt her and she'll run back to me. But I feel awful wanting that for her.

"How is Mr. Hemsworth?" I ask, barely masking the bitterness in my tone.

"It's just a confirmation of the party info," she says gently. "It's later this week. Saturday morning, actually." She shows me the text, and it's not as if I need to see it. It really is only a work message, and I feel like a schmuck for letting my misplaced jealously shine through.

But another note pops up on her screen.

Would you like to get a coffee sometime soon? :)

He used a fucking emoticon. I can't believe it. I want to punch the air in victory, because that is complete and absolute grounds for a revocation of his man-card. "What's with the smiley face?"

"It's cute," she says, and she sounds a little dreamy, like she likes him.

That's it. I snap. "Don't go. Don't fuck him."

She wrenches back and looks at me as if I've sprouted two heads. Snake heads, based on the vitriol in my tone.

She parks her hands on her hips. "What the hell does that mean, Nick?"

I scrub a hand over my jaw. I try to let go of the jealousy, but it's not a green-eyed monster for nothing. "Just not yet, okay? Don't fuck him while we're fucking," I say, keeping my words as crass as can be. I can't let her see that the thought of anyone else touching her eats me alive.

"I would *never* do that." Her tone is full of hurt.

"Well, how do I know?"

She pushes my chest, shoves me hard. "Get real. Seriously. I told you I haven't slept with anyone in a few years. I told you I barely know what I'm doing in bed. I'm not going to sleep with you and someone else at the same time. I'm not even going to date him right now." She slices a hand through the air. "I would never be with you and someone else. Never."

And I'm an asshole.

"I wouldn't, either," I say softly. "I don't want to be with anyone else right now, either, and I didn't mean to suggest you would."

She stares at me and exhales. Her eyes seem to soften, but she crosses her arms over her chest. I'm not forgiven yet.

I reach out and wrap my arms around her. She lets me hold her, but doesn't reciprocate. "It's just we never said we wouldn't while we do this." Whatever *this* is.

"I didn't think we had to. Isn't it obvious we won't? I won't. You won't. It's that simple. It's not even a rule we need to establish. It's just an is."

And fuck, the way she says that, so certain and determined, so clear on who she is, hooks into my chest.

I am so utterly fucked with this girl. And I don't just mean fucked in that way. I mean it in every way.

* * *

After I return to my home, I text her.

I'm sorry. I acted like a dick

I shower, slide under the sheets, and grab my phone. There's no reply, and all I can think is I screwed up badly.

CHAPTER 22

I wake up far too early for my taste. As I grab my phone from the nightstand, a twinge of hope rises in my chest. It's then dashed by the absence of a reply.

Shit.

I pull on shorts and a pullover, lace up my sneakers, and jam in my earbuds. I run hard in Central Park, my phone in my hand the whole time as the sun rises, waking up Manhattan.

Still nothing.

I hit the gym for a quick round of weights, then return to my apartment and down a glass of water. I'm wiping the sweat from my brow when my phone dings. I take a deep breath. I really hope she's not pissed anymore.

I unlock the screen, see her name, and click open her text.

Princess: Good morning :) :) :) :) :) :) :)

I laugh at the way she needles me with her flurry of emoticons.

I try to respond in kind, tapping out a *hi* and adding a smiley face. But. I. Can't. Do. It. And evidently, I don't have to. Another text arrives seconds later.

Princess: I crashed as soon as I walked in the door last night. Apparently multiple Os are the best recipe for a solid night's sleep. By the way, why is dick an insult?

I laugh as I lean against the fridge and write back.

That's a good question.

Princess: I think dicks should be used for good, and referred to positively.

Does that make you a dick ambassador? Spreading the word about the unfair use of the male appendage as a put-down?

Princess: Yes. It does. I'm going to start using dick as a compliment. Here goes. Nick, you're a dick. Also, I like your dick.

And she's come roaring back with her sharp-tongued, dirty wit. My texting Harper. My naughty magician. I tap out a reply, suggesting a new insult.

How about ass? Wait. Scratch that. Ass suffers from the same undeserved fate. It should never be an insult. Also, I like your ass. Though love might be a more appropriate verb to express the depths of my admiration for that particular body part of yours.

I hit send then quickly add another note.

Also, would you please let me apologize for last night? I was such a . . . jerk.

Princess: You said you were sorry last night, and we're good. I'm not upset. I swear. I'm just glad we're on the same page.

We are. So much.

Princess: There won't be anyone else.

Same here. Also, Harper?

Princess: Yeah?

Sometimes you ask me if something we do is okay, and I want you to know you've never done a thing in bed that hasn't turned me on . . . your mouth, your face, your hair, your body, the way you touch me, the way you respond . . . it's all one massive turn-on.

Her reply arrives seconds later.

Princess: Now I have butterflies . . .

And I grin like a fool.

I'm taking you out tonight. What do you want to do? Dinner? Movie? Trapeze lesson? Art show? Museum? Horse-drawn carriage?

Princess: None of the above. But I have an idea. I'd love to plan our date.

She texts me a time and tells me she'll send more de-tails later. As I get ready for work I send her a text. Something I've always wanted to say to her.

By the way, I can still taste you . . .

Within a minute, a response lands on my phone. I groan as lust thrums through me. This picture couldn't be more perfect—a shot of her legs, with her fingers on the waistband of a pair of light blue panties that dangle on her ankles. I don't know if the lacy garment is going on, or going off, but I know this much—I'm going to need a few more minutes alone with this photo before I leave for work, and in my mind the clothes are definitely coming off.

Ten minutes later, I catch the subway to Comedy Nation, feeling pretty damn good that not only do I have a date, not only are we going to engage in proper protocol, but she also felt butterflies.

I might not be as skilled at deciphering Harper's cues outside of the bedroom, but I know one thing for sure—butterflies are better than dicks.

And I mean dick as a compliment.

* * *

That easy breezy feeling carries me through the day. After a long session with the show's writers, then a meeting with marketing, Serena pulls me aside in the conference room. "I almost forgot to tell you."

Even her standard preface to a Gino request can't get me down. "There's a cocktail party at the end of the week. Friday night," she says, then gives me the details. Friday is just a few days before the contract talks Gino has scheduled with Tyler.

"I'll be there. Any rules?"

"Just be your usual charming self. But not too charming. You know how it goes."

"Can I bring a date?"

Her eyes widen. "Ooh, tell me more. Who's the lucky lady?"

I shake my head. "It's not serious. But she's the one who came with me to bowling a few weeks ago."

"Ooh. *The one*," she teases, with a big wink.

"I didn't mean it like that."

"Sure you didn't," she says, shooting me a knowing look.

"It's only temporary."

She rubs her hand over her basketball belly. "That's what I once claimed about Jared," she says, mentioning her husband. "Now look how permanent we are."

"Powerhouse couple, and you're ready to pop," I say, since her husband works in the TV business, too, at a broadcast network.

"So you never know about these temporary flings."

But I can't let myself entertain those thoughts. If I do, then butterflies will get in my head and mess with it. Be-fore I know it, Mister Orgasm will have turned into a love-struck fool by the end of the TV season.

A little after six, just as I'm stepping into the elevator, the hair on the back of my neck stands on end.

"Hold the elevator," Gino shouts from down the hall.

I swear the dude has a homing device installed to track me down, which is all kinds of creepy. He flashes a massive grin when he joins me, clapping me on the back.

"Nick Hammer. Just the man I was thinking of."

Words I never want to hear coming out of his mouth.

"That so?"

He nods vigorously and rubs his hands together as the elevator begins its downward trek. "I've been giving a lot of thought to our chat last week about the show. And I think I've got just the recipe to tone it down a notch."

Tension coils in me. "Okay." I wait for him to say more.

He rocks back on his heels. "But you know what? I'll just wait until I see Tyler Nichols next Monday, and I'll give him the down and dirty. Make it a surprise for him, and for you, too." He raises his eyebrows in an evil glint. "I do love surprises, don't you?"

"Like when a woman wears a red teddy under a trench coat? That kind of surprise?" I deadpan.

He clasps a hand to his belly and laughs as the car slows at his floor. "And that's what we pay you the big bucks for." He steps out, wraps his hand over the door, and pokes his head in. "Isn't that right?"

"Yeah. For red teddy jokes," I mutter as he walks off.

As soon as I reach the lobby, I dial Tyler and give him the down low. "What surprise is he talking about?"

"I'm meeting him a week from today," my lawyer says in a reassuring tone. "I have no doubt he's just posturing as we head to negotiations. This is his style. He's like a cat who likes to play with his food before he eats it."

I cringe. "Did you just compare me to cat food?"

Tyler laughs. "That came out wrong. But listen, man, we've got your back. Just go to the cocktail party in a few days, keep smiling, and we'll take care of the show when I see him in a week."

Easier said than done.

Because the show takes care of me. The show has given me this life in New York, the home that I own, even the shirt I'm wearing. It's given me everything, and I don't want to fuck it up.

It's who I am. It's a part of me.

But when Harper sends me the location for our date, the last thing on my mind is the show. It's why the fuck are we meeting a block away from Spencer and Charlotte's home?

CHAPTER 23

Harper waits for me on the corner of Christopher Street and Seventh Avenue South, wearing black heels, a light-pink jacket cinched tightly at the waist, a gray skirt, and black stockings. Immediately, I decide they have bows where the garters attach. Because of course she's wearing garters. Of course I'm going to be aroused the entire night. And of course I don't want to go to Spencer's apartment on our date.

I march up to her and park a hand on her shoulder. "Remember that time I said I liked everything? I'm going to amend that. The one kink I don't like is messing around at your brother's place."

She scoffs. "Relax. I just have to feed Fido. Spencer's house is right near where I've planned our date, so I figured we could do it on the way."

She spins around and starts walking to his house. I join her, covering the familiar block to my best friend's abode with growing unease as we pass the hip coffee shop, the shoe store, and the neighboring brick brownstone.

At his front door, that latent kernel of guilt shoves its way to the front of the line. As we enter the elevator, it lodges in my chest. "Harper, I feel like shit going into your brother's home like this."

"Like what?"

"You know. Since we're doing this *thing*." I gesture from her to me.

"He's gone for the week on his honeymoon, and we're not doing anything wrong."

"I know, but you're his sister. And I'm his friend. And I'm crossing lines."

She cocks her head to the side. "Do you want to stop?" she asks, worry in her voice.

"No more than I want to pound a five-inch nail into my head."

She winces as the elevator slows at his floor and the doors open. "Ouch. That hurts just thinking about it. But I'm curious—would a four-inch nail make a difference?"

I shake my head. "Nope."

"Then why are we discussing it?"

She makes a good point. A great point, actually. Besides, this is a temporary arrangement. One week only. Still, as we walk down the hall I picture myself as a man heading into a courtroom, ready to be judged. "Because you know how he is. He's protective of you."

She nods and shoots me a small smile as she reaches his door and grabs the key from her purse. "I do know, and I love him. But he's not the boss of my body. I'm in charge of who gets to touch me. Not him. Not anyone. Besides, you and I agreed this was just between us way back at Speakeasy," she says, reminding me of the nature of this relationship—to help her learn the ins and outs of sex and dating, and to never tell a soul.

"But more than that," she adds, running her hand down her chest to the top button of her jacket and undoing it to reveal a sliver of creamy skin. "I'm a grown woman, and I feel completely confident that I can make my own decisions about who I want to wear black stockings and a new lacy lingerie set for."

Just like that, I'm hypnotized. I'm under her spell, a cartoon character with glassy eyes, following the piece of steak he finds at the end of a string. No way can I resist her with that image planted in my head. I'll follow her and her lingerie and her kick-ass attitude wherever she goes. She's so fucking strong in her beliefs, in who she is, and it's a huge part of the allure.

She unlocks the door to Spencer's home, and we step inside. Fido scampers over to her.

"What kind of lingerie?"

"It's a surprise for you for later. But suffice to say, it's all part of my *thorough preparation* for your coursework, as you requested . . . Professor Hammer," she says, lingering on my new nickname in a thoroughly seductive tone as she bends to pick up the cat.

Her skirt rides up, giving me the sweetest, naughtiest peek of the top of her stockings, right where they meet her garters. Hello, hard-on.

"You darling boy," she coos to the cat as she stands. "Did you miss me?"

Fido meows at Harper in greeting, and offers her his chin for petting. "Aww. You little honey bear. I told you I'd be here to feed you your special tiger diet. I would never forget you."

He rubs his furry cheek against her breast, and I whimper. The lucky bastard. Then he has the audacity to stretch out his paw and rest it on the exposed flesh of her chest.

"I think Fido is trying to feel you up."

Harper laughs and scratches his chin. He snuggles even closer to her. Man, this cat has it bad.

"Come pet him. He's sweet," she says.

I move closer and rub his ears. As I stroke him,

Harper absently touches my hair. The cat stops purring. He stares at us, at her hand on me, as if he's cataloguing every move we make. Maybe I'm hallucinating, but I swear he narrows his beady eyes.

Harper puts him down, fills his food bowl, and sets it on the floor. As he eats, she changes the litter, and then washes her hands. After she dries them, she runs a hand down the cat's back. He arches into her as he chows down on the rest of his dinner.

"See? Fido won't tell our secret. He has a little crush on me, and all he wants is for me to come back tomorrow."

We head to the door, but when I glance back at him, he's no longer eating. He trots to Harper, meowing loudly and rubbing his side against her.

"I'll come back soon, handsome," she tells him as he turns around and rubs his other side on her calf, his tail swishing high in the air.

My eyes pop out. That cat is marking her with his scent. "Back off," I say to him. "She's mine."

Harper laughs. "You two having a swordfight?"

"Yeah, and I'm going to win."

We leave, and once we're in the elevator and safely away from the pervy cat, I press a kiss to her chest where his paw was.

"Are you actually jealous of a cat?" she asks.

Jealous of Simon. Jealous of a feline. Evidently, I'm the territorial one when it comes to this woman, and my possessiveness knows no bounds. "I would be if I wasn't completely confident that I'll be stripping you down to your bows and garters, and having my paws all over you tonight," I say, low and husky.

A feathery gasp escapes her throat. "I like your paws."

When we reach the street, I crane my neck to check out the sixth floor. Who's there but Fido, in the window, staring at us.

Probably preparing a report for his master. I swear, I'll quit when Spencer returns in a week. I will, I really will.

CHAPTER 24

Harper spins around, walking backward on the sidewalk, mischief tap-dancing in her blue eyes. A bus rumbles by, spewing exhaust, and a cab honks its horn as it swerves into the next lane. We're on the edge of the Village.

"Any idea where I'm taking you?" she asks, taunting, toying, playing.

I bring a finger to my lips. "Hmm. Did you plan a date at the drugstore?" I ask, gesturing to the Duane Reade on the corner. "Shopping for household goods, perhaps?"

She makes a buzzer sound. "Wrong. Guess again."

I check out the options across the street. There's a movie theater, so that's a possibility. But Harper's *I've-got-something-up-my-sleeve* attitude tells me she's not going for conventional. I cross off the sushi restaurant on the corner for that reason, too.

Then I spot it. A few stores away. I can't believe I missed it. Eden, a sex-toy shop. This is so very Harper.

"This might be my favorite date ever," I say as we near the entrance. "I don't know how I'm not going to buy one of everything."

She grabs my hand and laces her fingers through mine. "It's going to be impossible for you to resist."

"I'm game to try though," I say and turn into the doorway.

Like a dog on a leash, I'm jerked back. I nearly stumble into her. "What? Aren't we going here?" I hook a thumb in the direction of the shop.

"Oh God," she says, clasping her hand over her mouth. "I forgot that was here."

"Then where are we going?" I ask, since two and two isn't equaling four right now.

She points across the street to what looks like a huge bathroom store. "I didn't want to take you to the movies, or dinner, or bowling, or trapeze lessons, or a museum, even though I know we'd have the best time doing any or all of those things. I wanted to take you someplace you'd never been. Someplace that's very you," she says as we cross the street and reach the entrance to the Whiteman showroom. "And since the only thing you love more than drawing is showers, I thought you might enjoy checking out some of the coolest showers in the world."

For several seconds, I'm too surprised to react. This wasn't on my radar screen at all. I wouldn't even have guessed it, but as I gaze into the pristine windows at the displays of model bathtubs and showers with gleaming fixtures and earthy tiles, my heart thumps against my chest.

I don't think it's beating this hard because I love showers.

It's because I'm floored by her. Her lips are parted slightly, and her eyes are full of anticipation, as if she's waiting for my approval. I can tell she's the tiniest bit worried that I might think this is silly, or strange, or too different.

I don't. I think it's awesome. "I've never been on a date to a shower showroom," I say as I open the door for her, and we head into a paradise for the shower junkie.

"It's like shower porn," she says as we wander past the first setup with a waterfall theme and smooth stone tiles.

"I could spend a whole day in there," I say, sighing happily as I take it in.

"You could start taking shower naps."

"Trust me, I've tried that."

She laughs and squeezes my arm. I look at her hand and flash back to all the times she's touched my arm. She was always doing it *before*, a friendly little pat, or a punch now and then. Sometimes playful. Now, it's sweetly affectionate. Funny how she has all these different ways of touching me.

The next one bills itself as a spa shower, and the display is complete with low lights, dark tiles, and mood music. "Is this where they hose you down after you're all oiled up at the spa?"

"Just like this," she says, and steps inside and pretends she's soaping up under the showerhead.

"May I help you?"

Harper snaps to attention and meets the gaze of a sharp-dressed saleswoman in a navy pantsuit. Her sleek black hair is twisted in a bun.

"Why, yes," Harper says, adopting a businesswoman tone. "I'm in the market for the absolute best, state-of-the-art, top-of-the-line luxurious shower for the true shower aficionado. What would you recommend?"

"What price range are you considering?"

Harper laughs like that's the silliest question she's ever heard. "Money is no object when it comes to one's predilections."

I raise an eyebrow approvingly at Harper for her word choice.

"Then you'll want a wet room," the woman says, and gestures for us to follow her.

"*Wet room*," she whispers, nudging me. "Told you it was better than Eden."

I loop my arm around her shoulders. "Yes, so much better."

We weave through floor displays of glassless showers, and jets with more modes than Harper's fifty-speed wand, and claw foot tubs, too, until we arrive at the centerpiece.

"This is the Rolls Royce of showers," the pantsuit woman says and presents a shower that's bigger than my bedroom, and boasts a dozen showerheads, two on each wall, and four on the ceiling. She waxes on about the rainfall settings, the steam options, and the quality of the tile, harvested in South America somewhere. I couldn't care less about these details, because Harper runs her hand through my hair and asks, "Do you love it?"

I know she means the wet room. But when I answer her I mean something else entirely, and I want her to know that. "Yes. This is the coolest date I've ever been on."

Her eyes sparkle. "Really?"

This is Harper and all her quirks. This is the way she listens to everything I say, how she soaks up all the details, how she pays attention to every nuance, and then finds a way to be playful and fun.

"Don't ever change your quirks," I say, then I brush a kiss to her lips. She shivers against me, and the shower showroom portion of the date needs to end very soon.

The saleswoman holds up her finger. "Excuse me. There's something I need to take care of." She scurries off.

"Me, too," I say, but I'm talking to Harper. Looking at Harper. Wanting Harper. "Let's order in Chinese at my place."

She runs her thumb over my jawline. "Does that mean you want to get out of here now?"

"Yes."

CHAPTER 25

We stumble into my apartment, our hands all over each other. Her lips are bruised from how I kissed her in the cab, and her jacket is undone.

My fingers find their way to the hem of her V-neck sweater. I want to tear off all her clothes. "Can I see my gift now? I've been soooo good."

"You've been very good," she says, arching into me.

My hands freeze. I stop my travels, remembering my mission and why I'm lucky enough to have my hands on her body right now—to teach her. "We almost forgot your lesson tonight."

She pulls back and shakes her head briefly, as if she's clearing her thoughts. "Lesson. Right. Lesson."

It doesn't take long for me to devise one. Call it an easy lesson plan. Call it my own selfish desire to watch Harper bare all. Giving her an assignment is the easiest thing in the world, because I want her so much.

"Strip for me." Tossing my jacket on a chair, I park myself on the couch and lace my hands behind my head. "Do it nice and slow."

She nods, reaching for her jacket. "Everything, Professor Hammer?"

I shake my head as I rake my eyes over her. "Take off the jacket, sweater, and skirt. Leave everything else on. That's the lesson. How you can drive a man wild when you're half-naked."

"Do I drive you wild?" she asks, as she joins me in the living room and shimmies off the coat.

"So much," I say, my voice husky and my eyes never straying from her as I nod to her skirt.

She unzips it. She takes her time, pushing down one side of the skirt, then the other. I groan as a hint of the soft flesh above her panties is exposed.

"More?" she asks seductively.

"Take it off, Harper," I say, like a command. "Take off the fucking skirt so I can see you."

"Since that's what you want," she says letting her voice trail off as she pushes the fabric past her thighs. She lets it fall to the floor and all the breath flees my body.

Her stockings are sheer black, and the garter belt hooks into them with little bows on the snaps. Her panties are black lace with a tiny pink butterfly pattern. I drag my hand over my face. I'm an inferno. No, wait. I'm lava. Molten. I take a huge breath and rasp out, "Jesus fucking Christ."

"You like?"

I swallow and nod, because I can't speak. My throat is parched. I make a rolling gesture with my hand, indicating that it's time for the top to get out of the way, too. She crosses her hands at the hem of her sweater and slowly, seductively, lifts her top, revealing a matching bra, the kind that pushes her tits high.

"I picked this out today. I went lingerie shopping for you," she says, her soft voice wafting over me.

"You bought this for me?"

She nods. "I wanted something new to wear tonight. Something I thought you'd like," she says, a sexy hopefulness in her voice. "Do you like the butterflies?"

Was this what she meant this morning by butterflies? Was it a hint about her lingerie? I have no idea, and at the moment, I don't care. I walk over to her and kiss her hard, possessively, claiming her lush mouth with mine. My hand roams to her ass, and I squeeze.

She breaks the kiss with an excited *oh*.

"How should I fuck you for the first time?" I ask, letting the question linger in the air between us like smoke and heat.

She runs her nails down my shirt, working open the buttons. "How do you want to?"

I shake my head. "It's not about how I want it. I want to give you all your fantasies. I'm almost tempted to check out your Tumblr feed right now, and see what you looked at this morning."

Her fingers reach the final button. She opens my shirt and runs her hands over my chest. Her touch is electric. Her index finger traces Hobbes. As she pushes off my shirt, letting it fall to the floor, her hands roam across the swirls of ink on my arms, the stars and the abstract shapes and lines. Her eyes follow her touch, then she blinks up at me. "What do you think I looked at this morning?"

I tuck a finger under her chin. "One of your women bent over, ass in the air. That's how you want it."

Her eyes widen, and her lips part. She nods.

"That's what I thought. And since I distinctly recall you telling me you wanted to be fucked on the counter, I'm going to grab a condom and when I return, I'd like to see you bent over and ready."

She nibbles on the corner of her lips and says, "Yes."

I head to the bedroom, grab a foil packet, remove my glasses, shoes and socks, and return to find Harper has

202 · LAUREN BLAKELY

done exactly as I asked. She looks like one of her fantasies, and mine, too. She's all legs, and ass, and a gorgeous, flattened back. I close the distance, set the condom on the counter and take off my jeans. She looks back at me and watches the whole time.

When I push off my boxer briefs and my cock springs free, she licks her lips. "I want you," she says in a whimper.

Those three words send a heated charge through me. I bring my hand to my dick and stroke it as she stares. My other hand curls over one round, perfect cheek. She gasps as I touch her. I raise my palm to swat her rear when I catch sight of something sticking out of her purse on the coffee table.

"Don't move," I say, and I walk away to grab a thin black stick from her purse. "I'm so fucking glad you carry that giant bag around with your magic stuff in it."

"Are you going to spank me with my magic wand?" Her tone is laced with excitement.

"I absolutely am."

"Because I'm going to retire that one from use after you do it."

"You bet your sweet ass this little prop is reserved for our dirty tricks now," I say, and I raise the black wand and tap it lightly against her rear, testing her. She inhales sharply.

"More?" I ask, stepping closer to the side of the counter so I can bend to her face and dust a kiss on her lips.

She nods, the look in her eyes heated.

I lift it again and whack her other cheek. She flinches, but then a soft gasp follows, and I rub my palm over her soft rear. Just to be sure she liked it, I drag a hand between her legs. Holy fuck, this girl is my perfect dirty angel. "You're soaked," I rasp out, as I slide my fingers across the damp fabric hugging her pussy.

"Do it again," she begs.

I gladly comply, spanking my naughty magician with her very own magic wand and soothing her with my palm each time, one delicious globe then the other, then back again. Winding her up. Making her writhe. Drawing out the most delicious noises from her. I kneel and press kisses on her bottom, pulling at the lace with my teeth, inching it closer to the crack of her delicious ass, exposing her flesh. I nibble on her cheek, and she moans. I lavish attention on the other one, giving her everything she wants right where she wants it, nibbling, licking, kissing her soft, sweet skin.

As I worship this fantastic rear, Harper whispers my name. "Nick, I need you."

She wants me. She needs me. I have never craved being the object of both more than I do with Harper. I pull down her panties and help her step out of them.

My dick throbs as I look at her bare ass, her slick, wet pussy, her gorgeous legs, and her face, her eyes so full of desire. "You're incredible," I murmur.

She pushes the condom at me. She's so damn desperate. I cover my dick, curl a hand around her hip, and rub the tip between her legs. She shudders, arching her back.

"Oh, princess," I rasp, as I rub the head against her heat. "I fucking want you so much."

She pushes back against me. "I want you, too."

Like this, with her bent over my kitchen counter in a black butterfly bra and stockings, I sink into the woman I've been dreaming about for months, and I groan in pleasure. She's divine. So hot, so fucking snug.

The intensity of this moment radiates in my body like a hot flare. I'm *inside* Harper for the first time, and it's so good it's unreal.

She moans, and I lower my chest to her, pressing against her back, my lips near her face. "Harper," I say as I ease out then push in.

"Oh God," she moans, and it sounds as if she's lost in pleasure.

"Harper," I say again, my voice rough, commanding.

"Yes?"

"You're perfect like this."

I raise my chest, grip her hips with both hands, and thrust—slow, deep lingering strokes that have her squirming and begging, saying *yes* and *please* and *more.* I take my time, making her want it, rocking in and out of her. She circles her hips against me. Her knuckles are white from gripping the counter. I run a hand up her spine, grab a fistful of hair, and tug. She yelps, and the noise transforms into a low, sexy groan as I take her harder.

"Deeper," she begs. "I love it when you're so deep in me."

Sparks fly down my legs. Lust incinerates me, and desire spreads to every cell. She raises her ass higher, sinks lower, gives me more of her body. Each move she makes fans the flames, and I fuck her how she wants it. Deep, hard, passionate.

Her breath comes in shudders and reckless pants. Curling my hands tighter around her, I say, "Is this how you wanted it? All those times?"

"Yes. God, yes."

"Is it like your dirty pictures?"

"It's better. So much better."

I know what will make it the best. Her lips. I lower my chest to her back, cup a cheek with one hand, and turn her face to mine. This isn't the easiest position, but I don't care. I know what I'm doing, and I fuck her from behind as I kiss her madly, needing her lips, craving her tongue, wanting this connection. She's so wild beneath me, all moans and murmurs and thrusts, and her tongue seeks mine, her lips pressing hungrily to me.

Her pussy is my favorite place in the universe, and she grows even wetter with each kiss, and slicker still with every consuming thrust. We kiss like sloppy, crazed lovers, until she bites down on my lip. She cries out, lets go of my mouth, and utters a throaty, hungry series of *oh Gods* that are nearly my undoing as she comes hard, calling my name.

Somewhere, tingling in my body, I can feel the start of an orgasm. But I'm not ready to stop. I'm not done fucking my girl. I slow down, grit my teeth, and fight off my own release.

"I want you to come again," I tell her, my voice rough.

She just nods, and that's all I need to know she's game for multiples.

I pull out, my fingers tight around the condom, keeping it on. "Bed. Now. On your back. Legs spread. Leave the shoes on."

She's never been to my bedroom, but it's not hard to find, and in seconds she's on the navy blue comforter and open for me. I crawl between her legs, and shove back into her.

"Oh fuck," I groan, my cock surrounded by her sweet heat once more. "You're so fucking wet."

"You got me that way," she says, as I fill her.

"You're so fucking sexy. You feel so good."

"God, so do you. It drives me wild the way you fuck me," she says, and every word from her mouth gets me hotter. She wraps her legs around my ass, and loops her hands around my neck. This is how I want her.

"I want to watch your face when you come again. You're so beautiful beneath me. You're so goddamn gorgeous when you come," I say, and she trembles, gripping me tighter, pulling me farther into her.

I don't want this to ever stop. I don't want this night to end. I want her over and over. I roll my hips and thrust into her, finding a new rhythm. It's fast, but not frantic. It's intense, but not out of control. It's just fucking perfect, then more perfect when she raises her knees, sliding them up my sides, opening herself even more.

"You like that, princess?" I growl, as she widens for me, giving me her body in that position.

Her answer is a low, sexy cry of rapture. I drive farther, rolling my hips, hitting her in all the right places.

"I can feel you deeper like this. So deep that . . ." She trails off, her lips near my ear. She draws my earlobe between her teeth and nips. She moans against me, a sexy, beautiful noise as she whispers, "That I'm going to come again."

My favorite words from her. I'm so fucking turned on. So fucking crazy for her. "Do it," I groan as I pump into her, and she grips my ass, digging in, holding on. Her face is pressed to mine as she rocks up. Her body detonates, and she's like a Harper bomb under my hands, a beautiful explosion of lust and sensuality, and so much rapture.

That's it. I'm done. I chase her there, pushing deep inside at a fevered pace, my own climax tearing through my body as she shudders beneath me. Our cheeks touch as I come so fucking hard that nothing but incoherent noises fall from my lips, nearly as loud as hers. Because, holy fuck, it's so good with her. It's so incredibly good.

Her moans don't stop for a long time, and nor do mine as I collapse on her. My heart beats furiously. Beads of sweat slick my chest. And I'm so damn happy to have her in my bed, beneath me, with me, next to me.

I roll off her, tie the condom, and toss it in the bathroom trash. I return to her, and she's the most beautiful sight ever—mostly undressed and fucked senseless . . . by me.

"Take off the rest of your clothes. I want to feel you naked," I tell her, and I help her slide off the shoes, stockings, and the bra. She's in nothing, just like me. I pull her into my arms.

She feels too good to be true.

* * *

"So this is your bedroom," she says, glancing around a few minutes later.

My room is simple—blond hardwood floors, a king-sized bed, and a bureau with a handful of framed family photos, as well as stacks of sketchbooks and pens. On my wall is a drawing of a duck taped to bricks, aptly titled "Duct Tape."

"Maybe you'll show me your bedroom someday soon," I say, as I kiss her neck.

"Actually, you've seen it."

I arch a questioning eyebrow.

"My apartment is a studio. I sleep on the purple couch. It's a pull-out."

"I have fond memories of what I did to you on that couch yesterday. Had no idea it was your bed too."

She taps my nose. "Don't know if you know this, Mr. Brains and Beauty, but Manhattan is a teeny bit expensive," she says, holding up her thumb and forefinger. "Especially for an almost twenty-six-year-old magician."

I nod, aware that her situation is different than mine. We're both skilled enough to do what we love, but I've had bigger breaks.

"But I'm lucky to have that place," she adds. "My parents bought it years ago as an investment, so I basically rent from them. They wanted to let me live rent-free, but I insisted on paying."

"Hopefully they gave you a good deal."

"They did. For a place in the 90s, it's better than rent-controlled. And it lets me live in Manhattan, working kids' parties for the most part."

I prop myself up and run my fingers along her hip-bone. "Is that the end game? I'm not saying you should do more. I'm just curious."

"I'd like to do a few more corporate events since the pay is better, but for now, I'm happy."

"Would you ever want to do a big, grand show, like in Vegas?"

She shrugs. "I don't know. I really like working with kids. They're fun and appreciative, and they believe in the illusion. They believe it's all real."

"You have no idea how badly I want to ask you to show me how to do the pencil trick."

"You know I could never do that." She stretches an arm to my nightstand, grabbing a pencil. She presses her finger to my lips. "I'm not going to *tell* you how it's done," she says, then brings her right hand to her nose, while her left hand is curved next to it. In a flash, she puts the pencil in her nose.

Or so it seems.

Equally quickly, the writing implement emerges in her other hand, as if she pulled it out her ear. Even though I know she didn't put the pencil in her head, and even though I'm sure she hid it behind her hand, it's still a cool trick. Because it *looks* real. Her sleight of hand is that smooth.

"Want me to do it again?"

I shrug. "Sure."

This time she's just as fast, but she swings her leg over my waist as she does the trick, which rolls her an inch closer, giving me the slightest peek at her curved left hand, where she hides the pencil.

I smile, awareness hitting me of what she just did. It's a small thing, and a small trick, but it's pure Harper. Re-vealing, without exactly revealing. Letting me into her world.

"Now teach me the secret to drawing a great cartoon," she says, playfully demanding.

I raise my hand and brush her red strands over her ear. "Here's the trick. You have to *like* what you're drawing," I say, my eyes on her the whole time.

She has no clue what I've just told her. She can't have any idea that I've drawn her, and how much I like her. So much that it's way beyond "like" right now. She just smiles and says, "Good thing you like drawing a caped crusader who can make a woman arch her back and curl her toes in pleasure. Especially since you're so good at that, too."

Screw Fido. Screw that stupid jealousy. Fuck any jealousy. Right now all I feel is one hundred percent satisfaction over a job well done.

Speaking of jobs . . .

"Would you want to come to a work party with me?" I ask, then I explain about the cocktail party that Serena asked me to attend this Friday.

"Do I have to throw a bowling match this time?" She taps my chest. "Speaking of that, you still owe me a rematch."

"I promise you'll get one. But will you come with me? Gino is such a capricious ass," I say then hold up my palm. "Wait. Ass is good, we decided. He's a capricious weasel, and he's just jerking me around. But even so, I need to play the game and go. And I'd really like for you to be there."

"Of course I'll go. And as for Gino, fuck him."

I point at her, my eyes lighting up. "Hey. That's another one. Why is fuck an insult?"

"Hmmm. That's an excellent point."

"Right? Everyone says *fuck him, fuck this, fuck off.* But fucking is pretty much the greatest thing on earth."

"We'll start a new dictionary. We'll take back the word fuck, and we'll turn it into—"

"I know! We'll say it like a blessing." I soften my voice, and make it sound reverent and adoring. "*Fuck you, my child. Go in peace.*"

"Or," she says, her voice rising in excitement, "we can use it when we like something. Fuck can go into our dictionary as *like*."

I curl my hand over her hip. "Hey, you know what, Harper? Fuck showers."

I take her to the shower and introduce her to the tiled wall, as well as my bottomless appetite for her. She's pretty ravenous, too, and it's fantastic to have her again as the water slides down my back, and her legs wrap around me, and she falls apart once more in my arms.

When she comes down from her high, she whispers in my ear, softly, sweetly, "Fuck you."

I laugh lightly. "Fuck you, too."

CHAPTER 26

"I don't know how I'm going to resist her," Wyatt says with lustful longing in his voice the next morning in Central Park.

"Natalie?"

He shakes his head. "Little Cocoa Puff. Look at her. How am I not supposed to take her home? She can fit in my tool belt," he says, practically cooing as he gestures to the chocolate Min Pin he's walking. By my side is a dachshund mix.

"You don't even wear a tool belt," I say, as we turn down a path. "You just love to hold on to the *handyman* image, even though you're behind a desk half the time."

"What can I say? I'm good with tools, as well as juggling my growing empire."

"Then you should take Cocoa Puff home with you," I say, goading him on as I point to the pooch. "Think about how much help she can give you when it comes to women. She's a chick magnet, and let's be honest." I drape an arm over his shoulder sympathetically. "You need all the help you can get, Woody."

"Randy," he retaliates with a huff. "Our parents gave us the worst middle names."

I laugh. "Pretty sure they wanted to torture us, starting at birth."

He stops in the middle of the path and gives me some sort of knowing eye inspection. "But let's not talk about middle names. Let's talk about . . . hey, how about girls with alliterative names? HH, ahem."

"You know what alliteration is?" I ask, deflecting, as I wind the dog leash tighter around my wrist.

He shakes his head dismissively. "I do. In addition to a working brain, I also have a powerful nose to sniff out your bullshit," he says, and I pretend to be preoccupied with the dachshund's exploration of a bush.

Wyatt soldiers on, his voice stripped free of sarcasm or our usual trash talk. "When are you going to say something to Spencer?"

"About what?" I scowl. I'm doing an awesome job feigning confusion.

He laughs. "C'mon man. Drop the act. I know there's something between you and Harper. I saw you dancing with her."

"It was just dancing."

Just dancing. Just kissing. Just fucking. Just the best nights of my life. My chest warms with memories of the last few nights with Harper.

Wyatt sighs. "Nick," he says, and I can tell he's serious, since he's using my first name. "I saw her coming to your apartment last week. I saw you dancing with her at the wedding. I saw the way you looked at her on the train."

Alarm bells go off. We were so cautious. Could my brother tell something was up just by looking at us?

"If you like her, just say something," he adds, as if it's the simplest thing in the world.

I scoff.

Because it's not that simple. Harper and I aren't doing something that needs to be *discussed* or *approved*. We're not going anywhere beyond the bedroom. I don't even have to ask her to know her feelings on that topic. They're crystal clear, and have been from the moment I witnessed her secret language with men at Peace of Cake. Not only do her actions speak clearly, but so do her words. For starters, she acts normal around me. She's never once fumbled on words, or turned into a *hot mess* with me, as she does with Simon. On top of that, the woman has been amazingly specific when it comes to voicing what she wants. She asked me point-blank for dating help with other guys. Then she kicked it up a notch and requested lessons in sex and seduction.

She never expressed an interest in having me as her boyfriend, and that's one hundred percent fine with me. Best of both worlds. I'm having her in the bedroom, and we still can hang out together when these lessons come to an end after this week.

"There's not anything to say. It's just not like that with her," I explain with a casual shrug.

Wyatt brings his dog to heel by his side. "Listen, you can tell yourself it was just dancing, but you're not fooling me. The question is, are you fooling yourself?"

His question echoes. It sounds important, the way it lingers in the cool fall air, drifting through the leaves on the trees. But I've had my eyes wide open from day one. "Nope. I totally know the score."

He sighs. "Fair enough. But in a few days, Spencer will return," he says, reminding me of the expiration date. I hardly need the reminder. I'm well aware that Spencer makes landfall after his honeymoon in Hawaii after midnight on Sunday. Six nights from now. But who's counting? "And you need to think about the fact that you've got something going on with his little sister," Wyatt adds. "The sooner you figure out what it is, the better off you'll be."

But Spencer is out of sight, out of mind. He's on the other side of the world, and I don't need to worry about him right now, despite what his cat and my brother might think.

CHAPTER 27

The next few nights roll by in a haze of orgasms for Harper, and hey, I'm not complaining that I get to have plenty, too. Turns out Harper's quite a giver, and she insists on working on her blow job technique. Who am I to deny the woman her practical training? If she likes taking me in her mouth, she should damn well avail herself of the opportunity.

Blow jobs from Harper just might be proof that somewhere, in some other lifetime, I was a very good person. That's the only way I can possibly explain what I did to deserve the reward of her wicked mouth on my cock.

Like right now, on Wednesday night. She lies on her back on my bed, her head extended over the edge of the mattress, her hands clutched to my hips as I stand, deep in her throat, pumping my hips.

With her neck stretched like that, I can see the outline of my dick as she sucks. She loves trying new positions, like bent over the couch last night, like 69 earlier this evening—though it was closer to 61 since she was riding my face so blissfully, she couldn't keep me in her mouth. And this one, too—the upside-down blow job. The best part? It's not how spectacular this feels—though trust me, she sends me straight to some kind of ecstatic oblivion with her tongue and lips and mouth—the best part is I can tell how much she likes it by the way her back bows off the bed, and how she rocks her hips up and down. I'm loving everything, too. The way her hair spills wildly over the covers, how her nails dig into my flesh, and most of all, how when she moans, she's literally *humming* around my dick as she sucks me hard.

I'm moaning, too.

That's the problem. I could come in another minute if I let her go on like this. But I just can't. I'm not that selfish. I love her orgasms more than my own. Even as a fresh round of pleasure crashes into me, I find the will—Herculean task though it is—to pull my dick out of her lush mouth.

Her eyes are dazed as she stares at me, upside-down.

"Sit on me, Dirty Princess," I tell her as I sink down to the bed, grab a condom, and cover myself in seconds. I pull her up, then position her reverse cowgirl style on my cock.

We groan in unison as I bury myself in her. I loop my hands around her and cup her tits as she thrusts up and down, picking up the pace quickly, her back flush to my chest.

"This won't take you long, will it?" I whisper in her ear.

She shakes her head against me as she moans.

"Play with your pussy," I instruct her. "Touch your clit as you fuck me."

Her right hand slips between her legs, and she rubs as she grinds on me. "I've gotten off to you so many times, Nick."

Those words send me spinning. Lust spirals in me, torquing into something more potent and powerful. Something that's born of late-night fantasies and months of longing. "Me too, princess. I think about you all the time. I've fucked you so many times by myself."

"Was it this good for you?" she asks, her breath uneven as her fingers fly over her clit, and my cock pushes in and out of her tight, wet heat.

"No," I grunt, as her gorgeous back slides against my chest. "Nothing compares to the real thing with you." Because she is all my fantasies, only better, so much better.

"It's so good with you," she says on a broken pant. She shudders, her breath hitches, and her words come out in a hot whisper. "I'm going to come all over you."

"Do it, princess. Come on me," I growl, because she loves to talk, she loves to announce her orgasms, and she loves to tell me when she's coming, and I relish every single dirty, sweet, and filthy word to fall from her lips.

She circles her hips, rubs faster, and slams down hard as she cries out, "Oh god, oh god, oh god."

Her sounds and her shudders flip the switch, and I follow her to my own sweet annihilation. My entire body jerks as my climax crashes over me, assaulting me with pleasure. I groan against her neck. "You kill me, Harper," I say roughly in her ear. "I come so hard with you, you know that?"

She sighs, a sexy murmur telling me how much she likes hearing those words. "I love it when you come," she says, in a breathless admission. "I love hearing your noises. I love the way you grip me tighter, how your breathing goes wild."

It's such an intimate moment, unraveling for someone, letting go of all control. And, yeah, giving orgasms is my favorite hobby—but it's fucking awesome that she wants mine so much. Maybe that's why they're so good with her. Because I feel even more. More intensity. More vulnerability. Like she *knows* me.

"That's what you do to me," I tell her, brushing my lips to her cheek. "You make me go crazy."

218 · LAUREN BLAKELY

She leans her head back against my collarbone and loops her arms behind my head.

When her fingers play with my hair, I shudder. "I love that, too. What you're doing," I whisper.

"I know," she says, her voice so soft. "You've always liked it when I touch your hair."

Electricity sparks in my body, and I'm not sure if it's the aftershocks or some new high from what she just said. Because it's not just that she knows me. It's that she's figured me out. She's learned my likes (numerous) and my dislikes (so very few), and then my absolute fa-vorites, and she seems to want to give me as many of those as she can. She launched into this project ready and eager to discover what she liked, but she's quickly discovered me. And hell, I'm not picky—but I have my turn-ons, too. The lingerie she wears, the words she says, and the dirty things I can say to her, too.

"It's like you're studying me," I say, something like wonder in my tone.

"Maybe I am. Does that bother you?"

I scoff. "God, no."

She pushes her back closer to me. "I like giving you what you want."

I press my lips together, holding in my words.

You're what I want. All of you.

* * *

A little later, after we clean up, she takes my hand and tugs me to the kitchen. "I brought you a present tonight." Her eyes twinkle.

"Another present?" I ask, reining in a grin. I love her gifts.

She nods. "I slipped it into your freezer when I ar-rived."

"How did you do that without me seeing?"

She rolls her eyes and flashes her hands. "Nick, it's what I do. Sleight-of-hand. Misdirection."

She opens the freezer and takes out a pint of mint chocolate chip ice cream. "Your favorite," she says with a smile.

I can't help but grin, too. Because . . . this girl.

I wanted to just screw her out of my system. I desperately needed to just focus on the sex. But every little thing she does is magic to me—lingerie, ice cream, shower showrooms. And the way she talks to me in the heat of the moment, opening up, sharing, making herself so vulnerable, I nearly let myself believe this can go on, and that we can eat ice cream together every night.

Okay, maybe not every night. Gotta stay in fighting shape. But enough nights. Only, that's not what she wants. The here and now will have to be enough, so I'm going to just enjoy every second of this time with her until it ends.

With a sly grin, I back her up to the fridge, sneak a quick kiss, then steal the ice cream.

"No fair," she says, trying to grab it back.

"If you're good, I'll share," I tease as I hold the pint high, open the utensil drawer, and take out two spoons.

"You better share," she says, and then she eats mint chocolate chip ice cream naked with me on the couch. I kiss her, and yes, the taste of the ice cream on her tongue is as good as I once imagined.

Wait. I'm wrong. It's better. Everything with her is.

That's why I give her a gift, too. It's a small thing, but it's something she told me she wanted. I grab the Sunday crossword puzzle from my coffee table, and hold it up in front of my chest, as if it's a plaque I received to honor an accomplishment. "Voila. Finished it today."

"Is this for me?"

I nod proudly. "It is."

"Aww. You're like a kitty cat bringing me a dead mouse that you killed."

I laugh at her analogy. "Would you like to pet me in approval?"

"I would," she says, running one hand through my hair and talking to me the way she did to Fido. "You hunted all the words. I'm so proud of you." With her other hand, she turns over the newsprint. "What's this?"

I tense momentarily when I see a gray outline. What was I doodling on the back of the crossword? She tilts the page at me, and it's a cartoon of a puppet wearing a tight top, breasts spilling out. The bubble by her mouth reads: "*How to send naughty texts: a dirty puppet tutorial.*"

"*Nick.*" One corner of her lips quirks up. "I had no idea you learned all your skills from puppets."

I laugh, relieved that she didn't uncover a drawing of her, just of her co-stars in the doodles she inspired. I wiggle my fingers. "Don't underestimate the filth appeal to a cartoonist of something you operate with your fingers."

She laughs. "You are so bad. Tell me more about your puppets, Mr. Dirty Cartoonist."

"I would, Miss Naughty Magician, but it might be hard for me to talk when my tongue is all over your hot body," I say, then I spoon some ice cream onto her nipple and lick it off. Then on her belly, where I run my tongue across the cool dessert on her skin. She practically purrs.

Soon, the ice cream left in the pint is melting, and Harper is too, as I travel down her body and shut myself up in my most favorite way in the universe.

If I don't keep my mouth occupied, I'll tell her about all the times I've drawn her, and then she'll know how hard it will be for me to let her go.

Even though this isn't supposed to be difficult at all. This little fling should be the easiest thing in the world.

Only it's not.

CHAPTER 28

I'm beating her, and that drives Harper batty.

"I can pull ahead. I know I can," she says, as she joins me at the scoring bench, after only knocking over five pins in her frame.

We're at a bowling alley just above 101st Street, not far from her house. It's our rematch, and we decided it was best not to frequent Neon Lanes and risk running into Jason.

I blow on my fingers. "I'm on fire tonight, princess. It's going to be pretty hard to beat me." But before I can stand up to take my turn, Harper plops her adorable little ass on my lap.

She laces her arms around my neck. I shake my head. "Don't think you can knock me off my game by being so damn cute."

"Cute? I'm cute?"

"Hot," I whisper in her ear. "Hot, sexy, gorgeous, good enough to eat. Come to think of it, I kind of want to eat you up now."

She laughs, swatting my shoulder. "You want to do that a lot, Nick," she says.

"I know. I do. And I also know you're trying to make me lose by talking about this stuff. Let me play, woman."

She slinks onto the green vinyl seat next to mine, and I proceed to knock nine pins down, putting even more distance between Harper and me on the scorecard.

She shoots me a steely glare as I return to her. As she rises, I grab her arm and pull her back to me. "You tried to distract me. My turn to distract you."

"Ha. Just you wait 'til softball season returns. I'll really distract you then."

I smirk. "Too bad we're on the same team."

She sneers at me and snaps her fingers. "Damn it." Then she beams. "That's okay. I do kinda like watching you hit the homeruns." I straighten my shoulders because I am good at knocking in all the runners. Then reality smacks me hard. Next summer, I'll be playing on the same team with her when these lessons are over, and she's moved on. Maybe some other dude will watch her play, meet up with her after the games, take her out.

A wave of rabid jealousy rolls through me. I try to swallow it down, but I'm keenly aware that even if we haven't set an official expiration date on our project, there is one. Sure, we might like each other enough to bowl, to go out to dinner, and to share ice cream, but neither one of us expects to cheer the other on in softball next summer as secret lovers.

That's what we are now.

But when this ends, we go back to being Spencer's best friend and Spencer's sister.

I drag my hand through my hair as something like guilt mixed with shame takes up residence in me. Spencer's on his honeymoon, and I'm fucking his little sister behind his back.

I try to imagine his reaction if he walked in on this scene right now. We're snuggled up in a bowling alley, and he'd have every reason to be pissed. I'm not being honest with him, and the guy has been my best friend since the start of high school. I helped him brainstorm plans for the app he launched that made him millions, I went to opening night at the first Lucky Spot he started, and I stood by him when he promised to love Charlotte for the rest of his life.

What if he discovered this tryst and was so pissed that I lost him as a friend?

I fight like hell to push the unpleasant image from my brain.

But wait.

What if that didn't happen?

For the first time, I let the scene play out with a new opening act, with me saying something to him. What if I told him I liked his sister? What if he knew these crazy feelings inside me were real? Would he freak out if he knew I cared about her? Or not?

But, hell, I'm getting ahead of myself.

Harper isn't interested in re-upping after these next few nights. My chest tightens as the clock ticks in my head. It's Thursday, and we only have a few more days.

Better just enjoy the hell out of this time. No need to dwell on *what ifs*.

Harper runs a finger against my temple. "How well do you see without your glasses?" she asks, cocking her head to the side.

I laugh at her out-of-left field question. "I see okay without them, but worlds better with them."

"Did you ever want to try contacts?" She gently touches the frame. They're not special—just simple black glasses.

"I tried them. I don't really like putting something in my eyes."

"What about LASIK?"

I shake my head. "I like my eyes. What if I was the one percent it didn't work for and my vision was messed up?"

"That hardly happens."

"Hardly is not never."

"True."

"Do you not like my glasses?" I ask curiously, as the woman in the lane next to us nails a strike.

Harper's eyes widen. "I love them. I think they're panty-meltingly hot."

I groan from the mere mention of her panties. "Do they melt yours?"

She lowers her voice. "You know the answer to that. It's yes."

"Good answer," I say, then brush a finger along the edge of her eye. "What about you though? You had those glasses in your purse at the bookstore, but I've never seen you wear them before. Were they prop glasses?"

She shakes her head as the nearby machine scoops up the fallen pins. "They're real. But I wear contacts all the time. I have *horrible* vision without my contacts, so I bring the glasses along just in case I ever need them. I also carry a fake pair that I'm going to use for a new magic trick."

I tilt my head to the side, curious to hear what she's working on. "What kind of trick?"

She leans in closer and speaks softly in my ear. "The kind where I'm a sexy librarian."

And suddenly I have no interest in finishing this game anymore.

* * *

She shelves a book in her tiny studio. With her red hair twisted in a clip, she stretches her arm, standing on tiptoe in her heels, sliding a book back in place.

I catch a glimpse of her stockings. They're white, and she's slipped on a tight, white button-down, too, as well as a hip-hugging black pencil skirt.

"Oh my, I can't seem to reach the highest shelf," she says.

"Need some help?" I offer.

She turns around, roams her bespectacled gaze over me, and quirks up the corner of her lips. "Why, yes please. I would love it so much if you could grab that book," she says, pointing to the coffee table. She bends over, giving me the most fantastic glimpse of cleavage I've ever seen in my life. Her shirt is only half-buttoned, so I have a perfect view of the fuchsia lace bra that hugs those beauties.

I grab the book, never once taking my eyes off the creamy flesh and the swell of her tits.

"Now," she says, gesturing to the highest shelf. "I might need to stand on something."

I grab a wooden chair from her breakfast table, slide it over, and pat it. She runs her finger over my beard. "Such a helpful library patron. The helpful ones are my favorite."

I swing my eyes to her ass. "What I think would help you most is if you hike up that skirt."

"Would you be so kind as to do that for me?" she asks, batting her eyelashes.

So naughty. So playful. *So damn sexy.*

I tug her skirt to her hips then hold out a hand, watching as she stands on the chair, her legs and ass on display. She's wearing a fucking thong.

"Jesus Christ," I mutter, and I can't help myself. I'm nearly at face level with this gorgeous ass, so I bend and bite her cheek as she shelves the book. I groan and squeeze her flesh, my voice low and dirty, "The things I want to do to this ass. The things I want to do to your whole fucking body."

She trembles against my touch, gasping and breaking character—but hell, I've already broken it. She blinks at me, her eyes saying *holy shit*.

Then, she returns to the role, turning around, wagging a finger at me. "No touching permitted in the public shelves. That's only allowed in the quiet corner of the library, and only if you show the librarian"—she trails off as she bends down, cups a hand around my ear, and whispers hotly—"your long, thick cock."

This woman.

Wildfire twists in my veins, torching me. I'm up in flames, hard as steel, and aching to have her. In seconds, I strip to nothing, loving the way her eyes slide over my naked body, my chest, my arms, my abs, my dick. I drag a fist down my length, swipe my thumb across the head and the drop of my arousal there, and then press that thumb between her red lips. She sucks off a taste of me and moans headily around my finger.

I grab her hips, lift her off the chair, and set her on the floor. Then I park myself on the seat and nod at the condom on the coffee table. "This is the quiet corner of the library until you start making those wild, sexy sounds."

She grabs the packet and returns to me, opening it. As she takes it out, I yank down her panties, and lust seizes me as I catch my first glimpse of her pussy. So slick, and silky, and shimmering with evidence of her desire. She runs her hand over my dick, a purr of approval escaping her lips as she feels how hard I am for her.

"Nick, you need to show me how to put it on you," she says in a voice that's quiet, but full of heat.

Not gonna lie. I love that she's no expert in this. I take the condom from her, making sure it's going on the right way. "Pinch the tip," I tell her, and she nods and does as told.

"Now roll it down," I say, and with a small grin, she does the job.

I point to my hard-on and give her an order. "Now get the fuck on my dick." She shivers and then straddles me and sinks down in one smooth motion.

"Jesus Christ, Harper." A shudder wracks my body as she rises up on me, then strokes back. "You turn me on so much," I mutter, in the understatement of the century.

"Just like you do to me," she says on a gasp as she rides my shaft, her hands curling tightly over my shoulders. She's fully dressed except for her panties, and I'm completely naked, and I love the power exchange.

"So fucking hot. My sexy librarian is so fucking hot," I say.

"Why is this your fantasy?"

I can't think straight. Can't answer with any intelligence. But I don't need to when the answer is elementary. "Don't know. It just is."

I drop my hands to her bare ass, squeezing and drawing out a series of quick little gasps. "Why do you like it when I touch your ass?"

"I don't know," she answers with a broken breath. "I just do."

Just like. Just is. Just do. That's what we are. We are electric, and it's just that way. I bring my hands to her face and cup her cheeks. "Let down your hair for me."

She reaches up and unclips those red strands. They spill down her back in a soft tangle, and I thread a hand through them, my other hand gripping her hip as she moves on me. When I sense her getting closer, I grasp her harder, guiding her up and down, controlling her moves, watching her face contort in exquisite pleasure.

Her back arches, bowing into me, and then she cries out, a wild, long, intense moan that goes on forever. Grabbing her hair hard and twisting it in my fist, I fuck her through her climax, burying myself in her until my whole body quakes as I come undone, too.

Her arms grip me, her lips kiss my face, her hands hold me tight, and I don't want this to stop, I don't want it to end. I want Harper to want me this same wild and crazy way, like she can't get enough of me. Because, hell, it's become that way for me.

It just has.

CHAPTER 29

Gino holds a glass of champagne high and beams. "To the creator of the most popular show on late-night TV."

A sea of shiny, sparkly network executives, agents, advertisers, and other glitterati in the business of show-biz clap and join in the *hear, hears.*

I give a quick wave to the crowd. Gino grabs my arm and holds it up, like he's a coach and I'm his prize fighter in the ring. "This man is going places," Gino adds. "His show is going to be the biggest hit on all of TV soon. Just you wait."

More cheers come from the crowd at this posh, up-scale establishment on the Upper West Side.

"Just keep the viewers coming," I say with a smile, since Gino eats up those jokes like candy.

He fake punches me and then downs his champagne. He pulls me away from the crowd to the edge of the oak-paneled bar.

"Now listen, Hammer. I'm seeing Tyler on Monday. It'll all come together then. Good news is headed your way," he says, with a glint to his eyes.

"Whenever it happens is all good," I say, and cast my eyes to Harper waiting for me on a red velvet lounge at the edge of the joint, her drink on a low, dark wood table. She flashes a small smile in my direction, a little curve of her lips that's both sweet and sexy, and it feels entirely like a private grin just for me. I'm trying to savor these moments with her, knowing they'll run out of steam in about forty-eight hours.

Fuck.

I want to slow down time. I want to stretch the next two days and three nights into a year.

Gino follows my eyes. "*Oh.*" He says it in a salacious tone, as he licks his lips. "You've got your *friend* with you again."

I just nod. There's nothing I need to say to Gino about Harper.

He shakes his head in appreciation. "She is a sight for sore eyes." He lowers his voice and nudges me. "Is it true what they say about redheads?"

Oh no, he didn't. I jerk my head toward him. "What the . . .?"

He sighs longingly. "What I wouldn't give for a piece—"

My jaw clenches, and I meet his gaze straight on. "With all due respect, you really need to stop saying that shit every time I'm with her."

He raises his eyebrow. "Excuse me?"

I don't care if this pisses him off. I don't care if he won't re-up my show when Tyler sees him on Monday. I'm tired of his games, his dude-with-an-earring-and-a-Corvette insecurities, and his demeaning attitude. "It's rude. Have a little respect for women."

He adjusts his shoulders and mutters, "I meant no disrespect."

"Good," I say, though I don't believe him. "Now, if you'll excuse me."

I walk away, join Harper, and drape an arm over her shoulder. Not that Gino would have a chance with her even in the zombie apocalypse if he were one of the last men standing. But she's with me tonight, and she'll never be with him, and let him chew on that pill of bitterness as I get to touch her.

"Hey, handsome," Harper says softly, and her greeting surprises the hell out of me. She's not a *hey, handsome* kind of girl, but I enjoy the new term of endearment, especially since it's like a direct shot of that crazy, fluttering feeling in my chest. "You looked kind of insanely hot out there."

"You think so?" I ask, eating up her compliments, ready and willing for her to pile on more.

She nods, and her eyes draw up my body, lingering on my chest and arms. She runs her hand over my biceps, and all the time I've ever spent lifting weights pays off in the way she touches me. "I couldn't take my eyes off you, and your hair, and your scruff, and your arms. I was admiring the whole package," she says, letting that last word roll off her tongue, and it's like she casts a spell on my dick. She did the hard-on trick once again.

"You can admire my package with your tongue later, Princess Sex-In-Your-Eyes," I whisper as I lean in close, loving her filthy innuendos.

She feigns surprise, covering her mouth with her fingers. "Oh, my. Was it that obvious I was objectifying you?"

"No, what'll be obvious is how much I like your objectification when I stand up in a few minutes to get you out of here." I wave a hand in the air. "We need to get rid of this tent in my pants. Talk about pencils in your nose." I smack my forehead. "Shit, that turns me on, too, now that I've seen you do it naked." Another smack. "*Naked.* I said naked. This isn't helping the have-you-got-a-banana-in-your-pocket situation that you caused, Harper."

She holds up her finger excitedly. "I know! *Mashed bananas.*"

"Ouch. You're the erection devil. Thank you for that awful image."

"Happy to help," she says, as my ridiculously pregnant publicist waddles over to us, her hand pressed to her lower back for support.

I rise and help Serena sit, even as she waves me off.

"Isn't it time you actually took your maternity leave?" I ask.

"Oomph," she says, parking herself on the velvet lounge.

"When are you due?" Harper asks, concern etched in her eyes as Serena huffs and holds up a hand. She winces, grits her teeth, and seems to be counting.

"A year ago, it feels like," she says, her lips forming an *O* as she takes a deep breath.

"Can I get you a water? Do you need anything?" Harper asks.

"Just for these contractions to stop."

My eyes widen. *Contractions.* That's just one of those words that means business. "Serena, are you serious?"

She laughs. "I wish! I've been having Braxton Hicks for five days now."

I scratch my head. "Courtesy to speak English please?"

She pushes her curly black hair away from her face and gives me a side-eye glance. "You don't know what that is?"

"Serena, I'm a twenty-nine-year-old single guy in the city. I have no clue. Why don't you enlighten me?"

False contractions, Harper mouths.

"They're evil," Serena says with a hiss. "They're basically trick contractions. They make you think you're going to finally exorcise the demon from your belly, but they're just a constant false alarm."

Another one must come, because she winces and grabs the table.

"Serena," Harper says gently. "I think we need to get you out of here."

"Nah, I'm fine."

"You're a workaholic," I say gently. "It's not going to be good for the baby. Let's get you home."

"From one workaholic to another, I'm going to be fine. It's good for me to be here. Gives me something to do other than count the seconds." She breathes out hard. "But you know what? I think I need to pee again."

Serena pushes up from the lounge, holding on to the table.

"I do, too." Harper stands and accompanies the about-to-burst publicist to the ladies' room. I check my watch. Seems I've served my time at Gino's fête. I send Harper a text that I'll be waiting outside for her, and I make my great escape to the cool autumn air of Amsterdam Avenue.

I check my phone. No reply. I scroll through messages and send a quick note to Tyler, letting him know about tonight's less-than-Kodak moment with Gino. I glance at the door. Still no Harper. I click on Facebook and absently scan my wall. Thirty seconds later, Harper's voice lands in my ears. "They're so fast. Look! It's already here."

Harper's arm is wrapped tightly around Serena, and she motions wildly for me to follow them. Harper escorts Serena to a black SUV idling at the curb.

I run the few feet to catch up. "What's going on?"

"Her water broke," Harper says, her tone even and calm. "I ordered an Uber. It's here already."

"That's fast," I say, dazed, and I'm not sure if I'm talking about the car service, Harper's Uber-ordering skills, or Serena's labor.

I open the door to the car. Harper follows Serena, sitting in the middle and holding her hand. I join them. I've never dealt with women in labor, and maybe it's easy for anyone who has, but I'm really glad Harper is here shepherding this situation, because I haven't a clue what to do.

"Mount Sinai Roosevelt," Harper says to the driver, even though he already has the info from the app. "And step on it." She squeezes Serena's hand and says, "I've always wanted to say that."

Serena laughs lightly then shoves her phone at me. "Call Jared. Tell him to meet me at the hospital, stat."

That I can do. I dial her husband's number, and he answers immediately. "Hey, sweetie. Everything okay? I'm almost done with this contract."

"Hey, Jared. It's Nick Hammer," I say and dive right into the details. "Serena went into labor at the party. She's on her way to the hospital, and I'm taking her there with my friend Harper."

I hear the squeak of a chair and papers being shoved aside. "Thank you, man. I'll be there in ten minutes."

I hang up and turn to the two women in the car, in awe of how calm both of them are while my mind is topsy-turvy. Kids are Greek to me. I wouldn't know the first thing about holding a baby, let alone playing the role of the helpful friend as labor sets in. But Harper slides into that position seamlessly, clasping Serena's hand and guiding her through her breathing. A few blocks later, as the car swings into the right lane, Serena snaps her gaze to me. "I'm not naming the baby Uber if he's born in the car."

I flash her a grin. "Is Taxi an option?"

Serena smiles, and soon we pull up to the front doors of the hospital entrance on Tenth Avenue, help her out of the car, and take her into the emergency room. Her husband rushes in to greet her. He arrived fast. Jared is tall and sturdy, with thick black hair and glasses, too. I've met him a few times, since he's in the business. "Thank you so much," he says, his eyes wide and eager, a touch of nerves in them, too, understandably.

"She's the one to thank," I say, pointing at the woman by my side. "Harper got her here."

Harper waves off the compliment. "Good luck with the baby. I'm so excited for the two of you."

We walk away, and I'm honestly a little stunned by that change in tonight's lineup. I scratch my jaw, trying to come up with something pithy to say, but words fail me.

Not Harper, though. "Isn't it amazing that in a little while, maybe a few hours, maybe more, their lives are going to change massively, and they'll have a baby in their arms?" she says, with a glossy look in her eyes.

Oh no. Is she one of those girls?

"I love kids," she adds sweetly, and yup, there's the answer.

"Do you have baby fever?" The question comes out cautiously.

She rolls her eyes. "Yeah. I want to be a twenty-six-year-old single mom in New York City."

"But seriously. Do you want to have kids?"

"Um. Not tonight, Nick."

"But someday?"

She holds her arm out far in front of her, pointing. "Someday. In the future. When the time is right. Yes. I do. I like kids. What about you?"

I shrug my shoulders. "I have no idea. I've literally never thought about it."

She stops walking, parks her hands on her hips, and shoots me a sharp stare. "Bullshit."

"What?"

"I don't believe you've *literally* never thought about it. *Never* is a big word. And *literally* is, too. You mean the idea of kids has never once crashed into your mind?" she asks, tapping my head.

"No. It hasn't. I've been pretty focused on work, and my job, and the show. That's what my life has been since I graduated college, and I love it. I don't sit around and ponder kids."

She nods and takes a deep breath. "Right. Of course."

"You say that like it's a bad thing."

She shakes her head and flashes a smile. "No, it's not bad. Your work is your passion. I get it. That makes sense. I feel the same. But my work involves kids, so I guess it's natural that I'd think about it more. Doesn't mean I want to get knocked up anytime soon, though." She holds up a finger for emphasis. "However, I will most definitely want to snuggle that baby when Serena comes home with it."

Snuggling babies. Such a foreign notion to me. But this whole past hour has occurred on another planet—Babylandia—and it's not one I'm terribly keen to visit again soon. Even so, I'm still in awe of how swiftly she handled the situation. "How did you know what to do? With her?"

She laughs. "It's not that hard."

"Oh yes, it is," I say, nodding vigorously as we wander uptown. "I didn't even know what Braxton Hicks were. I can't imagine what happened when her water broke in the ladies' room. Please don't tell me what that was like." I hold up a hand like a stop sign. "I'm just glad you were there."

"Me, too. For her sake. And to answer your question, my friend Abby took a CPR and first-aid class when she started nannying a few years ago, and she asked me to go with her. I figured it couldn't hurt, since I never know in my job if someone will ever get hurt or sick. And that's one of the things they touched on. What to do if someone goes into labor."

"And you had the car right away, too," I add.

She gives a one-shouldered shrug and a smile. "As for my amazing Uber-ordering skills," she says, and wiggles her fingers, "all I can say is I've got some magic hands. They're quite fast."

I kiss her palm. Then each knuckle. "I'm quite fond of these hands," I say, and for the first time I'm not playing with double meanings. Especially when I slide my fingers through hers. "I like holding your hand."

"I love it, too." Then her eyes light up with an *I've got an idea* twinkle. "Hey! Want to go get a gift for Uber?"

I frown in confusion.

She nudges my side. "The baby, silly. We can stop at An Open Book. It's on the way to your house."

"Let's do it."

A little while later, we walk through the front door of the bookstore, and I do a double take.

Holy fuck.

I blink.

Blink again.

Long black hair. Haunting silver-gray eyes. Carved cheekbones. Ten, maybe fifteen years on me. She's as gorgeous as the day I met her. I'm not seeing things. There, in the romance section, running her fire-engine-red nails along the spines, is J. Cameron.

CHAPTER 30

From above the shelves, she catches my eye. A *what-a-nice-surprise-to-see-you* grin spreads on her face, and J. Cameron emerges from behind the display, dressed in tight jeans, black heels, and a clingy red top.

"Nick," she says, her voice smoky and befitting her profession. She drops a kiss on my cheek. I tense, hoping her touchy-feely ways don't tick off Harper.

"Hey, Jillian. How are you?" I ask, and the words come out dry and scratchy as I use her name, the one I always called her by. I glance at Harper. Her face is impassive, revealing nothing.

"I'm fabulous. I'm back from Italy. My new book just released, and I have a signing here tomorrow. I always like to get the lay of the land beforehand." She turns to Harper and extends a hand. "I'm Jillian, or J. Cameron. So lovely to meet you. I'm jealous of your hair," she says, and gestures to Harper's red locks.

"I'm Harper. I'm jealous of your fictional characters. They have the best nights ever," she says with a wink, and I nearly stumble.

Holy hell. The tension in me ratchets up because I do *not* want the conversation going in a direction where they casually tango near bedroom exploits of her imaginary characters.

"They do have quite a good time, don't they?" Jillian flashes another smile. "What brings you both to An Open Book tonight?"

"Harper helped deliver a baby," I blurt out, and I clasp her hand as if I'm proud of her. Then I realize I sound like Harper around Simon. My heart rate quickens, because this is too weird to be in the same five-foot radius as my ex-lover and my current lover. Harper knows all these things I've done with Jillian because of her book, and all I want to do is reassure Harper that it meant nothing, and no one can even hold a candle to her.

"How exciting!"

Harper downplays her role again. "All I did was order an Uber when her water broke in the ladies' room."

I shake my head, squeezing her hand. "No, she was amazing. She made sure that my co-worker Serena felt calm on the way to the hospital, and that everything was going to be fine," I say, and cast my gaze to Harper, trying to meet her eyes, to read her thoughts, to figure out how she feels right now—if she's jealous, or annoyed, or embarrassed. I want to tell her I don't think about other women, I don't fantasize about them, and she's the only one I've wanted in any way, shape, or form for months.

Harper points to the back of the store. "I need to run to the ladies' room. Never got to use it at the party."

She darts away.

And now it's just Jillian and me in the new release section, a slice of my past sliding into my present. "You look amazing," she says, and runs her hand briefly down my shoulder. Her touch does nothing for me. It's only friendly.

"So do you," I say politely.

She raises an eyebrow and then pushes a strand of my hair off my forehead. "Somebody's in love."

"You're in love? That's great," I say, flashing a smile, because I'm happy for her.

Smiling, she shakes her head then corrects me. "No. You are."

I frown. Make a huge *no* gesture with my hands. "That's ridiculous."

"No, it's not. I can tell these things."

"Because you're a writer?"

"You never looked at me the way you look at her."

I barely process what she's saying. It's not computing. It's too strange to hear my ex psychoanalyze me, so I turn it around. "You didn't want that. That wasn't what we were about."

"I know, but perhaps she wants it." Jillian tips her forehead toward the restroom.

I frown in confusion, trying to make sense of her comment. "Why do you say that?"

"Because I *see* it. In the two of you."

I roll my eyes, trying to show how much I want to brush off her suggestion. "Whatever you say."

But the truth is I don't want to dismiss the idea at all. She sounds wise and insightful, especially when she adds, "Think about it, sweetie. There's something there."

I latch on to her comments, wondering now if she's onto something. If she's figured out the puzzle of Harper in a way I haven't. It can't be true, right? She can't possibly be accurate in her observation. I should drop this conversation. Let it go, *poof*, like a disappearing rabbit. But the denial I practiced a few seconds ago vanishes, and now the idea takes hold, digging roots into some part of my heart that barely gets used. "Do you really think so?" My voice rises at the end.

Jillian parts her lips to respond then shuts them a few seconds later as Harper returns to my side.

"I should go. Get my beauty sleep before the signing. It was lovely meeting you," Jillian says to Harper then shifts her attention to me. "And to answer your question, yes, I really *do* think so." She takes a beat then adds, "I do think it will be a great turnout tomorrow, and I can't wait."

She spins efficiently on her heel, having answered my question about Harper and ensured, too, that Harper didn't know we were talking about her.

After Jillian leaves, Harper clears her throat. "So I was thinking about getting Uber *I Love You to the Moon and Back*. It's a great book."

"Can we add in a copy of *Harry Potter,* too? For when Uber is older?"

"That sounds perfect."

The weirdest thing is, buying a gift for a baby with her isn't weird at all. It feels right, in its own way.

* * *

"It's nice you're friends with someone you used to go out with," Harper says almost wistfully when we return to my place, the door clicking shut.

I shrug. "Yeah, it is. Though, I wouldn't say we're friends."

"But you got along so well at the bookstore," she points out.

"It was amicable. We never had deep feelings for each other." I lean against the kitchen counter and toss my jacket on a stool, then set down the bag with the gift for Serena's baby. Harper sheds her coat.

"Did it bother you to run into her?" I ask, reaching for her hand. She lets me hold it. "I couldn't tell at the bookstore, and I was hoping you weren't upset."

She juts up a shoulder. "I wasn't upset. But it was a little odd, to be honest." Her voice drops a notch. "Mostly because I feel like I can't compare."

I shake my head and pull her close, my heart lurching toward her. "Stop. There's no comparison."

"But you *chose* to be with her. You're just doing this with me because I asked."

My shoulders sink. "I can't believe you'd think that. This is not an obligation. It's the best time I've had in ages."

Best time.

Okay, maybe that wasn't the most romantic word choice, but I don't really know what this conversation is about, or how to properly reassure her that she's amazing.

"I've had a good time, too," she says softly.

I tilt my head, try to study her, to figure out what's going on in her head—but even more so, what's in her heart, and if it's even remotely close to matching what's in mine. I can't tell, and I desperately want to know. Because if there's a chance she feels the same, I should say something. I should let her know I don't want this time with her to end.

"What's going on, Harper? You seem pensive," I say and brush a strand of hair from her cheek.

She nibbles on her lip, looks away, then turns back to me, and the words spill out, piling on top of each other like clowns spilling out of a car. "I-keep-wondering-do-you-think-we'll-be-like-that?"

"What?" I ask, as my heart speeds up. She's *never* spoken that quickly with me. She's never used her awkward language, and it gives me this wild burst of hope. Maybe Jillian is right.

Holy shit, I hope Jillian is right.

Harper slows, takes a breath. "Will we stay friends?"

The burst of hope dies a cruel, painful death. All the air leaks out of me and I'm utterly deflated, even though I knew this was coming. I've known from the start. Her actions have always told me I'm not a guy she wants to date.

But I can't let on how hard this hits.

"Of course," I say with a big smile, trying to mask the disappointment rooting in my chest. Because as tough as it will be to not be intimate with her, losing her friendship will be much worse. Maybe *best time* wasn't such a bad description after all—Harper and I *do* have an amazing time together, and I can't imagine not having her in my life. These last few weeks have been the most fun, vibrant, and wonderful time I've had with anyone. If she were gone entirely in the wake of some breakup or weird romantic misunderstanding, that fate would be worse. "That's what you want, right?"

She nods. "I do want to stay friends. You and Jillian get along. And I want that to be us. I want to go to your signings and save you in line from women with magic bullets in their pockets and dangerous biker husbands. I want to get you detergent to clean the hot chocolate I spill on you. And if you need me at a bowling tournament to throw a few frames, I want to be the one tossing the gutter balls," she says quickly, racing through each sentence, barely breathing. "I want to see you at dinner with Spencer and Charlotte, or just walking dogs in the park with your brother. Or if you ever get a new shower, I want to help you pick it out."

God, her words kill me and lift me up. They make me feel so good, and so fucking awful at the same time. Because it's clear what she's saying. *When this ends*. Because it will end. It has to. It has a beginning, and it will have an end, like all the others who have come and gone. Even though I will miss this woman in a way I never have anyone else.

And I wish that I could tell her I want to be so much more than her wingman and buddy. But if I tell her that, will I risk losing her as a friend, too?

There's no answer key for me to follow on this count. I can read her cues in bed, but I haven't the foggiest idea what would happen if I told her I didn't want to be her teacher—I want to be her guy.

I choose the path I can see clearly. "Harper, you better always be in my life. It's just brighter and more fun with you in it. And if you need me to . . ." I trail off because what have I actually done for her? Offered dating advice? Mocked a dude who used emoticons? Or just introduced her to multiple orgasms? Is that the mark I've left? "If you need anything, I'm your man."

She smiles faintly, the kind of smile that doesn't reach her eyes. "Will you take me to the train station tomorrow? After Hayden's party that I'm doing," she says, and I force myself to blot out the reminder of Hayden's father, Simon. "I have to go to Connecticut in the afternoon. Remember?"

I nod. She told me she had some parties there this weekend for a few of the Manhattan moms she's worked for, who've since moved to the suburbs, and asked me to feed Fido on Sunday. I don't even know why she wants me to go with her to Grand Central. But I'll go. "Of course."

My chest is hollow. Taking her to the train station feels so inadequate for all that I'm learning I want with her. But I can't hang my hat on something a romance writer thinks. Jillian wants to believe in true love. She makes a living out of buying into storylines about how the little sister falls for her brother's best friend, and how lessons in sex turn into happily-ever-after. But this is real life. Real life is full of asshole bosses, and unrequited-ness, and guys who are lucky enough to have everything they've ever wanted when it comes to work, and life, and art . . . but who would be fools to think they get to have it all in love, too.

I'm not bitter. I'm not angry. I'm just realistic. Harper Holiday has always been a moment in time, and I've never been a love-struck fool. I'm a serial monogamist, and this series of nights with her is chugging to its inevitable end.

I reach for her shirt, tug her close, and bring her body flush to mine. "Harper," I breathe. "You have to know how much I've loved everything with you."

"Me too, Nick. Me, too." She plays with my hair then says, "Do you want to tie me to the fridge?"

I manage a small laugh. "No. I want something else."

"What do you want?" she asks, her eyes looking so vulnerable.

"I want to have you. As many more times as I possibly can."

She presses her forehead to mine, her lips brushing my lips as she whispers, "Have me."

That begins another night of bliss with her, even though I can't help but hear the ticking of the clock as we wind down.

CHAPTER 31

I pace up and down Sixty-Second Street. I drag my hand through my hair. I stare at my phone again.

I am not jealous that she's with Simon. I am not annoyed.

I check my texts again.

Princess: Running late. I helped them clean up and then had to grab a coffee after the party.

I will my teeth to unclench. I let go of the jealousy roiling inside me. Harper is a friend, and I won't lose her as a friend.

I think of my dad and his yoga mantras, his calm demeanor. The guy is unruffled, and he takes everything in stride. Yup. That's me. Life is good, I'm a lucky bastard, and I'm as cool as Saturn's surface with the fact that Harper is getting a coffee with Simon before I take her to Grand Central Station for God knows what reason.

Besides, I've got my own coffee. So there.

When Harper rounds the corner, clutching a paper cup, the Hemsworth dad by her side, his hand wrapped around into his daughter's smaller one, I take a deep, fueling breath.

Because you know what? He's better for her than I am. She likes kids. She wants kids. She's really good with them. I didn't even know what a Braxton Hicks contraction was.

If I'm going to be her friend, I have to let this envy go.

They stride up to me, and I paste on my biggest, brightest, happiest, shit-eating, nothing-is-fucking-wrong-with-me smile. "Hey Harper. How are you?" I turn to Thor and say hello. "How's it going, man? Was the party good?"

Hayden goes first. "It was the best ever. Anna the Amazing did the coolest tricks."

"She was incredible," Simon says, chiming in, and nope, I totally don't want to put chicken bouillon in the showerhead in his bathroom. Nope. I don't want to swap out his deodorant for cream cheese. Because *really,* I haven't done that shit since I was sixteen and pranking Wyatt.

I'm a grown man, and I don't need to beat my chest or stoop to that level. Besides, I can be Harper's friend, even if she dates this dude and wears her butterfly panties for him.

Smoke billows out my eyes as that image evilly taunts me. I crush the coffee cup in my hand, and the remnants of my drink squirt all over the sidewalk.

Oops.

Hemsworth: one. Nick: zero.

"Everything okay?" Harper asks as I toss the cardboard cup in the trash can then try to wipe the drink from my hands.

I laugh it off. "Shouldn't have upped the weights at the gym this week. Didn't realize how strong my forearms were getting."

"My daddy is strong, too," Hayden says and grabs Simon's arm and holds it up. Yeah, he's a candidate for arm porn, too. *Curses.* "He's a super star!"

"That's what she calls me," Simon says, in an "aw shucks" manner, and it is not fair that this guy looks like a movie star and is humble, too. It's like finding out your favorite athlete gives all his money to animal charities.

"It's adorable," I say, and I'm sure no one can hear the acid in my voice. I'm masking it so well. Besides, Harper won't even notice. She's probably blushing and unable to speak around the man she really wants.

"Simon," she says, turning to him. "Thank you for the coffee. And I know Abby is going to be so excited to hear from you. She finishes with her current family next week, and she's one of the best nannies so she'll be in demand. You need to snap her up." Harper snaps her fingers and laughs.

Simon laughs, too. "I'm calling her as we speak."

What the hell did I just witness? Harper didn't babble. She didn't speak in tongues. She didn't freak out.

"Well, not technically as we speak," she says, making a joke.

"You got me on that one."

"Okay, I need to run." She bends to Hayden and pretends to pull a pack of mini Skittles from her ear. "Special gift from Anna the Amazing for the birthday girl."

Hayden's eyes widen, and she clutches the candy. "I love Skittles! They're my favorite."

"I know," she says then waves good-bye to her. She shifts her gaze to her crush. "Fingers crossed that it'll all work out."

He twists his index and middle finger together.

"See you later, Harper." He extends a hand to me. "Good to see you again, Nick. Congrats on your show doing so well. Harper mentioned it to me. She's proud of you."

"Thanks," I say as Simon walks away with his daughter, and I cock my head, trying to figure out this strange

250 · LAUREN BLAKELY

creature in front of me with red hair, wearing Harper's clothes. Her massive bag is on her shoulder so I'm pretty sure she's not an impostor, but I have no clue how she pulled off that trick of acting normal. Unless . . . she's no longer into him. Which would be the best news ever . . . except she only wants to be friends with me.

But wait.

Let's think about that.

Let's add up all the facts.

Last night at my house when she was bent over the couch, she was a lot more than friendly. When she rode me into her third climax of the quartet I gave her, she was much more than cordial. As she cried out, *Oh Nick, no one makes me feel like you do*, that sounded a touch warmer than simple fondness.

And it felt like a lot more than lessons in seduction. It felt like much more than mind-blowing sex. It felt like we were falling for each other.

Maybe I should take another swing.

"Should we hail a cab?" I ask, thrusting a hand in the air. "Sometimes they come faster here than Uber."

"Good idea. Especially since everything ran late after the party."

An image flashes before my eyes of her working the kid's party. "Where's your cape?"

She pats the bag. "It's in here."

"You do wear a cape for your shows, right?"

She nods and smiles. "I do."

A bolt of lust slams into me. I can't help myself. I blurt out, "I bet you look insanely hot in a cape and nothing else."

"Generally, I don't wear my cape with nothing else," she says.

I raise an eyebrow. "Would you for me?"

"I would," she says, as the yellow cab arrives. I open the door and slide in after her. The door slamming rings in my ears, and it hits me. The game's not over until the final at bat.

"Can we talk about the elephant in the cab?"

Her eyes light up. "Sure."

I point my thumb behind us, in Simon's direction. "English. You've acquired full use of the language around Simon."

She nods happily. "I'm cured, evidently. Your lessons eradicated my little affliction."

"Oh," I say, my heart sinking as I strike out on pitch one. Guess that means she can behave normally around guys she likes. "We got rid of Princess Awkward. I'm gonna miss her though," I say, trying to keep the mood light.

"Yeah, me too," she says, sighing wistfully, then flashing a huge I've-got-a-secret grin. "But that's not the only reason I'm cured," she says, and wraps her hand on my arm.

I hate that sparks fly inside me from that touch. I wish they'd stop. "What's the other reason?"

She shrugs happily and squeezes my bicep. "I don't like him anymore. In fact, when he asked me out for coffee last weekend via text, I turned him down."

And we're back in business. Angels sing. The heavens burst open. Candy rains down from the sky.

"That so?" I ask, the corner of my lips twitching up in a grin.

"That is so," she says, all sexy and naughty and inviting. "The reason I was running late, as you probably ascertained, is that I helped clean up so we could talk about my friend Abby, since he needs a new nanny for Hayden. His ex-wife is hardly around at all, and he does most of the parenting. He bought me a coffee to say thanks."

"I did ascertain that. I also think it's incredibly hot that you just dropped a crossword-puzzle word into casual conversation."

"I did it because I knew you'd like it," she says, and runs her fingers up the back of my neck and into my hair. Those sparks? They don't just fly. They torpedo across my skin. They race through me. They live inside me with this girl. I'm so far gone for her, it's ridiculous.

How did I ever think I could just let her walk away? I can't, no matter who her brother is. I'll just have to sort out that little snag another time.

"I like it. I also really like that you're not into him," I say, as I lean my head back into her hand, turning my face to meet her gaze.

"Why does that make you glad?" She inches closer to me as the cab swings around the corner, nearing the train station.

"Because I'm a greedy bastard, and I want you to myself," I say, and it's not a full-on admission of all that I feel, but it's a start, and that's how I'm going to have to take things with her. Step by step.

"You have me. Don't you know that? I couldn't do the things we've done in bed and feel that way about anyone else. I swear, Nick, I haven't felt a thing for him since well before the night you kissed me. Since well before I sent you the pencils. Since before the laundry detergent, even. And I never ever felt a thing for Jason."

My heart thumps hard against my chest, fighting its way to her. "I fucking loved it when you gave me laundry detergent," I tell her, my eyes never leaving hers.

"I thought I wasn't your type. That you preferred older women," she says, on a whisper.

I shake my head, heat spreading across my skin. "My type is you," I say, and her blue irises glow with excitement, maybe even a wild kind of happiness.

"You're my predilection," she says, a little flirty, and fuck, now I'm even more turned on, and feeling like I can walk on water.

The cab squeals to a stop at the train station, and I thrust some bills through the window. I get out with her.

"I need to catch a train or I'll be late," she says, her tone full of longing.

"Come over when you're back."

"I get back really late tomorrow."

"I don't care how late it is. I want to see you."

"I want to see you, too."

I tilt my head to the side. "Why did you want me to take you to the train station?"

Her lips quirk up. "Because I *fuck* seeing you."

I crack up. "Harper Holiday, I *fuck* seeing you, too." I cup her cheeks in my hands and kiss her. This kiss is different. It's as hot as all of them have ever been, but there's something intangible in it, too, a quality that digs down deep into my chest, that burrows into my bones. An inevitability, and unlike last night, it doesn't feel like the end. It feels like a promise of more to come.

She breaks the kiss and turns to go, then she swivels around once more and slides her arm around my waist, tipping up her chin to meet my eyes. "There's one thing I want in bed that we haven't done yet."

"Name it."

"I'm on the pill," she says and knocks the wind out of me. I nearly sway on the busy street outside the train station.

"I'm clean. I've been tested," I add, my throat dry. The possibility of feeling her bare is almost too much. I'm not sure how I can function on any level between now and tomorrow night.

"Can we sleep together without a condom when I see you tomorrow?"

I nod. "I've never done it without one."

"I'll be your first?" Her voice rises with excitement.

"Yes." I'm dying to tell her that she's the first in so many things. First woman I've ever felt this way about. First woman I've ever cared about more than my work. First woman who's inspired a cartoon just for fun.

She presses one last kiss to my lips, murmuring, "I can't wait."

She leaves, and I'm pretty sure the next thirty-six hours will be the longest of my life.

Because . . . *bare*.

CHAPTER 32

I go to the movies with Wyatt that night, checking out a spy flick that numbs my brain with two hours of explosions, knife fights, and one badass motorcycle chase down a never-ending set of stairs.

He doesn't once ask about Harper or Spencer when we grab beers and burgers after the credits roll. I'm thankful for that, even though I don't know what to do about my buddy. I've got to hope Spencer will understand that the way I feel for his sister isn't cause for eyebrow-dyeing or hair-shaving.

Even if I haven't been upfront with him.

I push those thoughts away for tonight. Always the chatterbox, Wyatt tells me about his business expansion plans and how he needs to hire a new assistant. It's one of the rare occasions when we don't give each other crap the whole time.

I'm grateful, too, that I've survived the first day in the countdown to bare. When I return home that night, I head straight to my standing desk and draw a puppet with a stopwatch. He stares slack-jawed at the hot mechanic, who fixes brake pads in nothing but a cape.

I title it *Countdown to Bare*.

I know, I know. I'm pretty fucking brilliant. But as they say, a dirty mind is a terrible thing to waste. I turn off the screen, and when I slide under the sheets that night the last thing I do is check my phone. Again, karma loves me, because there's a photo from her. A close-up shot of her fingers, sliding under the waistband of her cranberry-red lace panties.

I swear, this woman will be my undoing. She's so goddamn perfect for me.

* * *

On Sunday morning I wake to my phone rattling on the nightstand. Must be another message from Harper. I grin in anticipation as I grab the phone.

A note from Serena pops up on the screen instead, with a picture of a baby sleeping.

Seven pounds of torture and I wouldn't have it any other way. Meet my baby boy!

An even bigger grin spreads on my face over the good news, and because I know Harper will like this picture, I forward her the note.

I freeze.

I just sent her a photo of a baby. To make her happy. What the hell has my world become? Who is this dude inside my skin texting pictures of a newborn? To a chick who sent me a dirty photo last night?

That's when the Road Runner drops the anvil, and Wile E. Coyote gets smacked with ten tons of obvious, and his head rings, and stars spin, but then everything becomes crystal clear. I want Harper to be happy in every way—in bed and out of bed. I don't just want to give this woman ten thousand orgasms. I want to see her smile more times than I can count.

Because . . . I've fallen in love with her.

I groan and flop back against the mattress.

This woman has upended my world. Once I only wanted to send her soaring, to bring her pleasure, to screw her out of my system. Now I want to make her feel joy in every way. I, Nick Hammer, self-avowed serial monogamist and Magellan of the female orgasm, have become a love-struck fool.

I wish there was a clue in the Sunday puzzle as to how to give voice to this madness taking over my heart. Knowing how to touch Harper, how to kiss her, and how to deliver ecstasy to every square inch of her body seems easy compared to reckoning with this strange, new foreign object occupying space in my chest. What do you even say to a woman you've fallen ass over elbow for? I scratch my head, coming up empty. Sex is my classroom, but love is a language I barely understand.

I close my eyes, letting my mind wander to all the things I know about Harper. She loves to entertain, to tell jokes, to spend time with her friends and family, to help people she cares about. She loves autumn, and cake, and bowling, and beating me in competitions. She likes taking care of Fido, and learning new magic tricks, and she loves to give gifts.

Most of all, she likes being understood.

I flash back to one of the texts she sent me. A non-dirty one.

I want to look into someone's eyes and feel like he knows me, gets me, understands me. I want him to see my quirks and accept them, not try to change them. I want to know what that's like.

This is a girl who has definite quirks. I latch on to something. Bits and pieces of our conversation back at Peace of Cake. Something she said about cheesy moments. What was it?

258 · LAUREN BLAKELY

I rub my thumb and forefinger together, as if that can stir the memory to the surface. It works, and I smile inside as I remember her offhand remark.

Does she write those cheesy sex scenes where the guy tells the girl he loves her while he's inside her or right after?

I might not know what to say, but I definitely know when *not* to say it. I get out of bed, brush my teeth, pull on my workout shorts and a fleece, and go burn off some of this energy, running all the way downtown to Spencer's house, where I feed Fido, trusting that this cat and his master will have to be okay with this turn of events, because I'm going to be so damn good to Harper. I'm going to treat her like the royalty she is to me. All I have to do is tell her.

I don't have a plan, a skywriter, or a bouquet of flowers, and frankly, I don't think she'd be impressed with any of those. That's not the kind of person she is.

But I know the most important part of my plan—there's no way I can let these lessons with Harper end. Not until I tell her I want to be so much more than friends with her, more than her teacher, more than her love coach. I want to be hers.

Too bad her train is really late that night. She texts me at ten to tell me it's stuck in Bridgeport for some sort of engine repair.

I write back immediately with the only possible solution.

I'll come pick you up.

Princess: Seriously?

You have no idea how much I want to see you.

Princess: As much as I want to see you?

Yes. THAT MUCH.

> *Princess: You won't use emoticons, but you'll use shouty caps?*

SHOUTY CAPS ARE MANLY. Get over here, woman. I need your naked body under me.

> *Princess: WHAT IF I WANT TO BE ON TOP?*

I DON'T CARE. JUST GET HERE. How's this? I'll order a car service. I'll send one to you. Whatever you want.

> *Princess: This is where apparating would come in really handy.*

Now you're really turning me on, talking Harry Potter and magic spells. But seriously, princess—can I send a car for you?

> *Princess: They say the train is going to start again in twenty minutes. I'll be there soon. If not, I might chew my leg off with waiting.*

Um, I like your legs. Please refrain from all chewing of limbs.

> *Princess: Ooh! We're moving again!*

A little later, I check the time. It's eleven, and a new text says she should arrive in Grand Central by midnight. I figure fifteen minutes in the cab will put her at my door at twelve-fifteen. I take a quick shower, brush my teeth, and wrap a towel around my waist.

A new text from her lands on my screen.

Princess: Ugh. Still more trouble. Train arriving at 12:45 now. Should I just go home?

My reply is instant.

NO FUCKING WAY.

I lie down, read a book, and drift off to sleep.

* * *

The ringing in my apartment is loud. I wake with a jolt, sitting upright in bed. I rub my eyes, orienting myself. I grab my glasses. It's a little after one. I get out of bed, and answer the phone. The doorman tells me I have a guest, and I say to send her up. I pad out of the bedroom, then slide the lock off the chain, crack the door a sliver, and peek down the hall.

The gears on the elevator crank, then slow, and the lift opens.

She turns and heads to me. Her hair is in a loose ponytail, and she wears jeans and her pink jacket. Her eyes widen as she nears me. They turn planet-size when she's inches away, and they drift down my body.

I glance down. Oh. Seems I'm wearing my birthday suit.

"I should always show up after midnight if this is my greeting," she says, her eyes roaming my naked body.

"You play your cards right, and that can be arranged," I say, raising an eyebrow. She doesn't know the half of it, though. She doesn't know how true that statement is. If she wants me, she can have me any time, all the time.

I grab her hand and tug her inside. She drops her bag to the floor as the door clinks shut.

I waste no time. I kiss her as if it's been weeks. Her tongue slides between my lips, and her hands travel down my chest, across my abs, down the happy trail, and I'm oh so happy that her journeys have taken her there. She skims her palm over my dick, and my breath hitches.

Her touch is spine-tingling. She dips her head to my neck, kissing me. I shudder, then bite my lip, because I can't let on all that I'm feeling for her yet. She kisses up my jawline, then to my ear. "I have to run to the little girls' room and pee. Wait for me in bed."

I salute her and retreat to the bedroom, following orders. I take off my glasses, set them on the nightstand, and park my hands behind my head. Slivers of moonlight slice through the blinds, and my room is cast in shadow. The water runs in the bathroom sink, then it's silent again. Her heels click on the floor, and three seconds later she stands in my doorway, illuminated by the moon.

She strikes a pose. If she was surprised by my attire, then color me ten shades of shocked by hers.

CHAPTER 33

"Holy shit," I say slowly. My jaw might be on the hardwoods.

Her hair falls loose on her shoulders. She's wearing a black cape, stilettos and white lace panties with pink polka dots. That's it. No bra. My mouth waters. My dick imitates the floor and is hard wood, too. My heart does a wild foxtrot as I sit up in bed and scrub a hand over my jaw.

I am so crazy for her it's ridiculous.

I stand up, walk over, and scoop her up. "You are my dream girl," I say roughly, and I carry her to the bed and toss her on it.

She squeals playfully as she lands. "So that's a yes then? The cape is good?"

I straddle her. "Let me put it this way. The way you look in that cape is scorching enough to launch a thousand new dirty Tumblr feeds. The Hot Redhead in the Cape. Wait." I shake my head then bring a finger to her lips. "Don't tell a soul. That's going to be the name of my next show. Only it'll be so hot it has to run in the early hours of the morning. On Cinemax."

She fingers the satin of the cape. "I guess that means you want me to leave it on then."

"For now," I say, rubbing my dick against her panties.

In a second, that naughty, playful glint disappears from her eyes. It's replaced by unbridled heat. She shudders and reaches her hands up to me, clasping my face. "Kiss me, please. Nothing turns me on more than your kisses, Nick."

"Kissing you is my favorite foreplay, too."

I bend to her and kiss her like crazy. She melts into my arms, just fucking melts like ice cream on a hot summer day, and she tastes even better. She's warm and snug beneath me, and she murmurs in my mouth, sighing against my lips, and her fingertips play with the ends of my hair in a way that makes me groan. She sucks on my tongue, nibbles on my lips, and then brushes that sweet, soft mouth of hers all over mine. I'm awash in a desire so wildly intense that the only way to quench it is to be consumed by it. To let it overwhelm me, like this girl has taken over my mind, my heart, and my body. I want her with every part of me.

She grinds her hips up against my hard-on.

Yeah, that part, too. *Especially* that part.

Another thrust of her hips, and that's all the kissing foreplay I can handle. A profound need crashes into me. The need to touch her everywhere, to kiss every inch of her body, to know her. I move down the bed and dip my thumbs into the sides of her panties. At the same time, she lifts up her hips.

My breath catches as she does that. It's such a small move in the scheme of things, but it tells me everything. She wants me to undress her as badly as I want to be the one to take off all her clothes.

My mind hooks on to something she said at the Italian restaurant, something she said she liked. *Seeing you undress for me.* Her voice plays in my head, and I hear those words in a new way. In a way that threads deeper into my heart, that means more than getting naked for someone. That means this is the person you want to strip bare for.

As I tug her panties to her knees, then her ankles, then off, I know with a bone-deep certainty that Harper is it for me. The road starts and ends here—with this magnificent beauty in a cape in my bed after midnight.

Kneeling at her feet, I slide off her shoes, circle my hands around her ankles, and gaze up at her face. Her lips are parted, and her blue eyes hold mine hostage.

"Hi, handsome," she whispers.

"Hey, beautiful."

Our voices sound different. She has to hear it, too. Has to feel it like I do. I bend to her calf and press a kiss there. When I raise my face, she gasps from that little touch.

"Harper," I say, my voice raspy.

"Yeah?"

"Want to know something I've learned about what I like?" I ask, repeating the words she said to me that night.

"Tell me."

"Seeing you undress for me."

"Oh God," she moans, and I spread her legs wide, part them in a *V*, and then I bury my face between her thighs.

There is nothing quite like that moan on the first lick. *Nothing*.

Her sounds fall on my ears like the most gorgeous song, and I love that she's learned how awesome oral sex is, because I can't resist licking her. I want to fuck her so badly, but this is my favorite thing in the world. Going down on my girl. Tasting her sweetness on my tongue, my lips, my face.

I love how slick she feels, and how much wetter she gets the faster I go. The more I flick my tongue across her flesh, the louder she moans, the wilder she writhes, until she thrashes under me. She doesn't even like fingers—all she wants is tongue and lips. She becomes this desperate, frenzied woman, her hands clutching at my hair, her legs widening then wrapping around my head.

I look up at her, and she watches my eyes dance between her legs, and then I do the thing she loves most. I dip my hands under her ass, and cup those luscious cheeks as I kiss her like crazy.

Oh God.

Yes!

That.

Oh my fucking God.

I squeeze and knead her ass as I kiss her pussy, and she's in paradise. I grab those cheeks harder, spreading them a little bit with my thumbs, and she bucks up into my mouth. I love her ass, and her ass loves me. We fit in every way, especially when she curls her hands tight around my head as if she's never letting go, and rocks into my face until she loses control and comes undone on a scream.

I slow my moves, letting her savor the aftereffects. Wiping my hand across my mouth, I crawl up her body, so ready to feel her in a new way. Her cape is all twisted around her, the tie yanked to her shoulder now. I quickly untie it, freeing her.

"I thought about you all day today. All night. All day yesterday," I whisper, as I rub the head of my dick against her slick heat.

"You have to know it's the same for me," she says, reaching for my hips, pulling me closer.

Electricity crackles down my body as I start to push in. I fight back the urge to tell her everything I feel. To let her know that this isn't just my first time without a condom.

That it's another first.

A bigger first. One that means so much more than the purity of pleasure. One that could tip over my future and turn it into a whole new color.

I ease into her.

"Harper," I groan. "This is . . ."

Words fail me. There just aren't any to convey how immense it feels to slide inside her. She wraps her legs around me, and, like that, I fill her completely. I brace myself above her as the sheer intensity of the pleasure ripples through me. I stare down at her face—her lips falling open, her blue eyes glossy as she looks into mine. God, this is almost too much. But I crave it like oxygen, this connection to her.

I thrust, and she rises up. I stroke into her, and she takes me deeper. We find a perfect rhythm, wrapped in silence for the first time. For two talkers, we're speechless, and I can't think of anything else to say. I can only feel. The heat of her body. The beating of her heart. The softness of her breath on my face as I lower to my forearms. She hooks her ankles tighter, and I pump harder, deeper.

She moves beneath me, our bodies like magnets seeking their opposites. "What are you doing to me?" I say on a thrust.

"The same thing you're doing to me," she says, running her fingernails up my back as she arches her hips.

"Tell me you feel it, too." I grit my teeth because it's so fucking good, and I'm so goddamn close, and no way am I firing early.

"Yes, God, yes," she cries out, and that's as much of a confirmation as I'm getting or seeking right now. She rocks up into me, hunting for more, and I give it to her. I give her everything she wants, taking her harder, because I want it, too. This deep connection. The physical that's so much more. I wrap my arms around her, and she pulls me even closer. We're chest to chest as my hands slide up into her hair.

"I don't want it to end," she moans.

"Oh God," I say, as a wave of pleasure crashes into me. Her words. They wreck me. They ruin me. "Please come. Please fucking come now."

I quicken the pace as desire assaults me. She clutches my shoulders then my face, running her hand over my beard as I fuck her and make love to her at the same damn time. She's so free with me, such a crazed little sexy thing, needy and hungry, as I ride her to the edge.

She buries her face in my neck, kissing me all sloppy and messy as her breathing turns wild, then she calls my name. The sound of it on her lips sends a charge across my skin. She cries out under me until she's boneless, senseless, and falling into me. That's how she feels. At last, I'm free to chase her there, and it's such a relief as my orgasm pulses through me, rippling in waves, gripping me as my shoulders shake, and my whole body jerks.

I groan, still high on her, breathing out hard. Another exhale, as I start to come down.

"I don't want this to end, either," I say, and my mouth claims hers. If I don't kiss her, I'll tell her, and now's not the time. She made that clear a few weeks ago, and I love her quirks. I swallow all the words with my lips on hers, but the whole time, they play in my head.

I'm so fucking in love with her, I can't stand the thought of this ending.

A few minutes later, I roll out of bed, and head to the bathroom to clean up. Grabbing a washcloth, I wet an end with warm water and return to her, all stretched out and sleepy-beautiful on my bed. Gently, I clean her, and she shoots me a sweet smile.

"Thank you," she murmurs and rolls to her side. I toss the washcloth in the hamper, slide into bed with her and pull up the covers. She's spending the night with me for the first time, and I hope it will be the first of many. I loop my arms around her and bring her close.

"I have nothing left to teach you," I say softly. "Maybe we're done with the teaching and it can just be us?"

She murmurs something that sounds like yes, then in seconds she's asleep.

I kiss her hair, run my fingers through it, knowing that tomorrow we can figure out what this means exactly. I can say the words in daylight, since I know that's how she wants it.

When I tell Harper, there needs to be no question about it for her. Harper knows I love sleeping with her. Harper knows she turns me on like crazy. I can't risk her thinking it's the endorphins steering the ship. The words I want to say need the weight of the sun behind them, not the wispy dark of moonlight.

Tomorrow, I'll tell her everything, and I'll have to tell her brother, too, that I've fallen wildly, madly, relentlessly in love with my best friend's sister, and I can't imagine living without her.

As her breath ghosts over my arm in a steady, even pace, I practice. Kissing her hair, I whisper, "I love you, Harper Holiday."

CHAPTER 34

Harper is a champion sleeper. I've never seen someone snooze like she can.

She's killing it in the starfish competition, too, and I'm not surprised at all, given the way she alternated all night long between octopussing me, and kicking me with her wild, wiggly legs as she slept.

Good thing I have a king-sized bed.

But even with all that flipping and flopping, the woman hasn't stirred once. Not to pee. Not to yawn. Not to raise an eyelid or burrow deeper under the covers.

Now, it's nine thirty in the morning, and I'm already showered, dressed, and drinking my morning coffee. I figured I'd take her out for breakfast and tell her how I feel, but at this rate, it might be lunch. Fine by me.

It's a Monday, and I'll work from home today. I head over to my desk, and as the computer whirs on, my phone rings. Tyler's number flashes across the screen. I answer immediately.

"Hey, man, what's the news?"

"The news is amazing. And I'm two blocks from your house. Get your ass downstairs and meet me for a coffee so I can tell you in person and congratulate you."

"Consider it done."

When I hang up, I grab a sheet of paper, leave a note for Harper that I'll be back soon and to wait for me, and head out of my building to a packed coffee shop on Columbus. Tyler waits at a standing table, his navy suit crisp and tailored, with two cups of coffee in his hands.

He thrusts one at me. "I won't even charge you my hourly for this, and the coffee's on me."

"For you to forgo your hourly, the news must be great, which surprises me, given how Gino was a dick on Friday," I say, and take a gulp of the drink. Since I didn't finish the one at my house, this will do as a replacement.

Tyler waves a hand dismissively. "Who gives a shit about that tiff? Listen to this, Nick," he says, parking his hand on my shoulder and clearing his throat. "They want to move the show to one of the sister networks on broadcast. Find you an even bigger audience."

My eyes widen. "He really thinks it'll fly on broadcast?"

Tyler nods proudly. "Ten p.m. timeslot is perfect for the show. And you know how broadcast networks are these days. They all want to compete with LGO," he says, mentioning the hottest premium cable network out there. "And this show gives them the edge. Plus, he doesn't even need you to make any major creative changes. Maybe tone down a filthy word here or there, but nothing that would compromise the integrity of the show."

I breathe a sigh of relief. Not that I planned to go all *artiste* on him, but it's nice to be able to deliver on the vision.

"That was all posturing from him?"

"Yup. Told you. He was just yanking you around. Trying to keep you on your toes. And hey, did I mention the best part?"

"No. Tell me," I say, eager for more good news, because this is way more than I expected.

"He wants to up the fee he pays you by thirty percent. *Cha-ching*."

I blink. "Holy shit."

"I know, right?" Tyler's smile is as wide as Central Park. "And they're not exactly paying you chump change now."

"No, they're not. Their checks cash well."

"That they do. And they want to make the move as soon as possible. They even mocked up some promos about the time change, and they're planning to make the switch at the start of the new year."

It all sounds amazing. It all sounds fantastic. It also sounds too good to be true.

When Tyler opens his mouth to deliver me the final bit of news, that gut instinct is confirmed. "Oh, and there's one more thing," he says offhand.

"What's that?"

"He's moving the show to Los Angeles."

It's like a punch to the kidney. I can't speak. My jaw drops open, and the words *Los Angeles* ring in my head. I grip the edge of the table to steady myself. "Los Angeles?" I croak out, as if I've never heard of this foreign land.

"That's where the broadcast network is based. He wants you there, too. Land of sunshine and palm trees. That's my hometown, you lucky son of a bitch." Tyler flashes a gleaming white grin. He's just served up a fantastic renegotiation package and tied it up in a perfect bow, given his love for the West Coast.

"Yeah, Los Angeles is great," I say, but my voice is hollow.

He must sense it, because he shifts into pep-talk mode, clapping me on the shoulder. "This is a game-changer, Nick. You're a star, and this is the kind of opportunity that shoots you into the stratosphere," he says, raising his arm up to demonstrate. "This is rarefied air, my man."

"It is," I say, monotone, as all my plans come crashing down. Not even anvil-style, just a heavy stone in my gut.

Because he's right. This is huge, so what's wrong with me? Work is what I love more than anything. My career is my passion, and this show has made all my dreams come true. But as I stand here in the middle of a coffee shop having just received the biggest news of my career, I'm not thinking of work.

I'm thinking of the one thing Los Angeles doesn't have.

Harper starfished on my bed.

Los Angeles possesses a complete lack of the woman I just realized I can't live without.

I take a swallow of the coffee, set down the mug, and ask a tough question. "This all sounds great. But there's one thing I want to know."

Tyler practically bounces on his toes. "Anything. Shoot."

"What if I say no?"

Tyler's mouth forms an *O*. Then his expression rearranges into *oh no*. "That's the thing. He's already signed on another show for your time slot."

I take a few seconds to digest that news. "Well, that does change the game, doesn't it?"

CHAPTER 35

Harper is twisting her hair into a ponytail when I open the door. She's perched on my kitchen counter, her legs crossed, kicking a foot back and forth. She wears jeans, a sweater, and boots. She must have everything in her wardrobe inside that giant bag.

A bright smile spreads on her face when she sees me.

"Hey, you." She sounds buoyant.

"Hey." My voice, by contrast, weighs two tons.

She frowns. "What's wrong?"

I take a breath and rip off the Band-Aid. "They're moving my show to L.A."

She slides off the counter, her boots hitting the floor with a loud thump. Surprise flickers in her eyes. "Really?"

I nod. I should be happy. I should be celebrating. "To the broadcast network. Better timeslot. More money. More viewers. More syndication opportunities. Yadda yadda yadda. Basically, I'd be set for life."

She nods and swallows. Then exhales. Inhales. Glances down. Fiddles with the sleeves of her sweater.

Harper is not a fiddler.

She lifts her chin. Her expression is tough, but in a flash, her face is the picture of excitement. Like, if you googled "show me an excited face" she'd appear in the results.

"That's amazing. That's so incredible. I always knew you'd be an even bigger star." She closes the few feet of distance between us and wraps her arms around me in a congratulatory hug.

It feels good to hold her like this, but all wrong, too. Because this is not how this moment should go. She's hugging me like Spencer's sister would hug me.

I separate from her. "I'd have to move to L.A."

"Sounds that way," she says, and I swear the chipperness in her voice is forced.

"Harper," I say, but I don't know what comes next. How is it that I can write and draw all these storylines every week, but devising what to say to this woman flummoxes me? Oh, right. Because my show is a comedy, and my life right now is desperately trying to imitate a romance, only I have no clue how those work. How the hell does anyone get from the shitty moment to the happy ending? "What about us?"

"What about us?" she repeats, her eyes locked on mine. Her body is a straight line, and tension, maybe anticipation, seems to vibrate off her.

"What happens to us if I go to L.A.?"

"Nick . . ." She takes a breath, like she needs it for fuel. "This is a huge opportunity for you."

"Yeah, I know. But this," I say, gesturing from her to me and back. Why doesn't anyone ever mention how hard it is to bare your heart? It's like peeling off a layer of skin. "This is just starting, right?"

She nods but says nothing. She closes her lips, and they form a ruler. She glances at her watch. "I, um, I have an appointment. I totally spaced on it. There's this class I've been taking. New tricks and all. I should go. And laundry. I have laundry to do."

No, I want to scream. *You can't go. Tell me not to go. Tell me you want me more than you can bear.*

But why can't I say those things, either? I try to speak, but nothing comes out. I try again. "Harper, I want a chance with you."

She leans against me, and I dip my nose to her neck, sniffing her. She smells like my soap. "Me, too, but . . ." She stops herself and raises her face. "This is an amazing offer. You need to take it. You need to go to L.A." She taps her wrist. "I really need to go. So late." She grabs her bag, shoves it on her shoulder, and heads for the door. "I'll text you later."

She leaves, and I want to kick myself for listening to her words in Peace of Cake. Cheesy moment or not, I should have told her last night how I feel. I should have told her before I knew about this twist of fate. Then I'd know for real if she felt the same.

Fuck the perfect moment. Screw waiting. I don't have a plan, and I don't care. I follow her down the hall, calling out her name as she presses the elevator button. When I reach her, I stop messing around and just tell her the truth. "I'm in love with you, Harper. If you tell me not to go, I won't."

Her eyes widen, and she blinks several times, then clasps her hand over her lips as if she's holding something in.

"Say it. Just say whatever you want to say," I urge, and I don't even know whether I'm asking for her to say *I love you* back, or to say *Don't go to L.A.*

Maybe both.

The elevator arrives with a soft ding. The doors spread open. She takes a step. I grab her arm to stop her. "Say it."

She takes her hand off her mouth. Raises her chin. Speaks clearly and simply. "I can't tell you not to go to L.A."

When I felt my heart sink in the cab the other day? That's nothing compared to now. This stupid organ in my chest craters, plummets to the floor like a meteor crashing to Earth. I want to stop her, to make her stay, to explain herself, but I'm frozen like a statue as the doors close. The elevator chugs downward, and Harper breaks my heart.

I kick the wall, and it hurts like a son of a bitch. "Fucking hell," I mutter.

I return to my apartment, march to the window, and stare at the street until she emerges from the lobby and onto Central Park West.

She wipes her hand across her cheek once. Then again. She picks up the pace, and soon she's a red blur, and my chest aches for her.

Love sucks.

I have no clue what to say, what she needs to hear, or what the hell I'm going to do. I don't even know who to turn to for advice.

But that matter is solved for me a little later when the doorman rings. Hope rises in me that she's returned. Only when I ask who's here, it's the other Holiday.

CHAPTER 36

Spencer yanks out a stool, parks himself on it, and plops a white plastic bag from Duane Reade on the kitchen counter. He says nothing as he opens the handles and methodically removes each item.

A box of orange hair dye and a razor.

"Shit," I sigh heavily as a new and equally nasty emotion crashes into me. *Shame.* I've lied to him, and he knows it.

He tilts his face, strokes his chin, and stares at me. "Tell me why I shouldn't shave your head and dye your eyebrows orange in the middle of the night."

I drag a hand through my hair and blow out a long stream of air. Then I just shrug. "Can't think of one."

He scowls. "Seriously? That's all you've got?"

I hold out my hands in surrender. "You are well within your rights," I say, my voice empty. Because really, who cares now?

He scratches his head. "You've been messing around with my sister, and that's all you're going to say?"

"What do you want me to do?" I spit out. "Deny it? Ask you how you know?"

"Umm," he begins, and he's speechless. He really did expect me to deny it.

"Look," I say, because I'm not in the mood right now. "I'm sure you figured it out. I'm sure you saw me dancing with her at your wedding. Right? Am I right?"

He nods, his green eyes registering some kind of surprise that I'm not tap-dancing around this confrontation. "Charlotte mentioned it, and I told her there was no way in hell. So we bet on it, and I came here to prove her wrong. But holy shit. Is there something going on for real?"

I nod, then shake my head. "There was. There's not. I don't know. Either way, take your revenge."

His eyes bug out. "C'mon. For real?" he asks, and he's the one in denial now.

"Look, I'm sorry, but I'm not sorry," I say, my voice rising as I lean against my fridge, frustration, anger, and sadness coursing through me.

He holds his hands out wide in a *what gives* gesture. "How the fuck did that happen?"

I give him a look. "I'm not getting into the details." The way it started is no one's business. I promised Harper I wouldn't tell a soul, and I'm not going to break that promise, even if she saw fit to slice my heart in two with her *feel-free-to-go-to-L.A.* send-off.

"You mess around with my sister, and that's your answer?" His tone darkens, and he's clearly pissed now.

"It's private, okay? It's private, and it's personal." I move away from the fridge and press my hands against the counter, staring him in the eyes. I thought I'd have to ask his approval to fall in love with his sister, but now I see that what happened with Harper isn't about his permission. It isn't even about him. I've gotten that part all wrong. She was only off-limits if I didn't care about her. I care about her so fucking much I don't know what to do with this surplus of feelings for my best friend's sister. It's time for him to know that. "It happened, and it happened again, and now here I am." I tap my sternum.

"I'm in love with your sister. So there you go. Get out the hair dye, shave it off. Whatever, man. It's not going to change the fact that I told her I love her, and she told me I'm free to go to L.A."

"Whoa." Spencer shakes his head like there's water in his ears, then he makes a time-out sign. "Back it up. I got *in love* and *L.A.* Start at the beginning."

Whatever anger was brewing in him seems to have quieted down.

I don't start at the beginning. I don't share the nitty-gritty. But I give him the basic ingredients of my lucky-bastard life and first-world problems. "Look, here's the truth. I've had feelings for her for a while now. I tried to deny them. I tried to ignore them. But the more time I spent with her, the tougher it became to fight it. I didn't ask you at first because what was happening was about her and me. I'm not saying that makes it okay. I'm saying that's how it went down, and I'm not sorry for how I feel. It all became clear when you were on your honeymoon. How much I care about her. And how much I'm in love with her. And the real rub in all this is now that I've told her, I can't even be with her."

He frowns. "Why?"

"They're moving my show to L.A. Gino already gave my timeslot to someone else. If I want to keep doing the show, it's California or it's over." I heave a sigh. "I don't expect you to feel sorry for me. I don't expect anyone to." Dragging a hand through my hair, I drop my voice. "I just want the girl, and I can't have her."

Spencer sighs, too. "Man," he says, sympathy in his tone. "It's not even noon, and we need to break out the Scotch because there is nothing worse than falling in love." He reaches for the hair dye and razor and drops them back in the bag.

"I get a reprieve?" I ask, with a quirk of my lips.

He nods.

"You're not pissed?"

He levels me with his gaze. "Dude, I fell in love with my best friend and business partner. I get it. Love just fucking happens and clobbers you out of the blue. And you—you fell for my sister. I can't fault you for that. I can't be mad at you for having good taste. Besides, you're suffering enough being in love without me being an ass."

I laugh once. "Love is a bitch."

"Don't I know how rough it can be. Which is why it's a damn good thing I can return these at Duane Reade." His expression turns more serious. "But listen, I need to say something. You know why I was a dick before about not wanting you to be with Harper?"

"'Cause you think I'm not good enough for her?"

"Fuck no," he scoffs. "You're probably the only guy who actually deserves my sister, and my sister is awesome."

I manage a small smile. "I know. She really is."

"I told you all that because if you break her heart," he says sharply, pointing a finger at me, "then I'd lose you as a friend. And I need you, Nick. But I'd still have to kill you for hurting her."

"That's kind of the nicest thing you've ever said to me. In a weird way."

"I know."

"But Spencer? I don't want to hurt Harper." I look him in the eyes so he knows I'm as serious as he was. "And I don't want to break her heart. I just want to love her. And you can totally mock me for saying that. But it's true."

He pushes back on the stool, stands up, and claps me on the back. "All right. I didn't want it to have to get to this, but clearly we need to call for reinforcements."

"Who's that?"

He shoots me a look, as if the answer is obvious. "Charlotte. You think I can figure out how to get her back? I'm lucky I convinced Charlotte to marry me. You need the big guns for this one."

* * *

Fido stares at me like he knows all my secrets while Charlotte listens to the tale of my unrequited love from her perch on the couch.

"Let me get this straight," Charlotte says on a yawn. She's jet-lagged from their trip but willing to tackle my pathetic excuse of a love life. Spencer is next to her. "She encouraged you to pursue the most amazing career opportunity you've ever had?"

"Yes."

"And she is well aware that your show is the thing you love most." Charlotte stares at me.

"It is?"

"Duh. Everyone knows that."

"They do?"

Her eyebrow rises. "Nick, it's not a bad thing. It's a true thing. You love your work, you love cartooning, and you love *The Adventures of Mister Orgasm*. I'm sure Harper knows how much you love the show."

"I guess." I flash back to our post-mortem after Harper's pseudo-date with Jason, when she asked what I was most afraid of. My answer? *That it will all fall to pieces. The job, the show, the success.* Then, after we took Serena to the hospital, and she asked me about kids down the road. My reply underscored once more that the show is my true love. *I've been pretty focused on work, and my job, and the show. That's what my life has been since I graduated college, and I love it.*

Which means . . . *ding, ding, ding* . . . Harper Holiday has every reason to believe I'd do anything for work. I'd go anywhere for my show. She has no reason to think anything else.

Charlotte confirms this with her next assessment. "She knows that your job—understandably—has been the center of your universe for all of your twenties."

I nod again, and Fido takes the opportunity to stretch across Charlotte's lap and flop to his back, offering her his belly for petting. He is such a manwhore.

"But," I say, shaking my finger as I trot out more evidence, "I told her I loved her and she said 'I can't tell you not to go to L.A.' She didn't say she loved me."

Charlotte waves off my concern. "That's not the issue. She's trying to show you she supports you. She doesn't want you to make the decision based on her."

"How would I be doing that?"

"By blurting out that you love her in the same breath as you tell her that you're moving to L.A," Charlotte says calmly as she pets Fido.

"And that means I'm making her make the decision?"

"Yes, and she cares about you, so she wants you to be free to make the right decision for *you*," she says, pointing at me.

I narrow my eyes. "How do you know that she cares about me?"

"When you told her about this new opportunity, she urged you to take it. Yet somehow you think that means she doesn't care about you? Am I understanding correctly?"

Spencer smiles widely and drapes an arm around her. "My wife is brilliant, isn't she?" Then to her, "So can you tell us what this all means?"

Charlotte rolls her eyes. "You two are such ding-dongs. And I love you both. In different ways, of course."

"Better be different ways," Spencer says with a huff.

Charlotte turns to me. "How did you feel when you were with her? Did it seem as if she felt the same way?"

Spencer covers his ears. "La la la. I don't want to hear."

As he continues to hum, I tell Charlotte more than I'd ever admit to him. "Yes, it did. Completely. We were in sync. You know? The way she looked at me. The things she said . . ." My voice trails off. I don't tell her how I felt in bed with Harper last night, but I know she had to feel the same way.

Tell me you feel it, too.

Just the memory of last night lights me up.

I replay the moments in the cab before she left Manhattan, and how we finally admitted how much we wanted to see each other.

I rewind to what Harper said after running into Jillian. I'd thought she was trying to box me up in the friendship zone. But what if she was trying to do the same thing I was doing—make sure we were something, at least? That we didn't lose each other? Because something is better than nothing. I replay all the moments we shared —her asking me to take her to the train station because she wanted to see me, her showing up after midnight in a cape, her bringing me ice cream, and giving me detergent and pencils, and taking me to the shower showroom, and coming to Gino's party, and throwing the bowling match, and giving me my librarian fantasy, and even wearing lingerie for me. My God, the fantastic, heavenly, unholy lingerie she wears that drives me out of my mind. She turns me on, and she makes me happy, and she inspires me and—

Charlotte interrupts my reverie. "I think the question isn't whether she should tell you *not* to go to L.A. The question is whether *you* want to go. If you do want to go to L.A., perhaps you should ask her to go with you."

She's brilliant. Totally brilliant. I've done this all wrong, and I need to fix the mess I've made. I stand. "You're right. I need to go."

I kiss her on the cheek, clap Spencer on the shoulder, and scratch Fido under the chin. He arches a haughty eyebrow, but I know he approves because we love the same girl. As I leave, Charlotte turns to Spencer and says, "I won. Gummi Bears are on you tonight."

When I leave, I cab it uptown to my house, grab some files, then head to Tyler's office where I tell him to call Gino's bluff.

CHAPTER 37

If this were one of J. Cameron's romance novels, the hero would hire a skywriter to pen the heroine's name across the blue canvas above us. Or he'd stop the airplane at the gate and profess his love. Maybe he'd even tell the woman he adores that he only had eyes for her on a Jumbotron at a packed baseball game.

But this is my life, and Harper's life.

One thing I know to be true about the woman I'm crazy for is that while she might like public kisses, she's not one for public declarations of love.

That's why I don't do any of those things. I don't buy flowers. Or chocolate. Or balloons. Or a teddy bear. I don't grab a boom box and play Peter Gabriel outside her window. Instead, with an eight by twelve envelope in hand, I head to her building and press the button for her apartment.

It rings, and it rings, and it rings.

I take a deep breath.

Maybe she's in the shower. I look at my watch. It's two in the afternoon.

I buzz again.

And it rings, and it rings, and it rings.

I grab my phone from my back pocket. Maybe I should have called first. I definitely should have called first. This was fucking stupid. She could be anywhere. She could be doing a magic show.

Okay, maybe not on a Monday afternoon.

Wait. I snap my fingers. She said she was taking a class. Then doing laundry. I slide open the screen to call her, and when I see a message from her, my heart goes into overdrive. Holding my breath, I click open the text.

I learn she's doing none of the above.

Princess: Where are you? The doorman is ringing, and ringing, and ringing.

That note is followed by another.

Princess: Oh, you could be anywhere. I guess I could call. My phone is bi-directional after all.

My heart soars at her words. She's at my house. Holy shit, she's at *my* house. I dial her number, but before I can hit send, my phone beeps. "I'm at your building," I say as soon as I answer her call.

"I'm at yours," she says, and I can hear something like lightness in her voice, like hope. I want to clutch the possibility of what it might mean tight in my hands.

"I have an idea," I say, thinking quickly. "Meet me in the middle?"

"Eighty-Fourth Street then?" She lives on Ninety-Fifth, and I'm on Seventy-Third.

"I love it when you do math. Yes, meet me at Central Park and Eighty-Fourth."

"Are you Ubering it or walking?"

"Walking."

Ten minutes later, I stand by the park entrance, under the bronze and wine-red leaves of a cherry tree, as after-

noon traffic whizzes by. I pace, waiting for her, searching for her, until I see her, walking fast, practically
running to me.

My heart beats like a wild bird, and I don't know how
it can stay inside my chest. I have no idea what she's going to say, or why she was at my house, or what's going
on, but she's here now. She came to find me, and the last
time she came to find me was the start of our first real
night together.

The autumn breeze blows her hair, red strands floating past her cheeks as she marches right up to me, looks
me square in the eyes, and says, "I'm in love with you,
Nick. If you ask me to go with you, I will."

And my heart, I swear, it jumps out of my chest into
her hands, where she can hold it forever because it belongs to her. I fall deeper into love with her in that
moment.

She cups my cheeks and says more before I can even
speak. "I didn't say anything when you told me this
morning because I wanted it to be your decision," she
says, her blue eyes fixed on mine. "That's why I left
right away, so you could be free to make the choice that
works for you. I didn't want you to worry about me, or
think you had to turn down something you love because
of me. But the whole time I was a wreck because I feel
the same way you do. And I know how much this means
to you, and you mean so much to me, and I want you to
know I'd go with you. Because I love you, too."

I can't not kiss her. I slant my mouth to hers, brush
my lips against hers, and kiss the woman I love, who
loves me, too.

New York and autumn. Harper and me. Love and
friendship.

I'm so damn happy it can't be contained. There's no
way I can hold all this joy inside me. We kiss, and we
kiss, and we kiss, and I can't stop. I thread my hands in

her hair, the soft, silky strands spilling over my fingers as I kiss her outside Central Park where I've met her in the middle.

Only, there's no need to compromise. There's no need for her to give up anything for me. When I break the kiss, I'm lightheaded and grinning like the love-struck fool I am.

"You can't go with me," I tell her, and her expression morphs as sadness flickers in her eyes.

"Why?" Her voice breaks.

I press a finger to her lips. "Because I'm not going."

"What?" She swats my chest. "Are you crazy? This is the opportunity of a lifetime."

I shrug. "Maybe it is. Maybe it isn't. I don't care about the show right now. The show has given me everything I could ever want, but it hasn't given me you. My whole life, I've loved to draw more than anything. It's been what I love most," I say, running a hand through her hair. "Until you."

She trembles. "Stop. That's crazy."

I shake my head. "It's not crazy. It's true. There can be another show. There won't be another you."

She brings her hand to her mouth, like she's trying to cover up the quivering of her lips. But the tear that slips down her cheek gives her away.

"Harper, I love you more than *The Adventures of Mister Orgasm*. And I can't ask you to leave New York."

"But I would. I would for you. I'm really good at what I do, and there are moms everywhere who'd hire me. One referral and I'd be gold in L.A."

"I know," I say softly, and it's true. She's right. She could relocate and somehow make it all work. "But I love New York, too. And I want to be with you here in Manhattan. This is our home, and you're the thing I can't afford to lose. Not the show."

"So what happens?"

I shrug. "I told Tyler to turn down the offer. Gino thinks he has me over a barrel, but he doesn't. Because here's the thing. Gino's a jerk, and I don't like working for him. He thinks he owns me because he found me, but the show is portable. It goes anywhere. Gino might own everything I've created so far, but whatever it becomes next"—I stop to tap my temple—"that's up here. It belongs to me. It's my creation. And Tyler and I both think someone else will want it. He's shopping it around."

"You decided that before you even knew about us? Before I even told you I feel the same?" she asks, astonishment coloring her tone as she curls her hands over my shoulders.

"Sometimes you have to go out on a limb and put your heart on the line. Like you just did for me," I say softly.

"Like you did for me," she says, her lips curving up in a smile that matches mine. Those lips—they're impossible to resist. And I don't have to resist her anymore . . . not that I ever earned high marks in that class. But now I have free rein to kiss the hell out of her. I capture her lips again with a possessiveness that comes from the certainty that she's mine.

When we break the kiss, I take her hand and guide her to a bench inside the park, where we sit. "There's this new idea I have. I want to show you. A certain sexy princess I love was my inspiration."

She feigns a look of curiosity. "Whoever would this sexy princess be?"

"I had this idea when we went bowling the first time," I say, and I reach into the envelope and take out the copies I made of the panels I've worked on. Though work is hardly the word. *Play* is better, because drawing Harper always felt fun. "I pictured you as this crazy-hot mechanic."

I show her the first one. She laughs, and looks at me. "That's me?"

I nod.

"I'm rather busty," she says kind of proudly, wiggling her chest.

"Yes, you are."

"And I'm a mechanic?"

"In this comic strip, you are."

"You do realize I don't even know how to drive?"

It's my turn to laugh. "Like I said, L.A. would be terrible for us. You're such a New Yorker."

I show her the rest of the cartoons I drew—the text message tutorial, the lube job joke, the mechanic in the cape, and many more. What began as random doodles has turned into the start of a storyline. Her eyes are wide and filled with something like wonder as she takes her time, studying each one.

"Remember when you asked me the secret to drawing a great cartoon?" I ask, reminding her.

She looks up from my work. "I do. You said you have to like what you're drawing."

"That's true. But I need to amend that. It helps even more if you *love* what you're drawing." I tap the last one, in which the puppet ogles the mechanic in the cape.

Her lips quirk up in a grin. "Is that you?"

I shrug. "Maybe. I don't know. But I have a lot in common with this puppet. He has a filthy mind and loves sneaking peeks at a certain gorgeous redhead."

She cracks up. "I love you, and your dirty cartoons, and your crazy brain, and the fact that you see me as a mechanic even though I'm a magician."

That last word reminds me of something I've never quite figured out when it comes to this woman. "Tell me something. I used to think you weren't into me because you were never Princess Awkward around me. Does that

mean your feelings changed when you said you were"—
I pause to sketch air quotes with my fingers—"*cured of your affliction*?"

She smiles slyly and shakes her head. "Nope."

"Then when?" I ask curiously.

"I've never had trouble talking with you." She runs her hand through my hair with a look in her eyes that's full of mischief. "Want to know the secret to that little trick?"

"Yeah, I do. That always kind of baffled me."

"Pay attention, because I don't give away how I do my tricks."

"I'm listening."

She raises her chin. "*Practice*."

"What do you mean?"

Her voice goes soft and vulnerable. "I've had years of practice. I've liked you since forever. You were my friend when we were younger, and you were always so handsome. I never felt awkward around you, because I've known you for so long. Pretending I didn't have a crush on you was the greatest trick I ever pulled off."

I let her admission soak in, and it makes sense, in a way, as I flashback to all the compliments she's given me in the last few weeks. Still, I'm kind of amazed, and awed, too. "Are you for real?"

"I've always had a thing for you, Nick," she says, as splashes of red color her cheeks.

A new burst of happiness spreads through me. "Do one thing for me, Harper."

"Name it."

"Don't ever break that spell."

"I won't," she says, taking my hand and threading her fingers through mine. She squeezes then adds, "That's why kissing you and making love with you never felt like lessons. It didn't feel like practice to me, Nick. It always felt real."

There's a warm glow in my chest, and I'm sure I'm the luckiest guy in the world to have this girl be mine. "It was always real for me, too," I say softly. "It was always true."

She dives in for another kiss, then gives me a dopey smile. "So you really love me, huh?"

I laugh. "I really love you."

"I am one lucky girl."

I sigh contentedly. "This has been a perfect afternoon. There's only one thing that can make this better."

"Cake?" she asks eagerly.

"That, and something else." I wiggle my eyebrows. "Want to get out of here?"

She squeezes my fingers. "Hell yes."

I take her back to my place, and as soon as the door falls shut, we strip each other, tugging off clothes and grabbing at hair and tumbling into my room.

In seconds she pins my wrists, lowers herself onto me, and rides me hard and beautifully as the sun dips in the sky. She takes control, her hips circling, her back arching, her lips falling open as she moves up and down. She sets the rhythm, and I follow her lead, watching every flutter of her eyelids, every bounce of her breasts. Soon, she bends lower, brings her face to mine, and whispers in my ear, "I just love you."

"I just love you, too," I say as I yank her closer, and the woman I treasure falls apart with me as we come together again.

We stay in bed for a little while, talking and touching, until my phone rings. It's Serena, and she's home from the hospital. A little later, we stop by to visit her and Jared and give them the baby gifts for their son. They named him Logan. Then Harper and I go to Peace of Cake to celebrate being together.

It's a date. It's definitely a date.

Wait. It's so much more. It's the start of a new story-line for us. The story of this great love of my life.

EPILOGUE

Several Months Later

They wobble. They sway. Then, with a resounding clatter, all ten bowling pins fall. Harper thrusts her arms high and struts over to me.

"Strike!"

I high-five her, even though she's walloping me.

"Say it," she says playfully, as she loops her arm around my neck.

"You kick my ass in bowling every single time," I say, repeating the truth of our life together. I've only beaten her once, in our very first rematch after the night she went sexy librarian on me. Every time since then, she's destroyed me, and I swear it has nothing to do with how absolutely distracted I get checking out her ass as she takes her turn in the lane. Nope, she's just really good, and she's about to clobber me for the tenth match in a row.

"And do I get a special present, like you promised, for beating you for the tenth time?"

I nod. I've been giving her gifts after each win. A new magic wand. Yes, *that* kind. A lingerie set. A satin bow for her hair that happens to have other uses too. "If you win you'll get a gift."

"And do I ever have to throw a game again?" she says, her eyes glinting.

"Never," I say, like it has ten syllables.

She gives me a quick kiss. "Never ever."

That's because I don't work for Gino anymore. My show's not on Comedy Nation. The deal didn't happen overnight, but a week after I turned down the Comedy Nation offer, I landed a new one. The show's new home is on the broadcast network Serena's husband works for —RBC.

I'm not saying helping his pregnant wife to the hospital got me the gig. Not at all. But it sure didn't hurt when Tyler needed to land a quick meeting with a new network. Jared greased the wheels, and Tyler did the deal, moving *The Adventures of Mister Orgasm* to the ten o'clock hour on RBC, where it's killing it in the ratings every week. Funny thing is the head of RBC doesn't play games, doesn't toy with me, and doesn't care if I beat him at golf, softball, bowling or anything else. What he does care about is that I deliver the best show possible, so that's what I do every week.

Well, technically I deliver two shows. RBC owns the cable network LGO, and LGO is now the proud home to the new five-minute cartoon short—*Naughty Puppet Theater Presents Dirty Girl Mechanic.*

It's early days, but viewers seem to like it, and there's talk of turning that show into a full-length weekly comedy. Seems I'm not the only one who likes a hot mechanic.

But the one in my arms is all mine.

And I want to make sure it stays that way.

That's why when the match is over, and she wins fair and square, I let her enjoy her victory dance for a few seconds until she spins around and finds me on one knee in the bowling alley.

She stops, freezes, and brings her hand to her mouth.

Once upon a time, I wasn't sure how to share my feelings, but now the words come out with ease, and I mean them with my entire heart. "Harper, I love you like crazy, and I want you to be the one I share detergent with, and bowling matches, and ice cream and cake, and dirty text messages, and showers, and love, and happiness, and inspiration, and all our days and nights. Will you marry me?"

She falls to her knees and throws her arms around me, knocking me onto my back on the floor of the bowling alley. "Yes, yes, yes, yes," she repeats over and over, lying on top of me, and this couldn't be a more perfect response to a proposal.

When she loosens her hold on me and we sit up, I slide a gorgeous, platinum, princess-cut ring on her finger as tears streak down her cheeks.

"I love you so much, I'd even take your last name, Nick Hammer," she says in between dabbing her eyes.

"I love you so much, I'd never ask you to do something that horrible, Harper Holiday."

I don't care if she takes my name, because I have everything I thought I'd once lost. I have the girl.

ANOTHER EPILOGUE

Ask me my three favorite things and the answers are so easy they roll off my tongue: kissing Harper, fucking Harper, and loving Harper.

Not gonna lie. That last one is my favorite, by a margin of forever. She's not just my best friend's little sister. She's not just the coolest person I know. And she's not just the inspiration for my newest show.

She's my wife, and loving her is pretty much the best thing ever.

Harper started out as the woman I lusted after one day in Central Park when we pranked her brother, and she became my buddy, my dating protégé, and then my student. But the truth is I learned just as much from her as she did me, if not more. I learned that loving with your whole heart is even better than racking up Os.

Don't get me wrong. I'm still a superhero of pleasure, but my mission is singular now—*her.* I intend to serve the terrain of her beautiful body for the rest of our days, because there's nothing better than being obsessed with making one woman feel amazing. But what's best of all is giving the woman you love everything—in and out of bed, and I do that every day for Harper.

My dirty mechanic. My caped beauty. My stockings-and-mini-bow-wearing, cake-loving, magic-wand-wielding wife.

Oh, and in case you're wondering, we have a dog now. We adopted a chihuahua/Min Pin who laughs at all our jokes, and we named him Uber.

I have a feeling he'll be the first of many little ones.

Now, you might be wondering if Harper took my last name. In a way, she did.

She's the one and only Mrs. Orgasm.

THE END

COMING SOON!

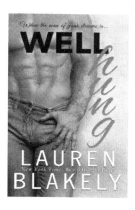

Coming Next! Get ready for Nick's brother Wyatt in WELL HUNG!

WELL HUNG releases in the early fall! To receive an alert when new titles release, **please sign up for my newsletter.**

Did you think I'd forget the hot single dad hero who looks like a movie star? Of course not! Simon is getting a book in SWEET IRRESISTIBLE YOU in the fall. And how about Tyler, Nick's lawyer? He's headlining THE HOT ONE. Stay tuned for more details!

ALSO BY LAUREN BLAKELY

Check out my contemporary romance novels!

BIG ROCK, the hit New York Times
Bestselling standalone romantic comedy!

The New York Times and USA Today
Bestselling Seductive Nights series including
Night After Night, *After This Night*, and *One More Night*

And the two standalone romance novels,
Nights With Him and *Forbidden Nights*, both
New York Times and USA Today Bestsellers!

Sweet Sinful Nights, *Sinful Desire*, *Sinful Longing*
and *Sinful Love*, the complete New York Times
Bestselling high-heat romantic suspense
series that spins off from Seductive Nights!

Playing With Her Heart, a USA Today bestseller,
and a sexy Seductive Nights spin-off standalone!
(Davis and Jill's romance)

21 Stolen Kisses, the USA Today
Bestselling forbidden new adult romance!

Caught Up In Us, a New York Times and
USA Today Bestseller! (Kat and Bryan's romance!)

Pretending He's Mine, a Barnes & Noble and
iBooks Bestseller! (Reeve & Sutton's romance)

Trophy Husband, a New York Times and
USA Today Bestseller! (Chris & McKenna's romance)

Far Too Tempting, the USA Today Bestselling
standalone romance! (Matthew and Jane's romance)

Stars in Their Eyes, an iBooks bestseller!
(William and Jess' romance)

My USA Today bestselling
No Regrets series that includes

The Thrill of It (Meet Harley and Trey)

and its sequel

Every Second With You

My New York Times and USA Today
Bestselling Fighting Fire series that includes
Burn For Me (Smith and Jamie's romance!)
Melt for Him (Megan and Becker's romance!)
and *Consumed by You* (Travis and Cara's romance!)

The upcoming Sapphire Affair series...
The Sapphire Affair
The Sapphire Heist

A Seductive Invitation

ACKNOWLEDGMENTS

Thank you so much for reading my books! I am so very grateful to each and every reader for making it pos-sible for me to keep doing what I love — writing romance. I am grateful to so many people for bringing MISTER O to your hands. First and foremost, a big thank you to my Brainstorm Princess, Jen McCoy. I am indebted to my cover mastermind Helen Williams, my chief strategist KP Simmon, my daily grind gal Kelley Jefferson, and all my editors and early, including Kim Bias, Dena Marie, and Lauren McKellar. A humongous thanks to my husband and kids! And as always, much love to my dogs!

CONTACT

I love hearing from readers! You can find me on Twitter at LaurenBlakely3, or Facebook at Lauren BlakelyBooks, or online at LaurenBlakely.com. You can also email me at laurenblakelybooks@gmail.com

52085323R00170

Made in the USA
Lexington, KY
15 May 2016